MANNFORD PUBLIC LIBRARY
P O BOX 193
MANNFORD OK

15445

15445

Angel on Trial

DATE DUE			
SEP 4 1999			

WITHDRAWN FROM MANNFORD PUBLIC LIBRARY

F
Ker
cd

Kerl, Mary Ann
  Angel on trial

MANNFORD PUBLIC LIBRARY
P O BOX 193
MANNFORD OK 74044

GAYLORD M2

Angel on Trial

Mary Ann Kerl and Jay d'Queue

North Sea Press
Fiction Division

Angel on Trial

Mary Ann Kerl and Jay d'Queue

Textual Editor: Jimmy B. Quick

Copy Editor: Jamie Clapp

Cover Art and Illustrations: Paul Locus, M.D

Cover Graphics: Michael Qualben

Copyright © 1996 LangMarc Publishing
First Printing 1996
Printed in United States of America

All rights reserved. Written permission must be secured from the publisher to reproduce any part of this book except for review.

Scripture quotes from The Holy Bible * NIV Study Bible
Copyright © 1985 by The Zondervan Corporation

Published by
North Sea Press
Fiction Division • LangMarc Publishing
Box 33817
San Antonio, TX 78265
Ordering information: 1-800-864-1648

Library of Congress Cataloging-in-Publication Data in Process

ISBN: 1-880-292-51-3 • $13.95

To Shirley Donaldson,
a special Earther friend,
whose godly love, concern, and support
have brightened many of my days.

Mary Ann

In Memory
of our brother
Phil

You made our family so proud
and filled out childhood home
with so much fun and laughter!

JDQ

Dear Reader:
Let there be no misunderstanding.
Both authors of
Angel on Trial
do believe in the existence of God's angels.

Angela Four, however, may have been
one of those angels
of whom Job 4:18 says:

He does not trust his servants,
and his angels he charges with mistakes.

What follows is based upon the Mission journal
"Angie" left behind…by mistake!

Publisher's Note:

If your spiritual life can't smile, please put this book back on the shelf—*at once!* What follows is not for the spiritually shaky. *Angel on Trial* is unique, we are told by booksellers, and not only because sound spirituality is woven throughout a humorous novel. It also spoofs science fiction, political and ethnic correctnesss, psycho-babble, New Agers, and lots of other silly stuff. Is there a niche in the marketplace for such a book? We'll see.

Read it, however, and we can guarantee you will find food for thought, practical insights into forgiveness, challenges to your imagination, and more than a few grins.

Learn while you laugh, as we have while publishing this book. *Angel on Trial* is published for enjoyment and enrichment, not analysis.

The Publisher

P.S. The Publishers are not liable for reactions to quotes from this book in sermons, Bible study groups, and—as Angie would say—other "churchy" contexts.

ONE

ZAP!

Greg Matthews heard the sound a split second before he recoiled. "Whoa!" He jumped from the sofa, grabbed a still-wet snow shovel and advanced toward the intruder. "How'd you get in here? C'mon, c'mon. Answers! Who are you?"

Angela Four's heart pounded. "D-d-don't hit me! I-I-I came to help you." Angie was terrified that she would goof up yet another Mission. A successful Mission was an absolute necessity for her to finally graduate from Mission Angel status. More than anything, Angie wanted to become a Heaven Angel. But for many millennia now she had been stuck at Angel University and Mission Control, where she faced tough professors and demanding supervisors.

That's why Angie had *Zapped* into Greg's apartment in Tulsa, Oklahoma on this New Year's Eve afternoon. "I-I-I didn't mean to alarm you." She was one stressed-out angel.

"You didn't mean to alarm me? What kind of a nut case are you, lady? Sheeezz." Greg glared at her. "How come my burglar alarm didn't go off?"

"The alarm didn't go off because I didn't come in through your door." She pointed to the floor. "I *Zapped* directly here because it's freezing outside." She shivered. "I heard this is the worst blizzard Tulsa has had in a hundred years."

"Forget the weather!" Still clutching the dripping shovel and holding it horizontally in front of him, Greg knew in his gut he could never strike this beautiful young woman. Beads of sweat gathered on his forehead. "You have exactly sixty seconds to explain how you got in here and what you want. At the count of sixty-one, I'm calling the cops. Give, lady. Start talking. Now! This better be good."

Angie's chest tightened with the same clutching anxiety she'd felt when she received the official ruling that she'd failed her previous Earther Mission with George Washington's good-for-nothing cousin, Wally Walla-wash. Before she could respond, Greg shouted, "Or am I having a nightmare?"

"No sir. No nightmare. And no cops." Angie knew she'd better talk fast. She tossed her ermine coat on a chair covered with discarded shirts and socks. She offered a handshake to Greg. He backed away, still clutching the shovel. Angie sighed deeply. This will be an impossible Mission if this Earther won't stop his hysteria, she thought. She brushed short blonde curls from her forehead and smiled meekly. "Relax. I'm Angie."

"Get real, lady. You just pop in here out of nowhere, and I'm supposed to *relax*? Sheeezz!" His eyes bulged as he pointed a thumb to his chest. "Suppose the next thing you'll want is to join me for tea and crumpets."

"That'd be super, thank you." Angie smoothed her pink turtleneck sweater and gray wool slacks before sitting on the sofa.

Greg squinted at the intruder. "What's that glaring bright light over your head anyway? Get that at some carnival or did you come from Chernobyl?"

Angie quickly pinched her nose twice, and her glowing halo disappeared. She hoped none of her supervisors noticed she'd broken Rule 210 by forgetting to turn it off. There were too many rules in this business. Too many gadgets. Too many supervisors. Too many complications.

Angie shifted to the soft vulnerable tone she'd mastered in her Earther Feminine Wiles course. "Oooo, Greg Matthews, I can tell you're a take-charge kind of guy. So rare in fellas as good looking as you are." She reached into a gray leather purse and pulled out lipstick and a small mirror.

Without taking his eyes off her, Greg leaned the shovel against a wall. This intruder might be a weirdo, he thought, but intuition told him she wasn't dangerous.

"If you didn't want to upset me, why did you just pop in here? How on earth did you do that anyway?"

"I didn't *Zap* in from earth." Angie paused. "I *Zapped* in from Mission Control."

"Mis-mis-Mission Control?" His words dripped scorn. "Are you from NASA or something?"

"What's NASA?"

"Everyone knows that. NASA launches rockets and controls satellites up there." He waved his hand upward.

"So they're the ones cluttering up Earth space." Angie imitated his vague gesture. "It's getting really dangerous to *Zap* down here through all that garbage."

"Where did you come from? Tell me now or you'll be telling the police. Now! Give, lady! Now!"

"Of course, I'll tell you." Angie glanced in the small mirror, smacked her freshly done lips together and put the make-up items back in her purse. "I came from Angel U. I meant to come sooner, but that's me. I procrastinate. 'No guts,' as you Earthers say. At least I'm here now, though."

Greg reached for a cigarette. He pulled matches from his denim shirt pocket. His hands shook so violently that he ended up striking four matches before he could align one with the cigarette. He glared at Angie as he puffed furiously on the Salem Ultra Light.

Angie wondered whether Greg might be into witchcraft when she saw the Salem label.

"Greg, I'm on a Mission. And you're it."

Greg pressed both palms to his temples. "How'd you know my name?"

Angie sighed. Angel friends had urged her to study up on Earthers before she *Zapped* in so she wouldn't make serious mistakes. They told her that today's Earthers act a lot differently from Mount Vernon days. For instance, she had to learn far more than to shift from saying, "Verily, verily" to "But of course." If only she had listened.

"Don't worry about a thing, Greg. I'm prepared to stay as long as I'm needed."

"Who needs you?"

"You do. I told you I'm here to help you. That's what my kind of angels do. I'm in the Mission Angel Corps. My Mission is to bring *shalom* to your life. You know, peace."

"Oh great! A Peace Corps fanatic."

"You Earthers have a Peace Corps? What is their purpose?"

"To encourage peace by helping people in underdeveloped countries build a better life for themselves."

"What a great idea! Was the Peace Corps here when George Washington was president?"

"Of course not."

"That's why I never heard of it. The last time I was here, George was in charge."

"George Washington?" Greg growled. "You're a loonytune, lady! You better tell me exactly what this Mission Angel Corps does." He waggled his hand. "And, where is it? I never heard of it."

"Mission Angel Corps isn't on earth."

"Oh," Greg mocked her, "I suppose it's in heaven, huh?"

"No, but it's in the neighborhood."

"This is getting really, really weird. Are you on drugs or something?"

"My supervisor at Mission Control told me to make sure to read the EE thoroughly before I came here, but I told him I already knew enough about Earthers to get by. I guess I was wrong."

"EE?"

"The—um—Earthers Encyclopedia."

Greg groaned. "Earthers?"

"At Angel U I'm taking a Double-E 101 course. It's not that I haven't been reading my Earthers Encyclopedia assignments. I have. But I keep getting stuck in the clothing section. I love clothes."

"Well, that's reassuring. Then I know you're a woman," he smirked, "but the angel part..."

"Tell you what. Get me a Bible. I can always explain things better with that. Or don't you even own a Bible?" Greg didn't move. He just stared at her. His mind spun. His jaw dropped. His eyes glazed. Angie feared she'd over-saturated this poor Earther. Too much revelation, too soon. She had broken the First Rule of Procedure.

Greg's face flushed. "Of course I have a Bible. What's more, I know a lot of verses by heart. 'In the beginning God created the heavens and the earth—' "

Angie held up her hand. "If you start rattling off the whole Bible, we'll be here forever."

"I wasn't about to quote all sixty-six books. I just want you to know I'm not ignorant about the Bible." Still shaken, he grabbed a chair, stepped up on it, and opened the cabinet doors above a built-in bookcase. Six dog-eared issues of *Playboy* and a rotten apple core fell on his head. Fumbling through magazines and newspaper clippings, Greg pulled out an old black Bible. "Here," he grumbled as he handed it to Angie.

She blew dust from the Bible and held its bound edge. Four dried flowers, two broken rubber bands and a paper clip dropped out. Angie flipped through the thin India pages, found the verse and cleared her throat. Her legs felt leaden.

Angie realized the odds were piling up against her. She might fail this Mission, too, just as she had failed her 249 earlier Missions. She had to succeed this time. Her eternal vocation was at stake. If she couldn't get Greg to shape up and start living in God's *shalom,* what was she going to do? Stay in school for all eternity? She shuddered at the thought. She really didn't like school after all these millennia. First, though, she had to convince Greg that he needed her help.

"Here it is." Angie's palms were sweaty. "Psalm 91:11. This verse was written for you, Greg. It explains who I am and what I'm doing here."

"I memorized that verse when I was a kid. 'For He will give His angels charge of you to guard you in all your ways.'"

"That's right! This may not be an impossible Mission after all. Don't you get it? I'm an angel who's going to guard you. I can protect you while helping you begin to walk on the paths of God's peace. What did you think that verse meant?"

He shook his head. "Dunno. Never thought that much about it. Never thought angels really existed. I memorized a lot of verses when I spent a year at Bible college. Going there was a condition in Grandma's will if I would receive my part of the inheritance." Greg frowned. "Are you sure this verse is for me?"

"Yes, of course, it is! This Bible is good for a lot more than just pressing flowers." Angie extended her hand for another try at a hand shake. "Anyway, I'm most delighted to meet you. My name's Angela Four, but my friends call me Angie."

Greg accepted the gesture and slumped on his sofa. "You mean to tell me you just popped in here from heaven?" Angie shook her head, swinging her blonde curls. Greg stared at her. "But surely you didn't come from, uh, from you know where." He pointed to the floor.

"I most certainly didn't come from hell, thank you very much. But I didn't come from heaven either. I told you, I've come from Angel U on special assignment from Mission Control. And you're it." Still staring at Angie, Greg fumbled in his shirt pocket for another cigarette. This time it lit on his second try.

"But there's no between place."

"No between what?"

"No between heaven and hell. So if you're any kind of an angel, you came from either one place or the other."

"Your Presbyterian upbringing is showing. I can assure you I see nothing wrong with Presbyterians. But the ones I knew back in Wally's day tended to see things in black and white terms with no red between."

"Red? Don't you mean gray? And how'd you know I'm Presbyterian?"

"I know all about you. Now I need to convince you I'm an angel who wants—no, actually *needs*—to help Greg Matthews, Case Number 6497102 Dash Three. Must I spell everything out for you?" She sighed again. "Mission Angel Corps works out of Mission Control, which is located in the southern hemisphere of planet Oreo."

"Planet Oreo? Like the cookie?" Greg snapped his fingers. "Got it. You're a kook from the cookie factory." She didn't smile. Greg shrugged. "Planet Oreo? Never heard of it."

"That's because Earthers haven't discovered it yet. It's several galaxies from here and, of course, not far from heaven. It's named Oreo because its polar ice cap circles the equator, and its vegetation is a brownish color."

> Planet Oreo's perfect circular orbit turns on an axis between two moderately-sized suns, Patty and Cakes. That, incidentally, explains why its northern and southern hemispheres are temperate, why its polar ice cap is around the equator, and why there is no night there. A third, more distant, sun orbits Oreo's circular course at right angles to the Patty-Cakes. Astrophysically speaking, a triune solar system is quite unique. *Editor.*

She smiled. "Now, how about that cup of tea you promised me?" Angie tossed several magazines off the sofa and crossed her legs. Greg's eyes studied every movement while he inhaled short puffs of smoke.

"Don't have any tea. Doesn't matter though, because my current squeeze is coming over in a few minutes. Kristin lives across the hall."

"Ah, Kristin. Good," Angie nodded. "I'm glad you mentioned her. She's one of the reasons I had to come here."

"This is ridiculous. You can't be an angel. You're a woman. A pushy broad. Probably a Libber out to torment guys like me."

She pressed her thumbs together and tilted her head. "It just might interest you to know I saved you from marrying

Susan. Remember that banquet honoring your father? I persuaded Susan to wear that pewter gray gown, which just happened to be identical to your mother's gown."

Greg gawked at Angie. "You?" How did she know this? He remembered that night. "Mumsie was so upset. That gown was the last straw." He studied Angie's face. "And you put her up to that?" He grinned. "On second thought, let's have a rum and Pepsi."

He shoved open a sliding door to display a small kitchenette. Dirty dishes were piled precariously high in both sinks. Greg was in his Chinese takeout phase, but not because he was that crazy about Chinese cuisine. When he ran out of clean dishes, Greg discovered he could eat right from the takeout boxes, using throw-away plastic utensils. A real plus for him, since his concept of housekeeping was based on trash bags.

Greg took a Pepsi from the refrigerator and his Bacardi from the cupboard. He handed the three-liter bottle to Angie. "Here, you have the Pepsi and I'll take the Bacardi."

"Go easy on the booze. That's another reason I'm here."

"Aha!" Greg shouted, snapping his fingers and slamming the bottle on an end table. "Now it figures. You're part of some crazy joke my ex-wife is pulling to get back at me." He slapped his forehead. "Uh-oh, I'm three days late with my alimony check."

"That has nothing to do with my being here. Marge has plenty of money."

"You know about Marge?" Greg picked up a dirty glass from the sink, wiped its inside with his shirt tail and held the glass for Angie to pour herself some Pepsi. He cleaned another glass the same way and filled it with rum. "Tell me more. What else do you know about me?" Greg settled back, his left arm on top of the worn sofa. "Just give it to me straight."

"It looks like you're already giving it to yourself straight." Angie glared at his glass. The nagging feeling returned. This could be a lot harder than she expected. She had to get Greg to stop boozing. Somehow. She quietly sipped her Pepsi. "I know you're a good man trying to earn a good living and do right by other people. But I also know how much harder you've been working lately, trying to sell your home security systems to meet alimony payments and other bills."

"Yeah," Greg said, taking a gulp of Bacardi. "Crime is down again this year. Seems like burglars aren't breaking into homes like they used to around here."

"It could be because Earthers like you have already installed so many security systems. I must say I'm surprised you have your apartment armed. I don't see many valuables here. Nobody could find anything in this mess anyway."

Angie eyed the apartment. Piles of dirty clothes were scattered on the floor, sofa, end tables, and coffee table. Art history magazines, back issues of *Guns and Ammo, Playboy,* and several scholarly journals were strewn helter-skelter on indiscriminate flat surfaces. Six half-empty coffee mugs sat on two end tables and on the TV. Several ash trays, heaped with stubs and ashes, were on a glass oval coffee table. An oil painting of a nude blonde hung lopsided on the wall. Several neckties and a pair of sweat socks lay on a lime green lamp shade. Greg's vacuum cleaner hadn't been used in two years, ever since a belt broke.

"You shouldn't worry so much. I also know you've got low blood sugar and high blood pressure. What should be down is up and what should be up is down. That's another reason I'm here. Your body needs some work, repairs here and there."

Angie cleared her throat. "Three items have priority on our agenda."

"*Our* agenda?"

"Yes." Her approach shifted to something she'd learned in her Motivational Tricks for Earthers course. "We'll be a team, a winning team. You'll see."

Greg buried his face in both hands. "Just three, huh?"

TWO

"Why would they put you on my case? I'm not such a bad guy. I know a lot of guys in worse shape than me."

Angie raised dark blonde eyebrows. "True. You're between. Sort of like I am. And between isn't good. Between is frustrating. But we're not talking about other Earthers. We're talking about you, Greg Matthews, Case Number 6497102 Dash Three."

"Drivers license, social security number, and now this. Sheeezzz! Another number. Just what I need." Greg moaned. "What's this Dash Three stuff?"

"A Dash Three assignment means an in-person Mission—here on earth. The first two tries were very long distance." Her palms opened to him. "All God's children have numbers."

Greg puffed furiously on his cigarette. "I'm one of them, a child of God's?"

"Of course you are. And that won't change. But *you* have to! I have to help get you moving toward spiritual maturity. Not just headed there, but on that road, traveling. Non-stop, too. Three things are involved."

Angie counted on her fingers. "One: You have to quit being such a boozy slob. Two: Open your eyes to what the Lord is doing in your life. Three: Forgive Marge."

"No way in hell!"

"Of course not. I'm talking about here," her finger jabbed the cushion, "on earth."

"But forgive Marge? Are you kidding?" He looked off into the distance. "I wish I could get her back."

"Marge?"

His face turned red. "No, my Bimmer. Marge totaled it—after she had totaled me. Sure, she was only a 300 series, but still, a BMW."

Angie had read about loss and grief among Earthers and was familiar with Kubler-Ross's stages. After two whole years, Greg wasn't just in some stage. He was mired in a rut over—can you believe it—a car. Not an encouraging sign.

"Marge was going to her mother's when she did it. If only, if only she'd stayed home to make supper like she should have, instead of...." Greg sighed deeply as he tried to calm himself. "I'll never forgive her for wrecking my Bimmer. Never!"

"Greg, this business about your BMW is a poison pill. Its poison will stay in your system as long as you don't let go of your anger and hand it over to the Lord. Otherwise, the rest of your life will be a mess."

"Woman, you're asking for the impossible. I can forgive just about anything. But not that. Never! What she did to me is way beyond forgiveness. Sheeezz, I miss my Bimmer." Greg took a deep breath. He glanced at his watch. "You've got to get out of here. Kristin will be coming any minute now."

"G never asks for the impossible."

"G? Who's G?"

"You know. We can't speak His name," Angie whispered as her thumb and head gestured upward. "It's too sacred to say. So we have to use substitute names."

"Such as G, huh? For the big guy in the sky?"

She curled her mouth in frowning disdain. "How crude."
Angie took a deep breath. "Yes, G, Adonai, and—um—other names too."

"Oh," was all he said. Greg's hands shot upward. "Look, whoever you are, I don't want to have to explain your presence to Kristin. I'm telling you to leave. Now!"

Angie had no idea Greg would be this obstinate. How could an Earther who is this sloppy also be so stubborn? Angie wasn't about to leave nor was she going to goof up this Mission. Not after pestering Archangel Michael for such a long time for this chance.

"Well, you can pop out as well as in, can't you?"

"You're talking to one very determined Mission Angel." She realized Greg would need some verification exercises if he were to believe she really is an angel. She stood up, raised her left hand, and tapped hot pink polished nails on a gold barrette she wore in her blonde curls. ZAP! Suddenly, Angie disappeared.

Three seconds later, ZAP! She stood in front of Greg again.

Greg gasped and got up slowly from his sofa. His eyes widened.

"See, Greg? I really am an angel. Only we angels can do Quickie *Zaps*."

"How'd you do that? Sheez!" He rubbed his eyes. "I've gotta get more sleep. Just gotta." Then Greg snapped his fingers. "I've got it! You're an illusionist. I saw David Copperfield pull a stunt like that once, but that sure didn't prove he's an angel."

"Please, Greg, I'm not an illusionist like your Coppermine person. If you want to know how I *Zapped* in and out of here, take a look at my barrette. It's my Zapper—my antenna to Zap Central."

"Zap...Central?"

"Yes, we Mission Angels can *Zap* back and forth in space. Zap Central is part of Mission Control. Our headquarters in heaven's—um—neighborhood." She pointed to her barrette.

"See? Two bars. I press this one for *Zap* Travel and the other for Talk. These access *Zap* communications."

"And you want to communicate with Zap Central because..."

"To get my Emergency Counsel Messages." She leaned forward, frowning. "ECM's are extremely important when, as you Earthers say, I find myself between a stone and a hard place."

"Not stone. A *rock* and a hard place. Okay?"

"Whatever..."

"Let me get this straight. You communicate with Zap Central to get emergency counsel messages."

"You're an intelligent man. You catch on quickly."

"Sheeezzz." Greg slid his forearm across his brow. "How do you get these little emergency messages from outer space anyway? There are local TV reporters who would kill to learn your secret."

Angie opened her right palm and pinched the tip of her little finger. "Come, sit by me so you can watch this."

When he glanced at her open palm, Greg gasped in astonishment.

"This is my Zapfax. This is how I get my ECM's, the printed out kind." Greg watched over her shoulder. On Angie's palm, bright red words flashed: "Mission Control. Zap Central, here. You're ever-ready Angel Bert on-line. How can we help?"

She tapped her left little finger across her palm and—presto! The red words were gone.

With her fingernail Angie wrote a message to Angel Bert on the palm of her hand. As she wrote, green letters appeared: Could you give us a small demo, Bert?

In a couple seconds, the green letters disappeared and red letters appeared: Bible verse for today is "For nothing is impossible with G. Luke 1:37."

"I can't believe this. It's impossible."

Angie shoved her hand closer to Greg's face. "Can't you read?"

"I know the Bible says that. It's just that I've never seen anything like this before."

With a tap of her left pinkie nail, Angie erased the message and wrote: Bert, I need to convince my Mission Guy, Greg Matthews, Case Number 6497102 Dash Three, that I'm really an angel. Can you help?

The green words disappeared, replaced by a message in red: No problem. Tell him about sex.

Angie erased the message as Greg studied her actions. She wrote: What about sex?

Bert Zapfaxed back: We don't have any.

"He's right. Angels don't have sex. There. That should prove that I'm an angel. Are you convinced now?"

Greg shook his head back and forth, grunted, and sipped more rum.

Angie was disappointed. Surely, she thought Greg would believe her by now. Such a cynic. She brought her right thumb to her lips and started whispering. A tiny microphone was embedded under the tip of her fingernail.

"Sucking your thumb. At your age? Sheeezz!"

Angie yanked the Zapmike away from her mouth. "Shhhh. I'm trying to speak with Bert." Thumbnail back to her lips, she called, "Angel Bert, come in please."

She opened her left hand, and suddenly, a voice boomed from the palm of her other hand. "Zap Central here. Angel Bert speaking. Need more assistance, Angie?" Hearing Bert's voice with ultra CD clarity, Greg's jaw fell open.

"I'm still trying to make my Mission Guy believe I'm an angel."

"So, do a Quickie *Zap*." Bert's voice had a nasal timbre to it.

"Been there. Done that. Maybe you should patch me through to a Mission Control supervisor for other ideas."

Suddenly a "barroom-barrah" sound came from her left hand. "We're receiving strange noises. What's that racket? Sounds like a goose getting strangled."

"Oh, that," Angel Bert laughed. "That's Gabriel."

"Archangel Gabriel?" Greg eyes widened.

"Practicing his trombone," Bert said. "Has a lesson in an hour."

"Trombone? What happened to his trumpet?" Greg asked as he spoke into Angie's thumbnail.

"Not any more." Bert cleared his throat. "He's really gotten into big sapphire rings. Two on each finger. Scripture stuff, all right, the sapphire bit, but the rings interfere with his valve fingering. So Gabriel recently took up trombone—with a vengeance. Look at it this way, Greg. At least that trombone keeps his lip in shape for Judgment Day."

Angie asked, "Speaking of that Day—any word on The Date yet?"

"Nothing definite. You know how Heaven Council likes to play stuff like that close to their chests. Is Greg still there?"

"Yes. Speaking." Greg's mouth returned to Angie's thumbnail.

"Greg, do you believe Angie's an angel?"

Greg stammered, "Hey, man, would you if you were in my shoes? All this is too bizarre for me."

"Maybe this will do it for you," Bert said.

ZAP! Suddenly an extinct—but very alive—saber-toothed tiger stood facing a panic-stricken Greg and a pleased Angie.

"Oh my God!" Greg gasped.

"Nope, not G. Just Evelyn," Bert said.

"She's so much bigger than tigers I've seen in the zoo."

Angie patted the powerful beast's forehead. "Well, Evelyn's been a growing girl for quite a while." She pursed her lips in an affectionate way. "Haven't you, pussy cat?" The tiger purred rather loudly.

"Please. Please don't do that," Greg pleaded. "My landlord. My lease. No pets."

"She's just purring. Like to hear Evelyn demonstrate a genuine saber-tooth roar?"

"Oh, my...G." Greg was getting the hang of proper angelic speech.

"Sounds like you're having a vivid spiritual experience, fella." Bert laughed. "Or would you like another miracle—

with a bit more size this time? Like a woolly mammoth? How about a friendly sperm whale? Right there in your very own living room, huh?"

"No, no. No way!" Greg shouted. He again leaned over and spoke into Angie's thumbnail. "If I get one more supernatural event in my life right now, I'm outta here. Pronto. Real quick!"

"Calm down, fella. Cool it." Bert's voice lost its jovial style. "We wouldn't want that. Are you with me, Angie?"

"I hope so. Thanks. May G be with you."

"Chiao, baby. Zap Central here, signing off." Click.

"What other powers do you have, and, can you get rid of this thing—what's her name? Evelyn? Please?"

Angie moved the thumbnail mike to her mouth. "Bert, you forgot Evelyn. She just—um—broke wind and..."

"Zap Central, Bert here. Whoops. Sorry about that."

ZAP! One saber-toothed tiger disappeared. Greg exhaled a sigh of relief as he waved a hand in front of his nose.

"Thank you." Angie's thumbnail left her lips. She turned toward Greg. "You asked about my other powers. While among you Earthers, that's about it. *Zap* travel and communication are about the only unusual things I can do."

She pouted. "Heaven Angels can do everything. The angels in my neighborhood just go to school, *Zap*, and get assigned cases like yours. Heaven angels have so much fun. You wouldn't believe all the neat things they do. Sing—lots of *a cappella* stuff. Party time, all the time." She ruffled her curls and glared at him. "And no Missions with unkempt Earthers."

There was a tap on the door. "Sheeez! You've gotta *Zap* outta here right now. Right now. Please. That's Kristin."

"Great! I want to meet her." Angie casually settled back on the sofa.

"Please, just *Zap* outta here for a few minutes. Come back when Kristin goes to work. Then we can talk."

Angie had no intention of leaving. If she left, she might be pulled off his case with no chance to return. Another tap on the door.

"Greggey, darlin', wheeere arrre you?" It was the first time Angie had heard a Texas drawl. Kristin spoke this way only when she wanted to affect that cute vulnerable manner many of her friends back home used to throw a guy off guard.

"What's that awful smell? Did you burn your breakfast eggs again?"

Greg was frantic. He shook his finger at Angie. "If you won't leave, I will. There's no way I can explain that horrible odor is from an extinct tiger."

Angie was frustrated. Why couldn't Greg get it? She couldn't leave and that was that. She had her heart set on graduating to Heaven Angel status, and her next chance wouldn't come for another two hundred years.

Angie was determined—success this time at all costs!

"Well then, go ahead and leave if you want. I'm staying and that's that." She cocked her head toward the windows. "Besides, it's freezing out there."

Greg shook his head. "This one's a real ditz."

At that moment Kristin sauntered into the room. Wearing a light green velour robe, she moved with the easy confidence of one who knows she has a great 'bod.' Long red hair bounced as she walked. She stopped abruptly when she spotted Angie. Hands jammed on her hips, she glared at Angie. "Who are you?"

Angie reached to shake hands with Kristin. "I'm Angela, but my—uh—colleagues call me Angie. Greg was trying to make me *Zap* out of here."

"Huh?" Kristin scratched her head.

"I was asking her to leave," Greg mumbled.

Kristin's hands jammed into her robe pockets. Each pocket had a red heart embroidered on it. "Greg" was sewn in yellow thread beneath one heart. Underneath the other heart, Kristin's name was in lime green. The snug-fitting garment suggested a full bosom.

"Please understand. There's nothing improper going on here. In fact, I have no romantic interest in him."

Kristin's eyebrows arched. "Most women fawn after him. He's the best hunk to ever come through the door at Louie's Place."

"What's Louie's Place?"

"A booze joint. Saloon. It's our home away from home," Greg said.

"Oh." Something else to confuse her. She turned to Kristin. "Hanky-panky is out of the question because I'm his Mission Angel. Besides, angels don't have sex."

Kristin turned to Greg. "I don't get it. What's going on here?"

"She's my cousin," he said, venturing an excuse for this awkward predicament.

Kristin studied each face. "Why didn't you say so in the first place?" She sashayed over to Greg, flung her arms around him and gave her him a long passionate kiss.

Angie gawked at the couple. "Fascinating. This is fascinating."

Kristin smiled at her. "Just remember, hon, you can do the angel or cousin bit, but the kissin' is my job."

Greg relaxed. His voice returned to normal. "I know, I'll fix us some brandy alexanders."

"Greg, darlin', y'all promised me you'd stop drinkin' in the mornin's."

"It's afternoon."

Kristin glanced at her watch. "Barely."

"Are those the drinks I read about in your files?" She stays on the sofa.

"Files?" Kristin's eyebrows arched.

"Recipe files," Greg said, too quickly. "An old family recipe. Turns out perfect every time." He opened the cupboard. "Sheezz. Out of brandy." He snapped his fingers.

"I know. Kristin and I can run over to Louie's Place for a bottle. When we get back, Angie, you can be gone. Can't you? Kristin and I are gonna have a nice private New Year's Eve together. Aren't we, babe?"

Kristin joined Angie on the sofa and plopped off her green furry slippers. "Darlin', I just don't feel like goin' any place right now. My feet are killin' me. Waitin' tables sure gets gruelin' durin' the holidays. Seems like nobody cooks at home anymore. Besides, it's rude askin' a guest to leave."

"She was leaving anyway, weren't you, Angie?"

Surely Greg had to be joking, Angie thought. She had just arrived on earth. How could she leave? So much was at stake for her. "Actually, I was planning on staying," Angie said rather airily. "At least a few weeks, maybe longer. It depends on the success or failure of my Mission."

Greg clenched his fists. His jaw set. He gritted his teeth. "Now don't you get difficult, cousin."

"Aw, come on, darlin'," Kristin drawled. "Angie doesn't have to leave. She doesn't even have plans for New Year's Eve."

"Of course she does." Greg stared at Angie. "Don't you?"

Angie crossed her legs and spread one arm across the top of the sofa. She twirled a lock of hair with her fingers. "Actually I was hoping to spend some time right here." She sensed that Kristin just might turn out to be an ally.

"There," Kristin said, "it's settled. Nobody should be alone on New Year's Eve." Kristin's affected drawl had disappeared.

"Hey, are you saying that our little trio is going to spend New Year's Eve chit-chatting and sipping brandy alexanders right here?"

"Course not, silly," Kristin brightened. "We'll all go to the shindig at Louie's Place."

"I thought your feet were killing you."

Kristin got up and swayed her hips. "Shucks, hon, my feet can always lose the pain for dancin.' That's just the kind of circulation they need to feel so fine again." She went to Greg, put her arms around his neck and resumed her cutsey tactic. "Aw, come on, darlin'. Don't be a stick-in-the-mud. We'll have a good time tonight."

Angie was fascinated by how Kristin used conversational Americanese. She also wondered how Greg could get stuck in the mud when everything was covered with snow and ice? She felt a growing uneasiness. Dancing? Louie's? Were these temptations to sin? Maybe she should leave Greg and Kristin alone for tonight, after all. She could *Zap* to her dorm room at Angel U and come back in the morning. She always handled things better after a good night of rest.

Kristin prevailed. She also announced that Angie would sleep in Greg's guest room but bathe in her one-bedroom apartment across the hall. Propriety did not dictate her decision. Sanitation did.

"Maybe Greg's right. Dancing isn't for me. Why don't I leave for the rest of the day and come back tomorrow."

"You'll do no such thing." Kristin touched Angie's arm. "Of course dancing's for you. Dancin's for everybody."

"But I can't dance. I don't know how."

"No problem, hon." Kristin laughed. "While Greg gets our brandy, I'll give you a few dancing tips. It's simple. We've got all afternoon. Besides, it'd be a sin for such a pretty thing not to party on New Year's Eve."

"A sin?" Angie perked up. "Are you sure?"

"Cross my heart and hope to die if I lie." With a sly grin, Kristin lightly jabbed Angie's arm. "Besides, have I got just the guy for you."

Angie wondered: what's a "guy" who is not a Mission Guy? Her backlog of questions to research in the EE was reaching critical levels. But now it was too late to *Zap* up to Angel U's library.

Greg tried again. "Angie really doesn't want to go dancing with us."

"But I don't want to commit sin either."

"Of course you don't. C'mon, Greg darlin,' it will be such fun. We haven't gone dancin' for so long. Besides we stayed in last year."

"Yeahhhhh."

Angie's palm covered her mouth. "That's right. You two did stay here last New Year's Eve. There are ten pages about it in your files." She said nothing about how those pages still baffled her. Earther couples are so strange and do such weird things when they think they are alone. Angie didn't know the half of it. Twelve scalding pages Angel Prissyla appended to her eyewitness report were deleted by Mission Control before Greg's file was posted in the Pending Earthers version Angie had read.

"Tell me, Angie, can I get you a date or not?"

Angie's heart pounded. What was she getting into?

"I, I really don't want to sin," she stammered, oblivious to the surprises that lay just ahead.

THREE

Although she had the day off, Kristin had too much to do in too little time. The first thing on her agenda was to get Angie a date for New Year's Eve. That didn't take long.

"Mission accomplished. I fixed you up with a blind date—my brother, Jimmy Goldfarb. Now to teach you how to dance. Come on. Hop up!" In less than an hour, the agile angel got into the swing of dancing. She was a quick learner.

What to wear tonight? Angie had a severely limited Earther wardrobe—in fact, she was wearing it. Slacks and sweater would never do. Kristin made it her New Year's Eve mission to get Angie in shape for a party-type evening.

They bundled up for the slippery drive to Loehmann's in quest of party dresses. As Angie slipped into her ermine coat, Kristin speculated about how Angie made her living to be able to afford a fur like that. She wondered if she was a prostitute or drug dealer? Do you suppose? Nah. She's too naive.

At Loehmann's, Kristin pointed to the crowded racks. "This is one of my favorite places." Noting her new friend's obvious surprise, she said, "Angie, hon, don't tell me this is the first time you've been in a Loehmann's."

"Okay, I won't tell you."

Kristin laughed. "Where do you shop for clothes?"

"Mainly on planet Oreo."

"Oreo? Ohh-kay." Kristin shrugged and led the way to racks loaded with cocktail dresses. "Let's get down to business, find us something foxy. How about this pink thing?"

"Pretty. I'll try it on."

Kristin picked out several possibilities for herself and suggested others for Angie. They headed to the dressing room. Angie gawked at the huge mirrors and bright lights. Over twenty women of all shapes and sizes were in a last-minute frenzied search for their New Year's Eve outfits. Angie slipped out of her slacks and sweater. Scantily-clad women discarded outfits helter-skelter. Most tried to wiggle into size-too-small possibilities.

Kristin glanced at Angie's figure. "You've got a nice 'bod,' Angie. So petite."

In bra and panties, Angie glared at herself in the mirror. "Five hundred years of bust development exercises and this is all I've got to show for it?"

Doffing jeans and sweatshirt, Kristin smirked. "I know the feeling. I did those exercises for years before giving up."

"At least you got some—um—results."

"Ha! Not from the exercises. These are from silicone." Several women within earshot snickered.

"Silicone?" Angie frowned, then relaxed. "Oh, you mean as in Silicon Valley—but why would you have them stuffed with computer chips?"

Kristin's jaw dropped open. "You're off the wall, Angie." She held a green dress against herself. "What do you think?"

"Sets off your red hair quite well." Angie slipped on a pink dress. She studied the mirror image from several angles. "This just isn't me."

After an hour in the dressing room, activity progressed from frantic to desperate. Women who were either putting on or peeling off clothes grew increasingly irritable. Two hours later, Angie and Kristin were tired but successful shoppers. Angie chose a red satin cocktail dress with spaghetti straps and scooped layers of chiffon at the hemline. Kristin selected a black velour sheath with a cowl neckline.

The two strolled to a sales counter with their party garb. A clerk scanned the ticket on Angie's dress. "With tax, your total comes to $59.36."

"So much?" Angie gasped. "This is no bargain. On Oreo a dress like this goes for not much over—um—twenty shekels. Twenty-five, tops. My coat didn't cost much more than what you want for this dress. But then, throughout our galaxy, Oreo is famous for its ermine ranch."

The sales clerk's quizzical facial expression prompted Kristin to try an excuse. "She has a wacky sense of humor."

"Wow! I can't believe how clothing prices have skyrocketed since George Washington was president."

"If you don't have enough money with you, Angie, use your credit card."

"Credit card?" Once more, Angie chided herself for neglecting her Double-E studies. She blushed. "I—um—don't have one of those cards."

"You can't be serious. Everybody uses credit cards." Kristin hesitated before making an offer. "Okay, for now we'll put it on one of mine. Sometime this week, we'll go to my bank and get you fixed up with some cards." The clerk packaged their dresses as Kristin signed for them.

Meanwhile, Greg and Jimmy knew Louie's Place would be crowded, so they went early to save a table. When Angie and Kristin arrived, they squinted until their eyes were used to the dimly-lit room.

The scene reminded Angie of several taverns she'd visited on her previous Mission, although that was in colonial Virginia and this was Oklahoma. Six large round red lights hung over the highly polished bar where several wooden bowls filled with nuts or popcorn were placed. A back-lit sign, framed by costly wood, dominated the wall behind the bar. In red letters, "The Time Is NOW" glared from frosted glass. There was a clock inside the large O.

Major renovations had been necessary to create Louie's Place. The facility originally belonged to the Zionist Gospel Tabernacle, which folded when the preacher ran off with two other women. Blueprints for the visible interior work and utilities had been duly filed with the authorities. Before the contractor started, however, a crew of faceless workpersons labored around the clock for a week, arriving and leaving in unmarked vehicles.

Angie was glad she'd come tonight. She thought Jimmy was handsome. His thick blonde hair was brushed back from a light-complexioned face. His blue eyes sparkled. When Jimmy laughed, his mannerisms resembled a schoolboy's, although he was two months past his thirty-first birthday.

Louie's head bartender, Nemmy, greeted the foursome. "Happy New Year's Eve. Greg, Kristin, Jimmy." He leered at Angie, "And who's this angel you've brought to us?"

Angie grimaced. How does he know I'm an angel? Did Greg tell him? If he did, why? She'd gotten the impression Greg wanted to keep prospects of her angelic nature a secret.

Jimmy eased an arm around her waist. "Angie, I'd like you to meet my man, Nemmy, one of planet earth's truly immortal bartenders. Nemmy, this is Angie."

"Delighted to meet you, Angie," Nemmy said, too-perfect white teeth flashing. Red light reflected from stylishly groomed black hair.

"Pleased to meet you, too," she responded politely, even though there was something about this man that sent chills through her.

Nemmy nodded to Greg. "I saved your usual table. Should get real busy later." The foursome sat at a small cocktail table. Nemmy lit the red candle. With a sly grin, he eyed Angie. "What'll it be for starters? Brandy alexanders all around?"

"A timely cure for shoppers' fatigue." Greg flashed Nemmy the OK sign. "Especially for these two victims."

Jimmy turned to Kristin. "Sis, you really came through this time. Angie's luscious, especially in her red little nothing."

"Well? What about me?" Kristin's face pulled into a pout.

"What about you?" Greg teased.

"How do I look in this l'il ole black thing?"

"Luscious, Babe. You sure do." He nuzzled her hair.

Angie leaned toward Kristin. "Your brother does see well enough to know the color of my dress. You said he was blind. What's the deal?"

Kristin laughed. "I'll explain later."

Nemmy served their drinks. "Since you're new, Angie, let me introduce you to some of our regulars." Overhearing their bartender's resonant voice, several customers turned on their bar stools. "The guy there on the left is Peter Chambers, better known around here as PC."

"Pleased to meet you, Angie."

"And I'm pleased to meet you." Her fingertip touched the dimple on her chin. "I know another Peter."

"Pretty popular name, even still," he nodded.

"The Peter I know is a real—um—saint."

A large man next to PC burst into laughter, shoulders bouncing. "PC doesn't even come close to any saint. He's persnickety, self-righteous, and a skirt chaser. No saint, that's for sure."

"But that's not enough to damn somebody." As soon as she'd said it, PC pounded the bar.

"Don't call anyone 'damned.' The phrase of choice is 'salvationally challenged.'"

Groans surged around the bar area. Angie tugged on Kristin's arm. "What's he talking about?"

Kristin rolled her eyes. "That's PC for ya. He's so dogmatic about politically correct terminology."

"What's your name?" Angie nodded toward the heavyset fellow.

"I'm Guy Schwartz." As he got up and headed toward their table with a Perrier bottle in hand, Angie wracked her brain. His name is Ghee?

"How do you spell your first name?"

"G-u-y."

Angie slapped the tabletop with glee. "Ah, Guy, I must have heard wrong."

"No, no, no. It is pronounced 'Ghee,' the French way."

"You're from France? Wonderful. I hear the French create marvelous women's fashions."

"Fashions? Huh? That's not it at all. My folks were Reform Jews. In those days, family policy was to become Americanized every which way. So they named me Guy. And my kid sister they named Heather." Schwartz sighed and slowly shook his head. "She lives in South Dakota now." He scowled. "She's hyphenated it."

"No!" Angie gasped. "You don't say. She can't have children?"

Schwartz seemed befuddled. "Wha...? No, no. Her name. She's hyphenated her name. Our name." He gulped some Perrier. "It's Heather Schwartz-Six Toes now."

"When did that happen? The hyphenating thing?"

"When she married this anthropologist. She was lucky to get him—Kenny Six Toes. Named for a notoriously strange but very wealthy ancestor who made big bucks in Beverly Hills real estate back in the 1920s. And your moniker, Angie? Your surname, actually?"

"Angela Four." One through Three had made Heaven Angel status, she mused. Maybe she would make it after this Mission, too.

Schwartz cupped both hands at his mouth and called to his bar buddies, "Fore." He gestured with the bottle. "See you around, Angela Fore. Time for a refill."

As Schwartz left, she took another sip of the brandy alexander. The smooth creamy beverage tasted so good. "This is a very fine drink." She lifted the glass toward Nemmy.

"Thank you, Angela. Most of our regulars like them." He arched a dark eyebrow Schwartz's way. "Some more than others."

Schwartz shrugged. "I don't guzzle booze because alcohol pickles brain cells. Just because you guys don't care about your bodies doesn't mean I shouldn't care about mine."

A woman wearing a strapless silver dress swirled on her bar stool to taunt him. "What's there about your body for anyone else to care about?"

While the others laughed, Nemmy beckoned Angie to the bar. "Angela, this gorgeous person is Rita. She's a lawyer," he gestured casually and grinned wickedly, "out there."

Squinting her large brown eyes shut for an instant, Rita hissed, "I *hate* to be introduced that way."

"You mean the 'gorgeous' part?" Nemmy smirked.

"I mean the 'lawyer' business. Mention that right off and most people jump to conclusions."

"Hellooo there," Schwartz pointed at her, "you are a lawyer."

"But I don't fit the stereotype. I'm not like other lawyers."

"What's wrong with being a lawyer?" Angie interrupted. "Moses was a lawyer. You remember Mount Sinai, don't you?"

Rita smiled at her. "Thank you, Angie. I like you already." She toyed with a strand of her shoulder-length auburn hair. "I'm more than an ordinary attorney, though. I'm a prosecutor." She sensed Angie's bewilderment. "I try cases for The People."

"You try cases? To see if they work?"

Rita laughed with the others.

"Schwartzie, here, tries big ideas," PC jerked his thumb at Guy. "He's a philosophy prof at the University."

"Oh? I go to a university too."

"In Tulsa?" Schwartz pushed black-rimmed glasses up from the end of a bulbous nose.

"No. Angel University."

Schwartz scratched his balding scalp. "Haven't heard of it. Is it—ahem—an accredited institution?" He winked at Rita.

"By the highest authority." Angie was visibly smug. "It's located near heaven. You know, not actually there but in the neighborhood."

"So you are an angel who goes to some Heavenly Angel University located in a suburb of Heaven, huh?"

"Not Heaven Angel," she pouted. "I'm still just a Mission Angel." Angie looked from face to face. "Why is it everybody around here already knows I'm an angel?" Those at the bar laughed again. She saw Nemmy wink at her. What was he up to?

"Angie, I love your wicked sense of humor." Rita patted her shoulder.

Nemmy resumed the introductions. "This is Tex. Another of our regulars. Tex is, let's see, how shall I say it? He's our guru wannabe."

With a slow grin, Tex tapped the brim of his black Stetson and drawled, "Uh, mighty nice to meet y'all, Miz Angie." Glancing at Nemmy, he pushed an empty glass across the counter. "Ah'm ready for another Laht."

"Laht?" Angie frowned.

"Yes'm. Millah Laht beeh. My favorite beeh."

Jimmy strolled over to Angie. "How about joining us for another round of brandy alexanders?"

"No more. A Pepsi will be fine."

"Oh, come on," Nemmy said with a sly grin. "I've already started making another batch." He snapped on the blender and flashed white teeth at her.

Angie hadn't consumed anything stronger than a Coca-Salsa at McAngel's Fast Food Joint, so Angie was dizzy now.

"Then a Pepsi it will be." Jimmy leaned toward Angie, squeezed her hand and gave her a gentle kiss on the cheek. Angie's heart pounded. She'd never been kissed before. What had she been missing?

Back at their table, Kristin whispered to her. "Angie, I haven't seen my brother this relaxed for months. I think Jimmy's really got a case on you."

"A case? He wants to try a case on me? The way she does?" Angie nodded at Rita.

Before Kristin could answer, Jimmy returned with two more drinks. "Nemmy says he's out of Pepsi. This is yours."

Angie hesitated. Nemmy called from the bar. "Go ahead, angel. It won't kill you."

Jimmy beamed. "Sis, you've goofed on a lot of blind dates you've arranged for me, but all is forgiven. This time you hit the jackpot."

Angie chirped, "I like people that forgive, but what's a jackpot?" Jimmy put his arm around her shoulder and kissed her neck. She blushed.

"She's an angel." Angie jerked her head. There, it happened again. Jimmy called her an angel, too.

The band started playing in Louie's ornately old-fashioned ballroom adjacent to the bar area. A large ball covered with tiny mirrors hung from the ceiling. As it slowly turned, reflections danced on the shiny hardwood floor. In that decor the ball's effect was like wearing work boots with a tux.

Angie accepted Jimmy's invitation to dance, hoping she'd remember Kristin's instruction. As she began, her sense of balance was unsteady. She stepped on his feet a few times, but soon she caught the beat and moved quite gracefully.

Jimmy drew Angie closer, and she leaned her head on his shoulder. She liked being close to him and, although she blushed each time he kissed her cheek or neck, Angie liked that too. He placed his lips on hers in a gentle kiss. She began to understand what those ten pages of files meant in Greg's report. She also remembered how other angels had warned her about such romantic Earther experiences.

"Don't take this Mission," her good friend and confidant, Angel Judy, told her. "A pretty angel like you will surely be tempted by your Mission Guy's lifestyle."

"But his lifestyle sounds like fun." Angie had pouted.

"You scare me. You're heading for trouble. Big trouble."

Regardless, Angie had been intrigued by the Greg Matthews Mission folder. She reminded herself that this Mission was doable and that if she pulled it off, she would graduate to Heaven Angel status. A big promotion. No more classes, no more books, no more professors' exasperated looks. She had just had it!

As a Heaven Angel, she'd be living the life of Riley. (Angel Riley had returned for a pajama party with Angie and her dorm mates at Angel U. She had filled them in on Heaven Angels' party-time-all-the-time schedule.)

When the four regrouped at their table, Jimmy said it was time for another round of drinks.

"No more for me." Angie hiccuped. "My head feels funny."

Greg groaned.

"Aw, come on," Kristin prodded, "let her have a good time."

"But you don't understand. She's been very sheltered up until now."

"Sheltered? I have never been homeless," Angie huffed.

"What I mean is that, well, you've lived a rather protected life."

Angie rested her head on Jimmy's shoulder. "You've got it all turned around. I'm the one that does the protecting and caregiving."

Jimmy nibbled on her earlobe. Twice. That doubled her Hearing-Power. With all the New Year's Eve party noise, the doubled din rattled her angelic skull bones. Angie quickly tapped her other earlobe to return the decibels to normal. Whew!

"Greg's right." Angie raised her head from Jimmy's shoulder. "I've got to be a good girl."

"But do I have to be a good boy?" His blue eyes gleamed.

Kristin rose quickly from her chair, grabbed Angie's arm and said, "Come on hon, let's go powder our noses."

Angie felt her nose. "Powder our noses? Why?" She didn't know what Kristin meant, but she followed her anyway.

She should have read at least the EE volume on conversational Americanese. Angel Peggy Sue had warned Angie that Earthers say things they don't mean, and that Earther language is most peculiar. Angie wished now she hadn't been in such a hurry to come back to earth. She had not anticipated such drastic changes since George Washington's time.

"Wait up, gals." Rita left her bar stool. "My nose needs powdering, too."

The ladies' lounge had red shag carpet. Six mirrors framed one wall. Make-up lights surrounded each mirror. Kristin, Angie, and Rita settled on small red velvet cushioned chairs in front of the mirrors. Rita opened her purse and pulled out a lipstick, eyebrow pencil, and eye shadow. Kristin dabbed at her lips with a tube of autumn rust lipstick that complemented her hair. Angie began brushing her blonde curls.

Rita excused herself. "Be right back." She went to a stall.

"Are you having a good time, hon?"

Before Angie had a chance to answer, a thirty-something woman stomped into the ladies' room. Angie was intrigued by the tattoos on the woman's arms, but not for long. She grabbed Angie's spaghetti straps and shouted, "You slut! Floozy!" Angie had never heard such words, but she was sure they were not kind words.

"Let go of my dress! It's brand new!"

"If I can't have him, no bimbo is gonna take my place."

The woman shoved Angie to the floor.

"Take that—stud-stealer!"

FOUR

"I'm not a thief." Angie jumped to her feet with angelic agility. "I'm an angel!"

"You're a witch!"

"Denise! Stop it! She's my friend," Kristin said as Denise shoved her aside. "Born To Fight" was tattooed on her right biceps.

"You stay out of this, Kristin. She's mine!" Before Angie knew what was happening, Denise socked her in the jaw. Blood oozed from a corner of Angie's mouth.

"Oh my God!" Kristin's palms pressed her cheeks.

"G, Kristin, G!" Angie yelled to stop Kristin from saying The Name out loud. Her jaw ached. Enough was enough. Mission or no Mission, she had to *Zap* back to Angel U to research her Double-E issues. The wages of ignorance had gotten to her—right in the jaw.

Angie touched the Travel bar on her *Zap* barrette. Nothing happened. She panicked. What was she going to do?

Favoring a classic boxing stance—rather than Mohammed Ali's open style—Denise came at her, fists cocked just below her chin. Angie's heart pounded. Onlookers backed off from the combatants.

Angie stomped on Denise's toes. "Take that, bad person."

"You little devil!" Denise hissed as one thumb swiped her nose.

"I'm not a devil. I'm an angel."

"Angel, ha! Stud stealer!"

Rita, a Taekwondo expert, burst from the stall, jammed her right foot into Denise's mid-section and yelled, "Kaaaaaaaaaachijah!" Denise's body made a loud thump when she fell to the floor.

News of the ruckus traveled quickly. Women swarmed into the lounge to watch the action. Foreclosed from exercising that ladies' prerogative, men could only cluster outside the open door.

"Will someone please tell me who this woman is and what she wants?" Angie pleaded. Denise lay semi-conscious on the floor.

"She's Jimmy's ex-wife, and I reckon she's trying to get even." Kristin wiped blood from Angie's cut lip with a tissue.

"But, but why didn't you tell me Jimmy has such terrible taste in women?"

"She seemed nice enough when they got married, but not more than six months later, family and friends noticed the change in her. Denise had fallen in with evil companions at the Catholic Sperm Bank where she works." Kristin dabbed at another drop of blood. "She's their refrigeration engineer, an Aggie grad gone bad."

"But, you should have warned me."

"If I'd told you about that spicy dab of family history, would you have come here with my brother?"

"Of course not. What kind of an angel do you think I am?"

"Come on, all of you, let's get back to the bar." Rita straightened her dress and hair.

Angie glanced at Denise sprawled on the floor. She actually felt sorry for her. If only she had known about Denise, she could have avoided this disaster by not agreeing to go on this blind date in the first place. "We can't go back yet. We've got to help Denise."

"We can't help Denise. Trust me. I know this woman, and it's best to get out of here before she comes to." Kristin reached for Angie's hand.

"But, but will she be okay?"

"Let me put it this way. You stay here, and she'll beat you to a bloody pulp."

"But a Good Samaritan can't just leave her lying half dead by the side of the vanity."

The drinks made Angie's head spin, knees wobble, and shoulders sag. That's why she forgot an important point: since she is an angel, there is no way she could be fatally injured. But that didn't preclude her getting beat up.

Potential disaster loomed larger. Angie tapped her *Zap* barrette's Travel bar again, hoping she could *Zap* back to Angel U. No such luck. No matter how hard she pushed on the barrette, she remained at Louie's Place.

Back at their table, Angie accused Jimmy. "Why didn't you tell me about Denise?"

"Angie just met Denise in the ladies' room," Kristin said. "Met her right fist, actually."

"Oh no. I'm outta' here. Sorry, Angie. Bye, hon." Jimmy gave his sister a quick peck on the cheek and hurried to the nearest exit.

Angie was bewildered. "How could Jimmy possibly have married that awful Earther woman?"

"Denise surprised us all. After those first six months, she started shooting pool, playing cards, getting tattoos on her arms and other strategic body parts, watching MTV. We should have known. I'm sorry about Denise showing up like that." Kristin patted Angie's hand.

"I never dreamed she'd be here," Greg said. "Isn't this her prayer meeting night?"

"I doubt she goes anymore since she started hanging out with bikers."

"Don't judge a person by their bike. Archangel Gabriel not only drives a BMW but is in the market for a Harley-Davidson. And he prays. Lots!"

Angie's attitude about the evening improved, however, when midnight came. Pink, yellow, blue, and white confetti swirled in the room. Everyone either blew a horn or kissed somebody. Angie discovered kissing was more fun than horn-blowing.

Kristin didn't know what to make of Angie, who was still unsteady as they entered Greg's apartment. "Come on, hon, I'll make up the bed and brew fresh coffee."

"Don't you know coffee has caffeine and caffeine's not good for the body?" Angie had one arm around Kristin's shoulder and her other arm around Greg for support. "Can I have another gregerick drink?"

"A brandy alexander has caffeine in it, too," Greg said.

"Ah yes, but it also has milk in it." Angie lifted a finger and waved it back and forth. "Milk's good for you." She hiccuped. "Did you know I designed cows?"

Kristin and Greg ignored her question, helped Angie to the sofa. She stretched out, her left leg slipping over the edge of the cushions. "I've never felt this relaxed." She frowned at Greg. "We must explain to Kristin who I am and why I'm here. The truth is I'm an angel, not his cousin. I'm a Mission Angel enrolled at Angel University."

"Greg, the woman needs help. She was talking crazy in the ladies' lounge, too. She told Denise that she's an angel when that sleezeball tried to kill her."

Angie jerked to a sitting position, her head clearing. "Not to worry. No one can kill me, Kristin. I've never been dead. I began when time began. When the Lord said, 'Let there be light,' He also said, 'Let there be Angela.' That should have been in a footnote for Genesis One. I wanted it in, but the editors voted against all footnotes. Anyway, when I was in heaven, I failed my first Mission, even before Lucifer showed up in Eden. You remember about Eden?" Kristin and Greg nodded.

"Anyway, the Lord decided we angels should make ourselves useful, do something besides sing praises all the time and fly hither and thither. So, on the day he was creating animals, he turned over the actual design jobs to us. Wouldn't you know, I botched mine."

"Which was?" Kristin asked.

"Cows. He told me to design cows. Made just two little mistakes. But I got everything else right."

"Which were? The mistakes, I mean."

"First, I goofed on udder placement. I figured a cow's udder belongs on her forehead so she could keep an eye on who's milking her." Angie sighed. "I forgot about the horns."

"Ouch!"

"M was able to fix it, though."

"*M?*" Greg laughed. "Sounds like that James Bond character."

"I'm talking about the Angel of the Lord. What did you say? M sounds like James who?"

"Bond. James Bond."

"M. Here, I'll write it out for you." Angie wrote MALAK on a slip of paper and showed it to them.

"Malak?" they chorused.

"Shush, you two. Can't speak his name. M is that close to G."

"G?" Kristin sighed.

"Explain to you later...K." Greg turned to Angie. "What was your second mistake with cows?"

"I made them blondes. Like me." Angie twirled a curl with her left hand. "A last-minute impulse, I guess, just before the production line started turning out my cows. Even then it all looked so good on the CAD printout."

"CAD? As in Computer-Assisted-Design? You had this technology way back then?" Greg gawked at her.

"You know about CAD?" With a sly look, she added, "I suppose that next you're gonna tell me you know all about the IBM two-zero-zero-gamma I used, huh?"

"Sheezz," Greg slapped a hand on his forehead. "IBM too."

"Intergalactic Brainy Mechanisms," she glanced from Kristin to Greg. "Ten trigs on the board, a real powerhouse."

"She means RAM, ten trigs of RAM."

"No, no!" Angie shook her head. "Angel Sophie designed rams, not me. As I was saying, those two mistakes short-circuited cows' genetic code and produced another defect that still persists. I'd designed cows so they could say to their farmer, 'Milk me, fella.'"

"And?"

"Instead, now all they can say is Mmooo."

Greg tried again. "Let me get this straight. Lucifer and his bunch fell from heaven because of pride. You fell for making several minor mistakes when you designed cows? That's what your telling us?"

"You have the first part right. But no, I didn't fall from heaven, like Lucifer and Nemesis and Hermes and the rest of their ilk. I got a demotion in status. The Bible Speak word for it is *menuddeh*. Like the publican praying in the temple, in that parable, demoted to a place in the back. I got demoted to Mission Angel status."

Angie took a deep breath and pursed her lips. "Heaven Council handed down my ruling right after the mess in Eden. That's when they realized they'd need lots of us Mission Angels. For Missions like you, Greg."

No one spoke for at least a minute. "Greg, you're my chance, my Mission. If we can succeed on all three parts of our Mission agenda, I'll graduate, gain Heaven Angel status. And—um—get my voice back."

"Your voice?"

"We Mission Angels suffer from *menuddeh* monotone. Voice lessons don't help." She shook her head slowly. "G knows I've tried."

"*Menuddeh*...monotone?" Greg asked.

"Sounds like Episcopalians chanting. Another demotion, this time in music quality." She leaned forward, lowering her voice. "It's a little known fact that when four Mission Angels were down here trying to help Ann Boleyn keep her head—you know, Henry the Eighth and all that— Henry strolls into one of his cathedrals while the four of them were practicing for their next monotone voice lesson with Gabriel. Ol' Henry was dumbfounded. He could actually understand the words they were singing.

"Turns out that *menuddeh* monotone matches the reverberation rates of old cathedrals better than just speaking. Almost as well as gangsta rap, in fact. *Voila!* Henry likes it. Orders his priests to use that monotone from then on. Only, because Episcopalians believe in Salvation by Good Taste, they call it chanting instead of its celestial term, churchy monotone."

Angie hunched her shoulders. "Frankly, I much prefer the gangsta rap style over churchy monotone because it moves. Gets things rocking, spiritually speaking. Know what I mean?"

Kristin said, "Incredible, Angie. Absolutely off the wall."

When Angie asked for another brandy, Greg and Kristin exchanged alarmed glances. His mother had been a recovering alcoholic for fifteen years.

"Alcohol can become a deception, Angie. Its relaxing effect, that is. A lot of drunks travel that road."

"Drunks?"

"People who use booze as a drug. As my sainted grandmother used to say, 'That's why boozers is losers.'"

Kristin giggled. "She never quite got the knack of connecting plural verbs with plural nouns. Never lost her Swedish accent, either."

"All they serve at the McAngel's is Coca-Salsa. I also like putting some on a cowburger now and then." Angie tried to snap her fingers. "Now I remember reading about drunkenness in Greg's files."

"There you go again about those files," Kristin said. "Angie, there's so much about you that baffles me." She leaned toward her. "But, I want you to know that both of us care about you, very much."

"That means a lot to me, knowing both of you care for me, too. Along with delivering G's messages to Earthers, our other main job as Mission Angels is to be Caregivers. Messengers and Caregivers, that's us."

As his grandfather's clock struck 4 A.M. Greg sluggishly wished everyone a Happy New Year and headed to bed.

Kristin sat by Angie on the sofa as the two sipped fresh coffee.

"You're such an angel to take care of an angel." Angie smiled and closed her eyes. "The Bible talks about entertaining angels, and that's what you and Greg are doing."

Kristin sighed. "Hon, I know that Bible verse. But right now..."

"You know that verse?"

"Sure do. I went through eighth grade in the Christian day school at our church back home." Kristin laughed. "Couldn't help but learn a lot of Bible. In Hebrews 13:2 it says, 'Do not forget to entertain strangers, for by so doing some people have entertained angels without knowing it.' "

Angie jolted upright. "You do know the verse." She squeezed her new friend's hand. "Kristin, you entertained an angel tonight but still don't realize it. Me."

Some time later, Angie slowly opened her eyes. She had dozed off on Greg's sofa. Kristin was nowhere in sight. She had returned to her apartment.

Angie's swollen jaw showed some black and purple color. But she felt happier than she'd ever been on any other Mission. She loved today's Earthers. Finally, she drifted into a deep sleep.

Angie heard the doorbell, but her response was a groan. She had never been a morning angel, jump-out-of-bed, hit-the-floor-running. No way. Not at all like Angel Peggy Sue, who was gung ho at the crack of dawn. Angie discovered that idiosyncrasy when the two bunked together during their most recent Mission Maneuvers camp-out on Oreo.

> Angie was used to hearing the rattling sound of dawn. On both the Patty and Cakes sides of planet Oreo, very large sunshades are hung on sky hooks, rolled back up at 6 a.m. Since there is no night there, the arrangement does help Mission Angels get some shut-eye. Engineering has yet to solve one minor problem, however. For their morning roll-ups, both shades zip up far too fast when the latches release.

So, Mission Angels hear the crack of dawn at a volume unknown to Earthers. *Editor.*

When the doorbell rang again, Angie realized she'd better answer it. It was Kristin. After the two chatted a few minutes, Angie prepared a robust, from-scratch hot breakfast for the three of them. She needed instructions on how to operate the new-fangled Earther kitchen equipment. She giggled when Kristin showed her how the stove turned on with just a flick of a finger. The microwave reminded her of some higher-tech features at *Zap* Central. It was refreshing not to have to draw water from a well and to have a big box that provided its own ice. Amazing.

Although Kristin and Greg invited Angie to join them for the day, she chose to remain at Greg's to see what inroads she could make on this pigpen he called home.

After they left, Angie made a list of cleaning needs and Zapfaxed it to Angel Bert. He had Angelic Custodial Services get the items to her by Priority *Zap* in less than ten Earther minutes. All were state-of-the-art stuff, (super)naturally, and environmentally orthodox. There was the Slime-and-Grime Flashlight; its rays immediately restored sinks, faucets, cabinets, and walls to spotless mint condition. The Buster Bar, when dragged across carpet or hard-surfaced floors, instantly vaporized all soils, dust, and stains within a foot of the thing. Angie placed a Vunder Valet in Greg's guest room. It not only cleaned clothes but automatically folded and stacked each piece in a collator-type gizmo alongside the machine.

When Kristin and Greg returned that evening, they were stunned to see an immaculate apartment. Not only had this miracle worker cleaned, but she had prepared a gourmet meal. Kristin added some candles and the three of them feasted on a seafood dinner that prompted Greg to smack his lips and rejoice with a "*Magnifico.*"

After eating, Angie encouraged Kristin to join Greg in the living room while she tried out his new-fangled dishwashing machine. Just as her new friends cozied up on the couch, Guy Schwartz dropped by to talk with Greg. He was impressed with Greg's talent and took this opportunity to offer him an exciting career change opportunity. It was a new MBA program at the University in Quantified Team Building.

Guy was stunned when he saw Greg's immaculate abode.

"Either you have a new girlfriend or Kristin suddenly turned into Susie Homemaker." Guy snickered as he jabbed his elbow into Greg's side. He sent Kristin a teasing wink. "Which is it?"

"Kristin's still my squeeze, but you wouldn't believe me if I told you how this apartment got so clean."

"Surely, little elves didn't do it."

"No, but you're getting close. An Angel U. student came in and cleaned."

"Honey?" Kristin tried to interrupt what she considered nonsense.

"Everything's okay, Kristin. A professor understands university students and their needs better than most."

"*What* U? Where did I hear of that school? Ahh. The beautiful blonde with you guys last night."

"Yeah. She goes there. She did all of this." Greg's hand swept around.

"Amazing. She's a remarkable young woman."

"Not really. Amazing, yes. Young woman, no." Greg grinned at the professor. Guy's jaw set, his eyes squinted. "She's an angel. Really, Guy. I'm halfway sure she's a genuine angel."

"Greg, I know you've been though a lot lately. What with your divorce and all, it's been a tough time. I've been divorced twice myself and, if there's ever any way I can help, just give me a call. Sometimes we divorced guys can get pretty messed up in our heads."

"Look at me. I've got to be the envy of every married man we know. I've got a terrific gal who loves me. True, Kristin may not be the world's best housekeeper, but that's where Angie comes in. She's great at fixing up a place and an excellent cook. She'd make Martha Stewart look like a slouch."

"This angel cooks, too?"

"Does she ever. She used to cook for George Washington's cousin. Angie's delightful. She squeals when she turns on the stove because she doesn't have to carry in wood. And you'd think my microwave was God's—excuse me," his eyes briefly shot upward, "G's gift to her." Greg grinned. "Couldn't be a better set up. Kristin won't be nagging me to take her out to eat like she used to, not as long as Angie's here."

"Right." Guy rolled his eyes at Kristin. "As I said, divorce can get pretty rough on some people. How about coming to our support group for divorcees? Some nifty chicks there."

"Support group? With what's going on here, who needs it?" Greg's manner moderated. "Truth is, I didn't think I was going to like Angie when she first arrived."

"Really?"

"Yeah. She just *Zaps* in here and starts telling me I need to get my act together. And that my doing so is her Mission." He counted off each finger. "First, she tells me, I've gotta get rid of Lucifer's deceptions cluttering up my life. Second, my eyes have to open to see what the Lord has been doing in my life. Third—and this is the toughie—Angie says I've gotta forgive Marge for what she did to my Bimmer."

Guy scuffed his black loafers first with one foot and then with the other. "I wasn't going to say anything about this, but, frankly, the guys at Louie's have been worried about you since the divorce. Maybe I'll just saunter over there right now for some bar-stool consultation."

"Fine." Greg slapped the arm of his chair. "Tell them I've got me a genuine angel, a career-change opportunity, and the best squeeze a fella could want. Let 'em weep, huh, Guy?"

"Have it your way. Just remember. We're your friends, and if you ever need anything, just let us know." With a casual wave, Guy left.

Kristin was alarmed to hear Greg still talking as though he really believed Angie was an angel. What's happening? Maybe Guy is right. Greg may be more disoriented after his divorce and disappointing career than she had realized. Angie has thoroughly conned Greg. Who is she—*really*?

The situation called for expert help, Kristin concluded. She'd make an appointment with a psychiatrist who'd grown up in her old neighborhood.

She knew Greg would never consent to therapy or Group, so she had to persuade Angie to attend so Greg would accompany her. She'd also tag along.

"Greg, your cousin really needs help. Do you remember a guy from Lubbock, Bill Billie, the psychiatrist? He isn't taking new patients, but I think I could persuade him to let Angie visit Group." Angie emerged from the kitchen.

"I was just telling Greg that I think you could use some help coping with life here in Tulsa. My friend, Bill, is a psychiatrist who mentors Tulsa's longest-running Group therapy operation. His Group could help you. I'll call to make an appointment."

"You'd do that for *me*? You are so caring. Um, what's a psychiatrist?"

Before anyone could answer, Kristin dialed the phone.

"Bill, is that you? Kristin Goldfarb. Listen, I've got a friend, actually two friends...I know you aren't seeing new patients. You owe me one. Get this. My friend thinks she's an angel and Greg believes her...uh huh...Really."

Dr. William Billie told her: "In my years of practicing psychiatry, I've had six Gods, ten Jesus Christs, four mother Marys, and six angels."

"But have you ever had an angel who attends a university in outer space, Angel U on a planet Oreo, which she claims is in heaven's neighborhood?"

"Bring 'em to Group at nine Monday morning. These wackos may be just what I need to cap off my next book."

"Greg, I made an appointment for you and Angie with Dr. Billie's Group therapy session on Monday. When I told him you believe Angie's a real angel, and she thinks she is, too, he said 'Bring them both in.'"

Angie was amenable to going simply to please Kristin. Greg's resistance melted under the high-voltage assault of another of Kristin's expert cutsey-lovey-dovey routines.

FIVE

Meanwhile, Zap Central was in an uproar. In the Crisis Response Clubhouse, one group of engineering angels huddled around Angel Bert at his console. They conferred after each new combination of switches failed to raise Angie through her *Zap* barrette. Another group worked at a large conference table. They studied maps and charts as they crunched torrents of data generated by the massive Lenox Dish Array as it scanned Oklahoma via Zap Central's viciously fast feral-neural computer.

Where is Angela Four?

They hadn't heard from her for several Earther days. Everyone at Zap Central worked on The Problem: how to locate Angela Four and reopen communication.

Over in the problem-solving corner of the large room, another team of angels tossed option darts at special electronic dart boards. A trio of angels wearing yarmulkes on their heads sought the Angie-solution through *pilpul* argumentation, a form of rabbinic logic.

A quartet of tonsured angels in brown robes struggled with the problem using medieval Scholastic logic, but they were hung up on whether Angie was only a Nominalist construct or a Reality to be located. The Hegelian foursome were banging their foreheads together trying to achieve synthesis, getting dizzier by the minute. (Hegel was a 19th-century philosopher who held that by butting thesis against antithesis, synthesis—the truth—would result. *Editor*) Yet another consortium of philosophers, the Contemporaries, were out to lunch, each eating alone.

Where is Angela Four?

Until Gabriel got back from an emergency session of Heaven Council, Raphael filled in as temporary Supreme Supervisor of *Zap* Central, ill at ease out of his usual bailiwick as Ultimate Coordinator of Field Work.

"Anything new?" Raphael asked Bert.

Bert shook his head. "We can't communicate with Angie via her Zapper, her Zapfax, or even make her Zapmike howl, Raphael, sir. At least not yet."

Raphael steered clear of the problem-solving clusters of angels. All of them already had celestial tenure. But, whenever they went into this academic mode, they kept forgetting The Problem they were supposed to solve.

Raphael stood in a corner and looked over the chaotic scene. Nearby, a janitor angel finished emptying another wastebasket full of paper wads into a large bag. "Sir?" Raphael didn't hear him. "Raphael, sir?" the custodial angel, who was shy and soft-spoken, persisted. "Could it be that Angela Four took off her *Zap* barrette while washing her hair and just forgot to put it back on? With all due respect, sir, angels in the Blondes Division have been known to do that. Your Ultimacy, sir."

"Set the switches to Barrette Vibration." Raphael's voice boomed across the room. "Crank them all the way up to the Annoy-the-Neighbors setting." He turned to the humble janitor, peering down at the name tag on the slight figure's coveralls. "Thank you, Willy. It just might work."

"What's that noise?" Greg was startled. A very loud buzzing sound came from the bathroom.

"My *Zap* barrette. I forgot to put it back on." Angie jumped from the couch and, seconds later, returned from the bathroom while installing the double-barred gold clip in her hair. With the final click of its fastener, a voice boomed from the palm of her left hand.

"Calling Angela Four. Raphael, here. Come in, Angie."

Angie gulped, blushing with embarrassment. To think she had forgotten to wear her Zapper. She raised her right thumbnail to her lips and timidly replied, "Angela, Four. Your Ultimacy (gulp), Sir." At the sound of Angie's voice, a roar of cheers came from the CRC at Zap Central.

However, the academicians continued their frantic mental work-out regimens. Two unconscious Hegelians, victims of their usual methodological concussions, were being carried out by Medic Angels while the remaining two kept banging their foreheads together.

A beaming Raphael went over to inform the rest that the problem of Angie's whereabouts was solved. But he was greeted with a storm of tenured protest. Since the Angie-solution had come from outside any of their parochial methodological parameters, the academicians insisted The Solution couldn't have happened, did not exist.

"Just listen." Raphael pointed to the happy cluster crowded around Bert's console. But the academicians' hands slapped over their ears to shut out the obvious. Their eyes slammed shut like errant toilet seats. Raphael threw up his arms in frustration and returned to the console area to get in on Angie's debriefing.

"Angie, you had all of us worried sick." Raphael scolded. "Why haven't you tried to contact us before now to keep us informed about your Mission?"

"But I did try. The first night I was on Earth, on New Year's Eve."

"Hummm. We didn't hear one scratch from you."

"But, I tried six or seven times."

"We heard nothing."

"Could there be something wrong with my barrette? I don't know what's going on, and I sure don't like it. I've got to communicate with you guys to work with me on my Mission here."

"Of course," Raphael quickly agreed. "Tell me something Angie. Had you washed your hair awhile ago?"

"Yes, (gulp) I did." Angie was embarrassed.

"Okay then. So naturally we couldn't communicate with you since you weren't wearing your Zapper. Anytime you take it off, you've got to put your Zapper back on as soon as you can."

"Yes, I'm sorry. But why couldn't I *Zap* travel or communicate with you on New Year's Eve?"

"I'm baffled by that one, too," Bert added.

"So am I," Raphael said. "We received reports that you had too much to drink and got in a fight at Louie's Place."

"Well, just go ahead and announce my mistakes to all the Mission Angels, or better yet, the entire Celestial System." Angie was annoyed that Raphael would do such a thing.

Raphael tried to speak in a comforting tone. "Something's wrong, Angie, seriously wrong. A properly-installed *Zap* barrette has gone dysfunctional. Impossible. This has never happened before." ☆ *See Angel Beepsie's End Notes*

Angie could hear the other Mission Angels gossiping about her in the background. But Raphael interrupted them.

"Please, angels, please, I must have silence so I can hear Angie when she speaks on her Zapmike."

"But how could my Zapper not work when I was wearing it?" Angie was as confused as everyone else.

Angel Barbie, the brainiest of the current crop of Mission Angels, bared her neglected, greenish teeth. "Look, are we going to sit on our butts talking about her Zapper, or do we investigate whether something else could be the significant variable here?"

Raphael spoke into his Zapmike. "We'll do everything we can at Mission Control to find out what's gone wrong, Angela. We're on it."

"Thanks." After several good-byes, Angie signed off. Her heart began pounding as she feared the worst. Was she stranded?

Meanwhile, Kristin and Greg cherished their new-found domesticated friend. Except for some strange quirks and weird notions, her unassuming manner was quite refreshing. Kristin enjoyed taking Angie shopping and showing her around Tulsa. Her naivete and off-the-wall ideas prompted much laughter.

It was fun to teach her about Earthers' taste, such as their passion for pizza. Cooperative, always. Uninformed, usually. One evening after Angie and Kristin had been shopping, Kristin suggested they buy a pizza.

"Sounds good to me." What on earth is pizza anyway? Angie remembered when the Lord made all kinds of food on the third and fifth days of creation. But where was she when G created pizza?

Kristin paid for the pizza with a credit card. Angie was amazed that Earthers could simply sign their names on a strip of paper to buy things.

Back at the apartment, Kristin opened the wide, flat box. Angie liked the aroma and came over for her first glimpse of pizza.

"Yuck!" Angie moaned, staring at the round thing. It reminded her of another food item she had once seen. That experience went back to another of her botched Missions: Lena, a sex-crazed Viking warrior princess back in the eleventh century. Then, as now, Norwegians liked to eat lefse, something like a thin tortilla but made from potatoes.

"Why do you say yuck? Everybody loves pizza."

Disdain contorted Angie's face. "Looks like somebody threw up on that lefse."

From her Swedish-Jewish ethnic heritage, Kristin knew about lefse and burst into laughter. "Angie, you're a stitch." She lifted a slice to demonstrate how to eat pizza. Handing another slice to her friend, she urged, "Try some. It's much better than lefse. Go ahead. Just close your eyes and try a bite."

Angie did. She nodded. "This pizza stuff does taste good. A lot better than it—um—looks."

☆ *Angel Beepsie's End Notes*
Zappers were perfected in the late sixteenth century, Earther time, and have never once failed since then. Through special dispensation, Heaven Council loaned its inventor to the Engineering Department. The design was the product of the greatest, but least known, genius of that century: Thomasius Quintillan Martinus Luthero. Or, TQM, for short.

He was the reformer's youngest and Katy's favorite child. Historians mistakenly regard him as such a cipher that Tommy Luther's existence is rarely noted, even in the most arcane of scholarly works. Tommy's entrance into their German home was memorable for Katy. Twelve pounds at birth, after a ten-month pregnancy. "No more hanky-panky, Doctor, without protection," she'd told her husband.

TQM's sole publication, *Toward Anfechtungen: A Techno-Theology of Bungee Jumping,* bombed in bookstores. (*Anfechtungen:* a very bad case of burnout.) Its failure not only turned him off from further authorship but precipitated his demise.

As history's first empirical scientist, TQM ventured to prove his premise by leaping off the spire of Leipzig's St. Thomas Church. However, his goat-intestines bungee line stretched just a teensy bit too far.

Michael recruited him soon after the youngest Luther took up Celestial residence, even before TQM had fully recovered from a substantial headache. Inspired by his mother's typical reflex of jamming one hand on her head whenever he'd stretched her patience too far, Luther the Youngest came up with the barrette concept.

He also radically simplified complex *Zap* functions and designed Zapper mechanisms in two models: the barrette and belt buckle versions. The buckle design responded to market research results that showed that Earthers giggle at male angels who wear barrettes. The real beauty of either design is that on-duty Mission Angels can access the mechanisms so casually.

SIX

Monday morning, our Tulsa trio arrived at Dr. William Billie's office shortly before Group's 9 A.M. "kickoff," as he encouraged members to call it. As an undergraduate, Bill Billie had turned into a fanatic fan of OSU football, abetted by his stint as Reserve Water Boy all four years.

They waited in the posh reception room where the morning sun streamed through beige venetian blinds onto a neutral carpet and beige leather furniture. Earth tone artwork was tastefully displayed on beige grass cloth walls. Marilyn, the bubble gum-chewing receptionist, sat at her desk enjoying her usual game of computer solitaire.

Dr. Billie was running late. For fourteen years now, he'd been working through Mommy issues in three 8 A.M. sessions a week with his own analyst, a throw-back orthodox Freudian specializing in Regression Therapy. Dr. Billie's tardiness resulted from the tail end of what his analyst proclaimed was a "real breakthrough," finally achieving their agreed-upon goal of two hundred such breakthroughs by the anniversary of their first session. Both analysts had sobbed for joy in each others arms for five minutes, delaying Dr. Billie's quick change from diapers back into street clothes.

William Billie, M.D., also had become a popular local talk show guest, especially after he'd gained a highly profitable Board Certification in Pet Therapy, specializing in unruly puppies. His nearest competition was in Oklahoma City. As the only puppy shrink in town, Dr. Billie's monthly bottom line was looking mighty healthy indeed.

Boogles of fees enabled him to assemble his pride and joy, the largest private collection of voodoo dolls in Oklahoma. Another collection revealed why he'd become a nationally-respected connoisseur of acrylic nudes painted on the black velvet medium, most items dating from the Regressive Realism school.

Dr. Billie wasn't only chasing big bucks. No sirreee. Ongoing diligence in retaining his research acumen was reflected in the nineteen papers on anal retentive behaviors he'd delivered at Tulsa's APA chapter meetings over the years. This also led to his longtime role and retainer fees as consultant to the Charmin Foundation.

"Marilyn, I want you to take notes for Group. I've got two new clients coming today. Miss Angela thinks she's an angel, and the guy agrees with her."

Marilyn glanced up from her computer and popped her bubble gum. She shrugged. "I'm not impressed. Need I remind you, Dr. Billie, in the years I've worked here you've had six Gods, ten Jesus Christs, four mother Marys, and six angels? Now we have a seventh angel. What else is new?"

Dr. Billie's baby blue eyes gleamed. "But this woman claims she's an angel who attends some university in outer space near heaven."

Dr. Bill Billie playfully pricked the next, unusually large bubble she blew, using a hidden hat pin. His favorite practical joke, it always set him off into an unprofessional fit of giggles. Peeling bubble gum from her nose and chin, Marilyn glowered at her boss.

"Oh? A college student? Actually, your new clients are sitting behind you. You're late. The rest are already in Group room waiting for you."

He approached the trio. Angie sat beneath a Post-Impressionist oil of a cat hanging from one paw on a tree limb. Across the bottom, in French, was the classic motto: *Dieu et mon droit* which, very roughly translated, amounts to "Hang in there, baby."

"Kristin, how nice to see you again."

She shook his hand and smiled warmly. "This is Greg, and this is my new friend, Angie."

"I'm so happy to meet you." Angie bubbled. "I don't know if Kristin told you, but I'm an angel. I'm having a hard time coping with earth this time around."

Dr. Billie suppressed a knowing grin and scratched his scalp. "As a matter of fact, Kristin did mention that. I'm pleased to meet you." He stroked a graying goatee. "Please, won't the three of you follow me, and we'll join the rest of this morning's Group."

As the four headed down the corridor, Marilyn chided, "Unh, unh, unh" while making a money gesture with her fingers.

Kristin blushed, returned to the desk, and opened her purse. She handed Marilyn a check. "I almost forgot."

"Fat chance. You know the rule: pay up front or go out back." Marilyn slipped the check into her bodice and blew a rather large bubble as she turned back to computer solitaire.

A sign on the door read: Bertha Billie Memorial Group Room. Bertha, Bill's mother, died not so long ago.

Large brightly colored bean bags arranged in a circle accented the Bertha Billie Memorial Group Room. Sunlight streamed through sheer multicolored drapes. Other clients of Dr. Billie's nested on the bags.

"Find yourselves a bean bag, and we'll get started," the erudite doctor gestured.

No sooner had the four entered when Angie got a whiff of an odor only angelic nasal passages can detect.

Her heart pounded. That unpleasant odor was a dead giveaway. Lucifer is in here. But which one of these Earthers was he? That immortal Master of Disguise liked to torment her by showing up in different forms on every one of her Missions. Angie realized he might even be the very bean bag she sank into. She was absolutely furious. No way would she have come if she'd known the devil was going to be here.

"This will never work," Angie stormed. "I can't attend Group if Lucifer—the devil—is part of it."

Dr. Billie smiled benevolently. "The devil, you say. Which one of us?" He feigned sincerity as he pointed to his chest. "Is it I?" Around the circle, in turn, everyone on a bean bag said the same thing, "Is it I?"

Angie's heart sank. She could smell him, but she'd be dinged if she would join him. However, since Lucifer hadn't chosen to reveal the form he'd assumed in this Group session, she had no option but to wait him out.

Rushing to the wall intercom, Dr. Billie bellowed, "Marilyn, get in here. Hurry, I need you to take notes *now*." Marilyn, yellow legal pad and pen in hand, jiggled her overweight way to a white bean bag. Dr. Billie continued. "You've already met Miss Angela. Take notes please. First of all, Miss Angela believes Lucifer, the devil, is in Group today."

"The devil?" Marilyn blew a bubble. "Doesn't that take all." She pulled her favorite practical joke on her boss, flashing both thighs his way. But since her copious thighs bore a striking resemblance to pink fire hydrants, there was nothing obscene to be seen.

Dr. Billie scowled at his receptionist and non-verbally scolded her with quick jerks of his head toward the others. He reached over and patted Angie's shoulder. "Later I can prescribe a tranquilizer for you, but for right now would you care for some coffee or a cup of tea before we begin? It might help you to relax."

"No thanks. But I'd love a brandy frederick. That's what'll help me relax."

"She means brandy *alexander*," Kristin said.

"We don't have alcohol here. Alcohol can be a crutch for too many people."

"A crutch?" Angie frowned. "How can you walk on liquid?"

Seeing Dr. Billie nod at Marilyn to write that down on her legal pad, Greg tried to clarify. "Angie hasn't kept up on her EE studies."

"EE?" Marilyn's eyebrows arched.

"Earthers Encyclopedia. It gives up-to-date information about earth and its inhabitants."

"Ahhh. Of course." Dr. Billie nodded again at his receptionist. More scribbling. "Are you saying then, Mr. Matthews, that you believe Miss Angela is an angel?"

"The evidence I've seen thus far would sure make that a reasonable conclusion."

"Evidence? Gimme some for instances."

While Kristin shook her head in dismay, Greg described her *Zap* appearance and demonstration of her Quickie *Zap*. Her Zapfax, Zapmike, and ZapCD, and that experience with Evelyn. Marilyn scribbled furiously. While Greg described Evelyn's breaking wind, an excited Dr. Billie caught Kristin's attention. With an exaggerated wink, he concealed his mouth and an index finger jabbing in Greg's direction. He mouthed the word "hallucinating" at her, arching his eyebrows to underscore the question. She pursed her lips and slowly shook her head.

Dr. Billie muttered to himself. "I need a cup of coffee." He retreated to a corner of the room where a small white table was set with a coffee pot and small bowls of sugar and cream. The doctor poured a cup of coffee for each participant. Dr. Billie cleared his throat and whispered to Marilyn, "Are you sure you're getting all this down?"

Marilyn looked up from her notes, shook her writing hand, and nodded. "Every word."

"If my next book makes the best-sellers' list, you can count on a raise." After Dr. Billie handed out the coffee mugs, he settled into his black bean bag. "Let's get acquainted. Please give us your name and the reason you're here. Who will begin?"

A middle-aged woman volunteered. "My name is Molly Meadows, and I'm here because I'm in the process of getting a messy divorce."

Angie gestured at Greg and told Group, "He's been there. Done that."

"I'm Sammy Summer," a young man spoke next, "and I'm here because I'm suffering from vocational distress. I'm a mortician and I thought I'd like working with the recently dead, but I don't. The silence nearly drives me crazy. About the only way I can go in my business is down—and I want to go up."

"So do I." Angie exclaimed, smiling. "Let's you and me see if we can graduate to heaven together."

Sammy studied Angie carefully. "Are you making a pass at me? Because if you are, forget it. I'm not that kind of male person." Sammy smoothed his hair and slacks in a motherly sort of way.

A woman in blue spoke to Sammy. "You said you don't want to go down. In your business, what's wrong with down?"

"Everything," he moaned. "I want clients to appreciate my best work. How can they when they're recently dead? I don't get any 'thank-you' or 'I'll be back again' from my customers."

"Theresa," Dr. Billie nodded to the lady in blue. "You're next."

She said, "I'm Theresa Triggah. I'm here because I left my couch potato slob of a husband, Trygve. So, I've gone back to my maiden name."

Marilyn gawked. "You're one of *the* Triggahs?" When she nodded, Marilyn asked. "Which brother's your dad? Phaulty or—phooey, my mind's not too sharp today—or..."

"Kwick. He's my dad."

"I'm Angie and I'm an angel. I'm here because I keep getting into trouble on earth. I'm a student at Angel U. That's on planet Oreo. Not far from heaven."

"I've been coming to group for eight years now," Molly Meadows interrupted, "and we've never had such an angel before. We've had ten Jesus Christs, but never, never a student angel that lives on another planet. How exciting."

"There's only *one* Jesus Christ," Angie said. "How could you have had ten?"

Molly Meadows laughed. "All ten were short a taco or two."

Angie was anxious to get Group's attention back to her problems. "I'm here because I'm trying to graduate to Heaven Angel status, but I keep getting into such messes. I do hope you Earthers can help me."

Dr. Billie's drooping eyelids snapped open. "What sort of messes, Miss Angela?"

"It all began with my cows...."

"Angie," Kristin interrupted, "not *again*."

"Okay. Okay. Whatever." She sighed. "I've failed 249 missions in a row, and..."

"Next!" Dr. Billie was in a tizzy.

"One question, please, Dr. Billie? I do like brandy alexanders," Angie said, "but tell me, you're the doctor: that doesn't make me an alcoholic now, does it?"

"Not necessarily," he replied, "but it could indicate you have a drinking problem."

Another participant who had been picking his nose till now, Alvin G. Angway, chanted in a sing-song voice, "Angie's got a drinking problem, Angie's got a drinking problem, Angie's got a drinking problem."

Angie jumped up and stomped her foot at him. "Cut that out. You're violating Group boundaries."

Sammy pushed Angie down into her pink bean bag. "Silly goose. Stop being such a passive-aggressive person. Think of my problem, please. Any emotionally mature person would agree it's bigger than yours. Every day I've got to work with the recently dead."

"So do we." Angie stared at Sammy. "Lots of us Mission Angels work with recently dead Earthers all the time, as their tour guides to heaven."

"No more fighting!" Theresa yelled. "We'll never get anything accomplished this way."

Dr. Billie reasserted his mentorship. "Let's get back to you, Miss Angela. I received an anonymous phone tip that you're having affairs with married men. Is that true?"

"Never," Angie shook her head vigorously. "Angels don't have sex."

"Hmm. I see." Dr. Billie's head bobbed up and down. He glanced at his employee. "At least I think so. Are we getting this down, Marilyn?"

"Yup." Marilyn was hunched over the legal pad jotting notes furiously. Beads of sweat dropped on her note pad, smearing the ink.

"Miss Angela," Dr. Billie continued, "tell us about your daddy." Dr. Billie closed his eyes, and his voice dipped to a hoarse whisper. "When you were a young girl, did he—or another male in your family—do naughty things to your body?"

"Young girl? Hey, I've always been twenty-eight. All of us angels are because too many Earthers don't trust anybody over thirty." Angie smoothed her curls. "And my father, G? I've never seen him. Only Heaven Angels get to do that."

"Marilyn? Be sure to jot that down. Abandoned by her father figure. Did some other adult male ever do something like, oh, say, play with your belly button?"

"Belly button? I've never had one."

"Come, come, Miss Angela."

She jumped up and pulled up the bottom of her sweater. "See?"

"Remarkable plastic surgery, I'd say."

"Now then, Greg, tell us why you came today. Was it to reinforce this young woman's delusion that she's an angel?"

"The only reason I'm here is because Kristin dragged me."

"That's true," Kristin admitted. "I did coerce him into coming. But someone's got to help us, Dr. Billie. I can't take much more. Both of them keep talking this crazy angel talk about Angie being a university student on planet Oreo. How can a Presbyterian like Greg believe something like that?"

Dr. Billie smiled and tapped a pencil on his note pad.

"Ahhhh," Kristin gasped. "I just remembered something. I don't know. It may be sort of private. Angie may not want me to say anything about it."

"How do you feel about that, Angie?" Dr. Billie asked.
"I want Kristin to say whatever she wants."
"Excellent. Kristin, you were saying?"
Hesitating, Kristin twisted long manicured fingers together. "Well, it's just that...I just now remembered something that doesn't make one bit of sense. When I took Angie shopping in Loehmann's the first day I met her, something strange happened."
"Which was...?"
"She didn't have a credit card. Not even one."
"Marilyn? A woman without credit cards." He made a circular motion around his ear with an index finger. "Clinically wacko. Got that down?"
Marilyn's pen kept moving at superhuman speed.
"And then one day at home," Kristin continued, "I asked Angie when her birthday was, and she said she didn't have one."
"Everyone has a birthday." Dr. Billie smugly rendered this professional conclusion. "Many women fudge about their age. Quite normal behavior."
"I don't mind telling my age." Angie shrugged. "It's just that I don't have a birthday. I'm an angel. I began before time began."
"You don't look twenty-eight." Molly Meadows frowned. "More like nineteen, I'd say."
"Twenty-eight," Angie said. She took a quick breath and muttered to herself, "plus a few millennia here and there." She paused, then glared at Dr. Billie. "The devil came here today. I can smell him."
He gestured impatiently at Marilyn in his patented "get it all down" mode. Angie's gaze swept the room—every Earther, furnishings, the walls, and drapes. Then, her arm shot out as she pointed at the wall clock. "Aha!"
The others turned to see what she'd discovered.
"Whoa!" Alvin gasped.
"Oh my goodness." Theresa groaned. "I'm hallucinating again, and I'd been doing so well on my medication."

"Finally. Just what I need." Sammy stomped his gilded shoes. "Excitement."

"It's too exciting for me," Molly groused, hurrying to the coffee table. She poured a cup of coffee and, when no one was looking, took a small bottle of Sunrise booze from a pocket in her voluminous skirt. She poured it into her coffee and casually slid the empty bottle into the wastebasket.

Dr. Billie sat with a stunned look on his face as he gawked at the large, antique clock. "Why is it doing that?"

The large hand was spinning around while the smaller one stayed on the present hour.

"Shh! Listen." Greg put a finger to his lips. Sure enough and no doubt about it: the clock was going TOCK-TICK.

A red glow seeped from various gaps in the clock's frame. And the glass over the pendulum mechanism was flexing like the stomach of someone breathing.

"Mommy's clock." Dr. Billie breathed heavily. "Someone, please tell me everything's okay. I thought I saw its front...moving."

"You did." Angie nodded. "That's the sort of gimmick the devil pulls when he doesn't take on an Earther's form." She snorted. "He still hasn't gotten the knack of using inanimate objects for secret habitation."

"I saw it, too," Kristin said. "That settles it. I'm going back on valium, Dr. Billie."

"Whatever you think is best."

"Come on, darling, let's leave." Kristin reached for Greg's hand. "You were right. We shouldn't have come here."

"Hold it." Greg refused her hand. "Angie can prove she's an angel to everyone here. Maybe that would help."

"Uh uh, not for me." Kristin got up to leave.

"Good thinking, Greg. I'm gonna show all of you some nifty angel stuff." Angie sorted through her options: Zapfax, Zapmike and CD, or Zapper.

"*Zap* functions are very left brain. That's why this is installed here instead of on the other side." Angie turned her lowered head from side to side and pointed to her *Zap* barrette. "This bar is for *Zap* travel, and this one keeps me in touch with Zap Central at Mission Control."

"I'm a Trekkie, too." Alvin slapped his knee several times.

Angie tapped the Travel bar with her left pinkie to effect what the technical manuals call a Quickie *Zap*.

ZAP! She disappeared from the room. Seconds later there was another *ZAP!* Angie was back in her bean bag. Except for Greg, all were stunned.

As was his way in high anxiety-inducing situations, Dr. Billie's right hand darted down to clutch his buttock, an early childhood development stress reflex. "This is bad science," he yelped. "Bad, bad, *bad* science."

"Evidence, Dr. Billie." Greg waggled an index finger at him. "Evidence."

"Let me show you my Zapfax." Angie leaned over and placed her right palm in front of Dr. Billie's face. She tweaked her pinkie tip. Green letters printed out: Angel Bert here. How can I help?

Dr. Billie gasped. "Oh, my God." Immediately, everyone left their bean bags and scooted over to see what was going on. The green message disappeared and a red one read: Zap Central here. Angie's an angel, genuine-like.

"No, no, no! This is naughty, *naughty* science. There must be some other explanation." Their mentor's jaw quivered.

Greg taunted him. "Doctor, I do believe you're manifesting paranoid behavior patterns."

A light bulb, figuratively speaking, of course, switched on over Molly Meadows' head. "We're hallucinating. Believe me, I know hallucinations when I see them. I've had more than my share. But this time, I've got company."

"Please, don't be baffled." Angie sensed Group was not coping well. When Angie stuck her thumbnail in her mouth, Dr. Billie put an arm around her.

"I get it. There, there. It's okay to suck your thumb, as when you were but a mere child. Regressing is good."

Yanking the thumb from her lips, Angie challenged him. "How can I regress to a childhood I never had?"

The doctor patted Angie's shoulder. "Don't confuse my coping categories. You obviously crave your thumb. I gave a paper on this a few years back: 'Is Searching for Plums in the Pie-filling an Oedipal Compensation?' Such desire always indicates childhood toilet training trauma in a dysfunctional family of origin."

Angie gawked at him. "You're nuttier than a fruit basket."

"Fruit *cake,* Angie. Fruit cake." Greg got a kick out of Angie's malapropisms.

"Whatever." She gestured at her thumbnail. "There's a microphone under here. I use it to chat with Mission Control. Angie moved the thumbnail to her lips. "Bert, are you there?"

With CD clarity, a voice boomed from her left palm. "Lay it on me, Angie."

Group gasped. Theresa Triggah put a thumb in her mouth, trying to imitate Angie.

"Is Mission Control anything like birth control?" Alvin G. Angway's disjunctive syndrome surfaced.

Ignoring Alvin, Angie spoke into her Zapmike. "I'm with some Earthers who don't believe I'm an angel. Could you send us a demo?"

"Happy to, Angie." Bert loved doing demonstrations. Loud trombone blasts of "When the Saints Go Marching In" burst in the background. Those swigs of Sunrise were raising Molly Meadows' consciousness. She got to her feet and began marching and singing.

"Molly, pulleeze. You're disrupting Group again." Dr. Billie chided her with his patented shrink shake, a gesture similar to a small boy flicking boogers.

"What is that terrible noise?" Sammy seemed stunned.

"Angel Gabriel," Angie said. "If you think his trombone sounds bad now, you should've heard it earlier." She scanned each face. "Bert is about to send us a demonstration." She put the thumbnail to her lips. "Ready when you are, Bert."

ZAP! A fully grown African elephant stood in their midst. The high ceiling's beams and light fixtures shook. Group shook, too, bonding through group dynamic trauma.

"Meet Gerald." Angie patted the elephant's trunk. Recognizing Angie, Gerald broke into a very broad smile, as his trunk nuzzled her blonde curls. She glanced at Greg. "He pals around with Evelyn."

Our playful pacyderm was a party animal. Gerald hated to miss out on a good time. With uncanny elephantine intuition, he seized the moment by seizing Molly. Deftly, of course, with his most significant schnooz.

SWISH! SWISH! Gerald whirled Molly as everyone dashed helter-skelter to avoid getting hit. Molly Meadows giggled, wiggled, and screamed with delight as she swung in Gerald's trunk.

Marilyn wrote so fast and with such vigor that she resembled a humongous bowl of Jello in an earthquake.

Dr. Billie frantically clutched his buttock. "Goodness me. Goodness me."

Crawling on the floor to avoid Gerald's fun-and-games gambit, Sammy went to his mentor. "Dr. Billie, during the past eleven years, I'd often wondered when to conclude Convalescent Therapy. You told me not to worry about it, that I'd know when the time had come. Frankly, I doubted it would ever come. It's here. No doubt in my mind. The recently dead may not be a vocational turn-on, but this is too much excitement for me. I'm gonna switch over to that new psychological massage parlor the Unitarians opened next to K-Mart."

Sammy Summer dashed to the door between Molly's orbits and, with a limp wrist wave, he said: "Bye-Bye, Group." Gerald released Molly Meadows, scooted his trunk up to the emigrant's buttocks, and shoved him out of the Bertha Billie Memorial Group Room.

"Now, do you all believe I'm an angel? Or do you need another demonstration?"

Vigorously wiping sweat off his forehead, Dr. Billie pleaded. "Please, please, get rid of that elephant. He's going to tear up this place. My insurance agent would have me committed if I told him an elephant did the damage."

"Okay, Bert. You can *Zap* Gerald back home now." She lowered her thumbnail and scratched the gentle giant's trunk.

"Thanks, Gerald. You really came through this time." Gerald was happily nodding his head at Angie when with a *ZAP!* he disappeared from their midst.

Dr. Billie breathed a sigh of relief and withdrew his hand from his buttock. "Excuse me. I've got to call the psychiatric ward to reserve a room."

"Oh no," Molly Meadows whined. "Please, don't make me go to that place again."

"It's for m-m-myself."

Marilyn kept taking notes. She suspected she might have to write Bill Billie's book herself.

After the ambulance came for Dr. Billie, Ms. Triggah picked up her purse. "Does this mean Group is over for today?"

From the stretcher, Bill Billie babbled incoherently, comforted in the security of his custom-tailored beige strait jacket.

"Don' worry, y'all. Dis shrink'll get shrunk real good," one ambulance attendant assured them.

Dr. Billie's clients walked briskly as they left the premises.

The wall clock returned to tick-tock shape.

SEVEN

In the days following, Kristin helped Angie open charge accounts and get credit cards. Kristin had lost touch with reality amid her credit card sprees. Banks were the only ones coming out ahead. Way ahead. Nonetheless, she led Angie on shopping binges at the pre-inventory sales.

Angie took her housekeeping chores seriously. One morning after cleaning the apartment, Angie nestled on the sofa with her shoes off and feet curled under her. Kristin stopped by before leaving for work. Angie pointed at a large book on the coffee table and asked Kristin about it.

"That's a scrapbook with pictures and clippings about my family."

"Do you mind if I look through it?"

"Sure, hon. I'm real anxious to hear about your family too."

Angie wondered how she would explain her angelic family of origin to Kristin. She began reading the scrapbook's news clips, letters, and diary pages. Blessed with the standard-issue angelic photographic memory, Angie learned a lot in a very short time about the woman who was looking more and more like her best ally on this Mission.

She had concluded already that Kristin had to be a remarkably decisive and effective manager. Her current job as a waitress had to be a stopgap, of course. Angie's reading confirmed this hunch.

Kristin had been senior vice president for marketing at Luigi's Pasta Specialties, Inc., a firm wholly owned by the Goldfarb family. Luigi's is based in Lubbock, Texas, where Kristin was born and raised.

Luigi's was founded in 1942 by Grandpappy Goldfarb, an ingenious broker of this and that. He bought, but couldn't sell, two boxcars of North Dakota durum wheat that somehow got hooked onto the end of a Southern Pacific coal train that derailed outside Lubbock. When Grandpappy heard that Dakota durum wheat gets re-christened as "semolina" when it arrives in Italy, he set up a small spaghetti factory on the edge of town.

Early on, the family realized they were onto something: the effect of Texas Panhandle sun and field dust on freshly-racked spaghetti imbued it with a distinctive bouquet utterly lacking in bland imported brands. He turned the enterprise over to his elder son, Sven, who was better known as Daddy Goldfarb. Sven led Luigi's to modest success during his tenure as CEO and also, later, as chairman of the board.

The breakthrough that turned Luigi's into a household name came from Kristin's creative genius less than eight months after her graduation from Gustavus Adolphus College. A medieval history major, she had joined the family business as its first-ever marketing person.

Angie was intrigued. There was more under Kristin's mop of hair than just red roots.

First, Kristin came up with the concept of making pasta in designer colors. The idea probably wouldn't have taken off the way it did if it hadn't been paired with her brilliant strategy of having Luigi's new pasta specialties hustled by a hitherto loosely organized group of effeminate waiters in Italian restaurants throughout New York City. All were members of a dissident (homophilioanthropic) faction in the Italian-American League, an organization that lobbies to have the name Verazzano put on ferries and bridges and other public stuff. Because of these waiters' considerable gastronomical influence, the word spread around town fast: Luigi's was the "in" pasta.

Of course, no housewife, house-husband, or "significant other" across America would dream of ignoring New York trend-setting fashion. The rest is history. Indeed, Luigi's meteoric rise to pre-eminence became a classic case study at the Harvard Business School.

So why, Angie wondered, why is Kristin a waitress now instead of a senior manager for her favorite pasta label?

Angie read on. It seems the fault rested on the shoulders of two men: Daddy Goldfarb and his younger brother, Billy Bob, who was the corporate Chief Financial Officer at Luigi's.

Daddy suffered an obsession: beating his kid brother at golf. Daddy's demise was a tragic result of this obsession and epitomized his competitive nature.

After losing 146 rounds in a row to Billy Bob, that fateful day they came to the 18th tee with Daddy Goldfarb holding a one-stroke lead. Billy Bob had the honors, but hit a lousy drive. A long-repressed slice problem resurfaced, rather severely. Daddy followed with the best drive of his life—long, low, with that picture-perfect little hook as it sank toward the lush grass. Galloping bounces, straight and true.

Just then a frolicking pit bull came out of nowhere, streaking across the fairway to attack Daddy's tantalizing Titleist. In full stride, the canny canine scooped up the still-rolling sphere in its jaws and ran toward the 16th fairway, then on to the 14th. There, he was distracted by a strolling rottweiler bitch and dropped the ball, 740 yards from the 18th hole.

Meanwhile, Daddy Goldfarb tore into hot pursuit as soon as he'd divined the pooch's intent. He screamed as he bounded off the tee after his ball was snatched. Eyewitnesses commented they had never seen such a seriously short fat guy move so fast.

When Daddy's heart joined the outrage, he was in the rough at the 14th fairway. A ladies' foursome later noted that "it looked like he was doing the Hari Kari bit with that club." The club was Daddy's beloved 4-iron. Daddy keeled over. The family buried him with the very same 4-iron in his adamant interlocking grip. It was a '55 MacGregor Tourney, 90 shaft-stiffness rating, the model he'd claimed all the pros use.

Angie was enjoying this scrapbook. Shifting to a business magazine article, she learned that with Daddy Goldfarb gone, nobody was left to keep Billy Bob in line. When the board named him temporary CEO, this also-CFO turned into a veritable snake. Billy Bob had always resented signing off on these under-the-table payoffs to the New York waiters, and he used that contractual obligation to hassle Kristin at every turn.

Two months after the funeral, while Kristin was in New York to focus group with the Italian waiters, Billy Bob seized the moment. During a board subcommittee meeting, he produced documents he'd counterfeited to support a scheme to get his niece fired. It worked.

Kristin moved to Tulsa within the week and got a job with Giorgio's J and G, the trendiest restaurant in town. But why Tulsa? Angie wondered. Good question.

The next day, Angie learned even more about Kristin's background. She'd been especially intrigued by the linkage of Swedish first names with Goldfarb.

"There's some little-known history behind that." Kristin helped clear the breakfast table. "Goes back to around 1600."

"Earther years?"

Kristin nodded. "In Sweden, King Gustavus Adolphus contracted with some Jewish management specialists in the Netherlands to come to Sweden and overhaul his government and military organization. Governmental expertise among Jews went back as far as Joseph in Egypt, remember? Anyway, they did such a good job that he gave a leading family of those Dutch Jews, the Axelrads, some land and made them titled nobility."

"How could that be? I mean, my Double-E readings say Jews were kept separate from the—um—political setup back then. Jews, officially, were a *tertium quid,* Double-E said, a 'third thing.' Neither Christian nor Infidel but in their own category."

"Except for my ancestors in Sweden. The Axelrad branch probably was the only Jewish landed nobility in all of Europe."

"So, why would any of them want to leave? Come to America? To Texas and Oklahoma?"

"All those who left Sweden, Angie, were younger children. According to a cousin who lives in Norway, even today the eldest child has the first right to inherit the family farm or business. That's why my great-grandfather, who was the youngest child in his generation of Goldfarbs, left Sweden and eventually settled in Lubbock. He gave Goldfarb children Swedish first names to honor and remember an important part of our family's history."

"Is Billy Bob a Swedish name?"

"Hardly. My uncle's legal name is Willem Robbheim Goldfarb."

"Is there a synagogue in Lubbock? If so, is it anything like Kashi's?"

"I don't know about that. You see, back around 1650, most of the family became Lutheran. Over here, we're in the Missouri Synod version." She laughed. "Lutheran Jew is not as strange a combination as it sounds, Angie. Ask any three American Jews to tell you what 'Jewish' means, and you'll get at least five different definitions."

Several evenings later, Angie was loading the dishwasher while Greg stretched in a recliner and leered at the centerfold of the latest *Playboy.*

"How shall I go about it?" Angie asked.

"Huh?" Greg glanced up from his magazine. "Go about what?"

"My orientation. About getting used to living here on earth. It's not easy you know. A lot has changed since George Washington was president. I don't know how to cope."

"Maybe you could try to meet some more people your own age."

"Yeah, right. That would be mission impossible. It's going to be hard to find any Earthers my age. Remember, I'm twenty-eight plus—um—a few millennia."

"That's right," Greg laughed. "I forgot. You certainly don't look your age, Angie. How do you do it?"

"Thanks for the compliment, but angels don't age." Angie finished loading the dishwasher. She was overjoyed that she didn't have to heat water to wash dishes in a pan. This Mission was a breeze in the housekeeping department.

"Earther women would love that setup. No night cremes. No face lifts. No cellulite."

"Why would they lift their faces and wrap them in cellophane? Beauty's not so important to me except for—um—I could use a little silicone. They really did a nice job on Kristin's bosom, don't you think?" Before Greg could answer, Angie said, "I've been considering the same surgery. I mean I've done bust development exercises for five hundred years and have so little to show for it."

"Oh really? You want to have them enlarged?" Shaking his head, Greg smiled. "I think you look just fine, but then I'm a man. I thought Kristin looked fine before her surgery last year. But she said it's what she always wanted, so I encouraged her to go for it."

Raising her knee slightly with both hands, Angie pursed her lips and nodded. "I think I'd like some of that silicone, which brings me to my main problem now."

"Which is?"

"Money. How to get enough Earther money to pay my bills—and get that silicone job done."

"Welcome to the third planet from the sun," Greg said. "Money is everyone's problem on earth."

Angie was not amused. Beyond her centurally allowance, money wasn't needed at Angel U. She had no living expenses there. And her clothing purchases were covered by the standard fifty-shekel-a-month Options Allowance. She had almost fainted when she got a credit card bill of $3,568.32 for her recent clothes-buying binges. When she asked if she really had to pay for all those clothes she put on credit, Kristin said, "Of course." She also felt obligated to help pay for groceries and other household expenses.

A job. She needed a job. So, that night at the dinner table, Angie asked Kristin about waitress work.

"What do you have to know to be a waitress?"

"That depends on what kind of waitress work you're talking about. For example, working as a waitress in a restaurant is more complicated than cocktail work."

"I really do need a job. Could you help me find one?"

"A job?" Greg and Kristin reacted in unison.

"Yes, I just can't go on living here without contributing toward my keep. Both of you have been so kind."

"Now hon, don't you worry none. The way you keep up this place, you're worth your weight in gold."

Angie took a sip of tea. "No, Kristin, I can't possibly live here any longer without contributing. And that's not all. My credit card bills are huge." She smiled sheepishly. "And I'm not even done shopping."

"Show me a woman who's ever done shopping," Greg said.

"Sure, I've got lots of dressy clothes but nothing for casual wear. I really need blue jeans and some Air Jordanians. I want to get into fashion with Earther women."

Kristin grinned. "I've wondered why you were always dressed up. You don't have a single pair of jeans?"

"No, I don't. Angel U's dress code is so prim and prissy."

"That settles it. We'll go down to the nearest Getajob agency first thing tomorrow. Every woman has an inalienable right to wear designer jeans."

And so they did. At Getajob, Angie filled out forms. She admitted to zero words per minute in word processing. She listed Angel University as her previous residence. How long? Since WBBC.

Ms. Fergunson, Getajob's employment director, sat stout and straight behind a large desk. She frowned at Angie.

"What's WBBC mean?"

"Way back before Christ."

Ms. Fergunson blinked at her. She looked through the rest of Angie's application. "I see you don't do word processing."

"Correct. At least I don't think I do. I—um—don't know what that is."

Ms. Fergunson removed her red-framed glasses and stared at her. "And why not?"

Angie gave a noncommittal shrug. "No course by that title was offered at Angel U."

"Angel U," Ms. Fergunson said weakly, slightly dazed. Angie nervously reshuffled her legs. She had to get a job right away through Getajob. But how? She leaned toward Ms. Fergunson.

"I'm a Grade A cook and housekeeper."

"Oh?" Ms. Fergunson regained some interest. "Tell me, what is it you do best?"

Angie thought for a moment. "Well, the thing I've learned to do best of all since I got here is to make brandy gregericks."

"Brandy what?"

"I mean—um—brandy alexanders. I make great ones."

Ms. Fergunson leaned back and picked up her glasses. "Tell me more."

"Well, I'm not bad at hammers either."

Ms. Fergunson put on her glasses. "Hammers?"

Angie was flustered. How she had prayed this interview would land her a job. She knew she was blowing it. "I mean—um—screwdrivers. That's it. I make a good screwdriver."

"Hmm. Interesting. Maybe our agency can help you after all." Ms. Fergunson noticed the puzzled look on Angie's face. "I may have just the job for you."

"Great." Angie leaned forward in her chair. "I'm anxious to go to work so I can make lots of Earther money." Ms. Fergunson rolled her eyes.

"There's a bartender job opening at a saloon near here. Louie's Place."

"Been there, but haven't done that."

"It's minimum wage, but good tips. It's hard to find someone who can make good drinks—and look as good as you do. I'll give the manager, Mr. Nemmy, a call. He might be very impressed with you."

Angie clasped her hands together. "Like I said, I make a super brandy frederick."

"Brandy alexander. It's brandy *alexander*."

"Yes, yes. A brandy—um—whatever. Surely, Ms. Fergunson, the Lord will reward you if you can get me this job."

Ms. Fergunson sighed. "Believe me, all I want is the commission."

While dialing, Ms. Fergunson nodded at Angie and actually smiled. Angie nervously twisted her hands and tapped her right foot. She didn't say anything, but she had one concern about working at Louie's Place: Nemmy. Angie still didn't know why, but nervous chills went down her spine when she was around him. But, if she could make enough to pay her bills, she could tolerate that. All Angie could think of was how lucky she would be to have a job and make money.

"Hello. Yes, this is Ms. Fergunson. I may have just the person for that bartender position we discussed the other day." There was a moment of silence. "This woman's name is Angela Fore."

Angie waved her hand vigorously. She wrote on a blank sheet of paper and held it up so Ms. Fergunson could read the large block letters: FOUR. ✱ See *Angel Nebbie's End Note*

"Excuse me, a correction. That's spelled F.O.U.R. And she says she makes an excellent brandy alexander." Ms. Fergunson nodded several times as she listened. Bright sunlight filtered through emerald green blinds and reflected from the muted-tone carpet. "Yes, I'd say Ms. Four is very attractive and is in her mid-twenties."

Angie leaned forward and whispered, "No, no, I'm much older than that. You'd better be honest about the age part. I helped the Lord create cows, I go back so far."

Ms. Fergunson shook her head furiously, covered the receiver with her hand, and whispered through clenched teeth, "Trust me, Ms. Four. I know what I'm doing."

Angie sighed as she leaned back in her chair. Ms. Fergunson probably did know what she was doing, but how hard it is to wait. She had no idea that she'd need so much of this Earther thing called money.

Ms. Fergunson resumed her telephone conversation. "Send her right down? Fine."

An hour later, Angie was at Louie's Place working as a bartender. It was some kind of miracle, Angie thought, that she got this job so quickly through Getajob. She hoped that working in a saloon wouldn't compromise her spirituality.

Little did Angie know.

✺ *Angel Nebbie's End Note*
You may be wondering, Dear Reader, why Angie keeps noticing spelling and punctuation errors in how Earthers *talk.* The reason is quite simple: Angie—simultaneously—reads what she hears. Another little-known Mission Angel quirk. *Editor.*

EIGHT

Raphael was horrified that Angie had accepted a job at Louie's Place. He knew she had placed herself in harm's way.

She had a lot to learn about bartending, but her photographic memory made her a quick study. Once she learned the recipes for various mixed drinks, it was a pretty mindless job. To compensate, she concentrated on getting to know the customers.

It certainly wasn't hard, for example, to remember Tex's passion for Millah Laht beeh. Tex enjoyed talking with Angie almost as much as he loved his Laht.

Tonight would be one of those evenings when Tex would insist on schmoozing. With the refilled glass before him, his manner turned earnest, somewhat conspiratorial. "Y'all said something a while back, New Year's Eve, that's been bothering me. About Moses and Sinai? Y'all into spiritual stuff like I am?" Tex cleared his throat. "In it, deep-like?"

"You might say so." Angie didn't know how to answer him.

"Wonderful. I just wanna share with y'all about what happened to me last night?"

Nearby regulars groaned. PC taunted Tex. "You're always sharing your wacky experiences."

"That's okay." Angie smiled at Tex. "Good people freely share what they have."

"You don't know what you're in for," Rita said.

"Just leave her be. Just cuz you don't want to be a spiritual person, Miz Rita, shouldn't exclude this young lady." He leaned closer to Angie. "Now, about last night? I got some real interesting vibrations while doing my spiritual exercises."

"Exercises?"

"Yeah, ya know, spiritual. The warm-up kind. Kinda like foreplay before the consummation." His eyes closed. He took a deep breath and exhaled slowly through pursed lips. "It is so good, getting in touch with my inner child." His earnest tone returned. "Y'all like me to teach you them exercises so y'all can get in touch with your inner child?"

"My inner child? Why would I want to do that? I'm not pregnant." Eavesdroppers burst into laughter. Angie blushed, baffled by the situation. "And, what's this about consummation?"

"Let me walk y'all through the matter, Miz Angie?" Angie had never met an Earther who ended so many sentences with question marks.

"It'll help y'all to know I've become a Melchizadekian." Tex anticipated her question and quickly added, "It's the latest New Age rage." Angie was drawing blanks, and it showed. He took another deep breath and resumed. "It really has taken off with us New Agers because it opens up a whole new dimension for channeling."

"Channeling?" Finally, Angie could relate to something in Tex's babble. "Been there. Done that."

"Ex-cuzzze me?"

"I've sailed on the Channel," she said rather smugly, "the English Channel."

"She gotcha, Tex." Rita laughed. "Good show, Angie."

"I'm talking about another kinda Channel, Miz Angie. Channeling is a way to communicate, to reach out and touch someone who can't come to the phone."

"Oh." The corner of her mouth turned up in bemusement. "But what's this got to do with Melchizadek? I've never heard him speak of such things." No one picked up on her comment.

"Melchizadek was this guy way back 'who was defined by neither birth nor death,' like the brochure says."

"I know him." Angie beamed.

"Whaaaat?"

"I mean, I know about him."

Before she could elaborate, Tex continued. "Anyway, the brochure says he was regarded as being in a higher order of priesthood than traditional religion." He pressed a hand to his chest. "But the biggest attraction of Melchizadekianism, for me anyway, is that y'all can channel *future* folks, not just dead ones. Like, I've channelled my teenaged daughter a couple times already."

"Daughter? Tex, you don't have a daughter," Rita said.

"That's what I'm trying to explain, sweetheart. She's a future tense person, like the brochure says."

"What do you—um—channel about with her?" Angie frowned, as she took another sip of her drink.

"I'm hoping she'll give me stock market numbers for twenty years from now." He smirked. "I'd be a heavy hitter in the market with that kind of info. Make a killing or two, believe me." Tex drank some of his Laht, then shook his head. "But it turns out my future daughter's a real ditz."

"What else, if she's your daughter." Rita said.

Tex ignored her. "Y'all see, Miz Angie, when I channel my future offspring, all she'll talk about are the boys in her life."

Just then Greg and Kristin entered Louie's Place. They sat at their usual little round table near the bar. That way they could turn off the regulars' conversation or participate in it.

"Channelin's great stuff," Tex said, giving Angie his complete attention. "Y'all got to get into it, Miz Angie. When I heard y'all mention Moses, I thought, 'Now there's a gal I want to talk with. There's a woman who will understand a spiritually gifted individual like myself.'"

"It'd surprise you, Tex, if you knew how much spiritual awareness Angie already is into," Greg called from the table.

"Yeah? Y'all into New Age too?" When Angie opened her mouth to respond, Tex took over the conversation again. "Now let me tell you, I can really get into channeling some nights, especially if there's nothing on TV."

Shaking a finger at him, Kristin spoke harshly. "Tex, will you get off it? That stuff freaks me out, talking to dead people. And now, it's future people, too? Gimme a break. That's one reason I stopped dating you back in Lubbock. I didn't want to hear such nonsense then, and I don't want to hear it now. Just, just get lost, will you, Tex?"

"I'll vote for that," Rita said. Kristin hadn't realized how loudly she'd spoken.

After another sip of his Perrier, Schwartz said, "Angie, if you're a real angel, how about making Tex disappear from here?" Others seconded the motion. Except Tex.

"Well, if you really want me to." Angie smiled at the prospect of showing off her angel powers to these Earthers. Maybe it would help her credibility with Greg and, with that, improve her chances of a successful Mission.

Ignoring everyone else, Tex shook his head in dismay and gazed at Angie. "I'm real good at figuring people out? Matter of fact, some days I think I missed my calling. When I'm out on the ranch riding my Arabian, I wonder if I should've gone into psychiatry instead of taking over the ranch after Daddy died?"

Kristin laughed. "A psychiatrist? A redneck like you?"

Redneck? Angie wondered why Kristin called him a redneck when Tex's neck wasn't red. Earther jargon was so confusing.

"I've been sitting here feeling some good vibes, Miz Angie," Tex persisted, shifting his Stetson. "Maybe y'all can feel them too?"

"Sure, I feel them. Especially after a drink or two, I feel lots of spirituality coming upon me." She was trying to "make a funny," as Angel Dusty termed it, but nobody picked up on her attempt.

"Then, let's get y'all channeling. Tell me, Miz Angie, what do you see right now?"

Tex paid no heed to the others. He focused intensely on Angie. "Like I was saying, just close your eyes and feel them vibes."

Closing her eyes, Angie said nothing.

"I'm still with y'all, Angie," Tex encouraged. "What's happening? What dead relative do y'all got on channel?"

"Nobody." She sighed and then opened her eyes.

"You sure about that?" Tex's diction was normal.

"Positive. I can't channel dead relatives."

"Why can't you channel a dead relative or two?"

"Quite simple. Angels don't have dead relatives." The others laughed at what they assumed Angie meant as a joke.

"Let's forget about dead folks for now, Miz Angie." Tex remained serious. "Shift into the future. Just close your eyes and see if y'all can connect with some future tense person?"

She closed her eyes. Both hands pressed her temples, her breath heavy. Tex leaned forward, expectantly.

"Coming through to y'all? Who's getting through? Who?"

She kept massaging her temples. "What's coming through is that I feel woozy. Whew." Angie opened her eyes. "I need a break and some fresh air." She headed for the ornate entry to Louie's Place. Tex followed her. Outside, Angie leaned against the pole that held a neon sign for Louie's Place with its familiar motto: The Time Is NOW. Angie was refreshed by the milder southern air that had arrived when yesterday's cold front passed. She closed her eyes again and nodded when Tex asked if she felt better.

"I just connected."

"With who?"

"With your daughter, Tamara. She's going to be six next month."

Tex's eyes widened, his voice hoarse. "No one else knows about Tamara except her Mommy and me. How did y'all find that out?"

Angie opened her eyes and gave an angry response. "You just lied to me. The judge also knows about it."

"Judge? What do y'all mean?"

Closing her eyes again, she continued. "I mean that I see some numbers. You owe exactly $53,568.32 in child support." Her eyes snapped open. "Dead Beat. And if you don't stop harassing me about that channeling baloney, I'm going to announce those facts to everyone back there." She smirked at him. "Plus other sordid details about the—um—matter."

The blood drained from his face as Tex hurried back inside. He paid his bar tab and left. Greg and the other regulars stared as Angie sauntered into Louie's and returned to her bar station.

"What did you say to him?" Greg said. "Tex has never left here before closing time. Tell us your secret."

"It's really not a secret, except for some closed minds and hearts." Angie pursed her lips. "I'm curious about something. Does Tex have a last name?"

Several regulars shrugged. Nemmy spoke from behind the bar. "His last name is Roncowiscz, first name Stanislaus. But everyone calls him Tex, although he was born and raised in New York City. Family moved to Amarillo when he was ten, then to Lubbock a couple years later. That was where he made Kristin's acquaintance."

"Unfortunately." Kristin stared at her drink.

"But he sounds like such a real Texan," Angie said.

"Honey, beneath that Stetson is just another Borough Kid, as they say in Brooklyn. Don't get me wrong. He dearly loves his adopted state and is fiercely loyal to Texas. But, in Lubbock we have a saying that folks who try hardest at looking and sounding Texan, ain't."

"Hey, Angie, how did you get Tex to leave?" Guy Schwartz pressed the matter. "What's your secret?"

"I'm an angel. *Zapped* to you Earthers. On a Mission." She gestured to Greg, "and he's it."

"Right." Schwartz sighed.

A gust of fresh air came through the door as an oriental man hurried to the bar.

"Hey, Kashi, how's it going? We've missed you. Glad you're back." Rita's face lit up.

Angie turned to see who it was. She was astounded.

Toshio Kashihara was taller than most of his Japanese contemporaries, a shade under six feet. That wasn't why Angie gaped at him, however. She had never seen an Earther rabbi before, except in several Earther Encyclopedia photos. But here was a real-life, walking, talking, Hasidic rabbi. Wow!

While the EE photos showed male Hasidim with large beards and frumpy black clothing, Kashi's suits and frock coats were custom tailored for him whenever he went to New York City for a Rabbinical Alliance of America occasion. No facial hair, though. The black frock coat and fedora otherwise followed custom, as did the exquisitely embroidered white-on-white prayer shawl that showed below the coat's hem, its multitude of tassels swaying with the liquid freedom of ultra-fine fabric. On each side of his face, long black forelocks bounced with each step, their shiny curls contrasting with the rest of his utterly straight black hair. Angie wondered whether he had to use a curling iron on those forelocks.

As he reached the bar, Rabbi Kashihara smiled and made several exaggerated bows to nearby regulars. "Greetings and felicitations, my good friends." Settling on a bar stool, he shot his usual high-five benediction Nemmy's way. "The usual, m'boy. Sunrise, straight up."

> Sunrise is one of those splendid regional secrets, a 110-proof delicacy distilled at various home business locations between Ganado and Refugio, Texas from long-grain rice grown in the area. Kashi suspected it was this long-grain feature that gave it a bouquet utterly lacking in the saki of his Osaka youth. *Editor.*

Although his Hebrew and Yiddish dictions were flawless, Kashi's English suffered occasional lapses with his R's, but only when he spoke of personally stressful topics. Members of his congregation, *Chabad ha-Tulseh,* couldn't care less since he rarely had to use this language in their presence. Most male members of his flock toiled as oil field roustabouts. They made a good living at it, too, especially after last year's catastrophic earthquakes in the Persian Gulf region drastically cut Middle East oil production and sent Oklahoma crude prices through the roof.

Kashi's Hasidim had to speak "American" at work. His flock's American linguistic habits were so contaminated that most *Chabad ha-Tulseh* Hasids hesitated speaking American in polite company or around shul (synagogue). And then only at considerable risk. A foul word or phrase, so essential even for burly Hasidim during a hard day's work in the oil fields, could slip out too easily.

On the plus side, this risk reinforced their reliance on the Lord's—blessed be he—own mother tongue, Hebrew, and its boisterous companion, Yiddish.

"Hey, Kashi, save any souls today?" Rita teased.

Kashihara raised two fingers while taking his first sip of Sunrise, then broke into an easy, high-pitched laugh. From smiling faces around the bar, Angie could tell that the regulars enjoyed this man. It was Rita who beckoned Angie and introduced her.

"Kashi, this is Angela Fore. Angie, meet Rabbi Toshio Kashihara, spiritual director of *Chabad ha-Tulseh*."

He extended a hand. "Pleased to meet you, Angie, and congratulations on the excellent Hebrew, Rita."

Shaking hands with him, Angie glanced at Rita. "It's spelled F-o-u-r, Rita, but that's okay. I'm used to it and have been for—um—a long time."

Kashi studied her left hand. "No rings." He glanced up. "And blonde." He clasped her hand in both of his. "You also wouldn't happen to be Jewish, would you?" Before she could answer, his gaze shot upward. "Please, Lord. Puh-leeze."

"Kind of, but Christian, too." Kashi was so easy to like, so out front, so without guile. She leaned closer to him. "You see, I'm an angel."

"You sure are." Still holding her hand, his eyes searched hers, silently, intently. Then, he shrugged and his cheery manner returned. "You're single, too?" She nodded. "So am I, unfortunately."

"A fun, good-looking guy like you? Still single? Why, I'd think every mother in your congregation would be trying to make a match with you for her daughter."

He nodded, twisting his mouth. "They try. Oy, they do try." He laughed. "All zeros. Zip. Worse, not a blonde in the bunch."

"Hey, Kashi, what's so special about blondes?" Rita asked. "I'm of the school that says they're overrated."

"Hear, hear. Definitely overrated," Kristin called from the table.

"Friends, reality check time." Kashihara smiled tolerantly as he released Angie's hand. "This is your friendly rabbi speaking." The lid of his right eye began to twitch. "The leality is this: a labbi with a blonde lebbitzin—"

"He means *rebbitzin*," Angie interrupted.

"That's what I said." His eyelid twitched more noticeably. "A labbi's wife." He glared at Angie, "A lebbitizin. Anyway, if I mally a blonde, I can get me one of those rich suburban shuls." He beamed confidently at her. "See? I can say it your way—suburr-ban. A rich suburr-ban conglegation."

"Kashi, I find it hard to believe you haven't found yourself the perfect woman," Angie said as she suppressed a giggle. "She deserves you."

"You really mean that?" He smiled again. "So nice of you. For years," his eyelid resumed twitching. "I've played to the Lord—blessed be he—that he'd bring me together with my wife in his fullness of time. It's time." His palms open, his arms shot upward. He nodded around the bar and the regulars applauded.

"Maybe I'm lushing it, though. I tell myself: 'Kashi? It's only six months since you gladuated from the seminally. What's the lush? The light one will come along in the Lord's—blessed be he—good time.'" He shrugged. "Maybe not in Tulsa, but the light one for me is out there somewhere." Pausing, Kashi took a deep breath and glanced upward. His eyelid stopped twitching as he gestured at his lap and laughed. "It's time. Fullness has come."

During the hoots and laughter he'd provoked, Kashihara reached inside his coat and withdrew an eel leather case. Opening the flap, he removed two hand-carved pieces of ivory, each with a solid gold hinge. His fold-out chopsticks were exquisitely crafted by a Lubovitch exile from Tibet he'd met at a *ladtke* festival in Brooklyn two years earlier. He snapped each one into place with a somewhat studious expression on his face before flashing a smile at Angie. Then he used the elegant utensils to pluck a bar nut from the nearest bowl and pop the pecan into his mouth. He chewed. Squinted. Announced. "Ah, San Antonio. Last year. Northeast side. Excellent vintage for pecans."

"How's the other business doing, Kashi? That sideline investment of yours?" Schwartz's tone was sincere. Kashihara's eyelid twitched briefly.

"Slow. Leal slow. You'd think Kashi's Kosher Sushi Bar would do a lot better on the beach at Miami."

"The help?"

"Oy! Still. The help. Can't find help who'll insult the customers. Ruins the ambiance. How can customers feel at at home—like at a New York deli—without the insults? Am I asking so much? For twelve bucks an hour they could insult a little?" One curled forelock tangled with the chopstick as Kashi muttered, "*Goyim!*"

The phone rang at Greg's apartment. As Greg picked it up, sparks flew from the receiver. "Oh my God. Oh my God."

"G isn't on the phone. There's only one character who calls like that." Angie cringed.

"Who?" Greg asked. His face twisted with pain as he rushed to the kitchen sink. He grabbed the cold water faucet, turned it on full blast, and held his injured hand under the cooling water.

"Lucifer. You know, the devil. I wonder what he wants now." Angie made several quick circles around the small kitchen looking for a pot holder.

"Greg, I need a pot holder."

"Helloooooo. Anyone there? I detest waiting." A loud voice squawked from the phone.

"Is that him? Is that the devil yelling over the phone like that?" Greg gestured at a lower drawer where the towels and insulated mitts were kept.

"It sure is." Carefully, Angie picked up the telephone receiver with her protected hand.

"Angie sweetheart, how've you been? Hear you had a little fun New Year's Eve." Lucifer accused her with his raspy baritone voice.

Oh no, Angie thought. The devil found out I was in a fight and drank brandy alexanders and enjoyed an Earther male's affection. I've given the Accuser grounds to charge me with the Triple-Play Error (fighting, boozing, and unangelic affection) in the Celestial Circuit Court of No Appeals.

"Fun? What fun?"

"What fun? Angela, Pussy Cat. One of my demons saw it all. You were a naughty, naughty girl. New Year's Eve is one of my more productive occasions. More Earthers enter my kingdom that night than any other."

"So what if I had a little fun?"

"So what if you had fun? Angela, my blonde yum yum, you were visiting my kingdom. And I'd love to change that from visitor to citizen status."

"We have all sinned and fallen short of the glory of G," she replied, quoting Scripture, as she tried to sidestep Lucifer's insinuations.

"Especially on New Year's Eve." The devil laughed at her. "Angie, baby, everyone down here is gossiping about you. Just how many brandy alexanders did you have?"

"You mean brandy gregericks."

"It's brandy *alexanders,* I can assure you. I should know. The original recipe was concocted by one of my more creative demons, Alex. He's the genius who has invented lots of stuff that fulfills my triune principles of expensive, out of touch, and inept—Congress, church conventions, free agent athletes."

"Why are you calling?" Angie asked as Greg walked briskly down the hallway to his room.

"Sugar Plum, I've got great news for you."

"You just happen to have another opening in your operation and want me on staff? You've tried that one before. I may not be the brightest angel, but I'm not that stupid."

"C'mon Angie, we've got the best of everything down here. No tomorrows to worry about. No yesterdays that matter. Everything's now, always the present moment. My kind of place."

Something clicked in the back of her mind but too vaguely to register. Angie focused on Lucifer. She knew he was so tricky that coping with him required her fullest concentration. "That's hell, all right, where everyone's trapped in your Kingdom of Get-It-Now."

"That insight doesn't sound like you, Angie. Maybe you didn't sleep through as many courses at that Sky Seminary of yours as word has it." His laugh sounded like an obscene cackle. "No job offer this time, baby. Just wanna be helpful."

"Ha! You? Helpful? Give me a break, Lucifer."

NINE

"Actually, I've uncovered something of momentous value to all Mission Angels, including you, sweetie. It could mean the end of your frustration, your humiliation over all those failed Missions." Lucifer knew he had her attention. "What's your little Mission this time? Greg, is it? Ha. Mission number 250. After 249 times of getting your hopes up only to fall flat on your face?"

His tone grew more secretive. "My simple but highly secret discovery will mean the end of all your millennia of failure. And Angie, Sugar Lumps, it could bring instant graduation to Heaven Angel status."

"*Pour moi?* Me? Angela Four?" Instant had an inviting ring to it. She'd already discovered instant on this Mission. Instant pudding. Instant potatoes. Instant rice.

"Yup." Lucifer sensed her eagerness. "Instant. No more of that Mission Angel hassle for l'il Angie. No more boring courses at Angel U. No more having to run for your life to avoid getting mowed down by Gabriel in that beat-up old vehicle of his."

"Beat up? Old? It's this year's model, a Bimmer 500 series." But she had to agree on one matter. "It only looks old."

"Tell me, sweetie. Why does Gabriel's BMW keep going into the body shop? I hear he's been in so many fender benders that it's beginning to look and drive like a Yugo."

"Well—um—he still insists on aiming that plastic Jesus on his dashboard at the center line of whatever road he's on."

"Uh huh. And what's this I hear about him taking up the sousaphone? No more trumpet?"

"You heard wrong, Louie." Again there was this vague click in the back of her mind. She quickly shook her head to concentrate. "He wanted a sousaphone. But it wouldn't fit into his BMW. So, he got a trombone. Gabriel is taking trombone lessons at the Slow Learners Academy of Music. You know, in the Angel U Annex."

"Where Beethoven teaches Conducting Gangsta Rap for the Hearing Impaired?"

"Right." She felt a surge of courage. "So the great Lucifer made a mistake about the new horn Gabriel's blowing. This ends your track record of 100 percent accuracy on inside information, Slimeball."

His voice turned silken. "Not at all, Angie Sugar. I specialize in what Earthers and angels *want*. I couldn't care less about what they get, about what actually happens. Your Big Boss in the sky wouldn't give me what I wanted so I quit. Left. Blew the joint."

"Quit? Lucifer, you got booted. Ejected. Out of the ballpark."

"On a technical foul. Believe me, Angie, I only bumped the ref."

"Oh no, fella. You bumped the big boss of the whole franchise." She felt more assertive as she took a deep breath. "So what's the deal, Lucifer? About this discovery of yours?"

"Discovery? Yes, the reason I called. Phone inputs to a hundred other Mission Angels on Earther duty this afternoon, and I'm dilly-dallying. Sorry about that, sweetie. Here's my discovery, Angie bubby."

Angie noted another pause at his end of the line.

"In fact, you can start shopping for your Heaven Angel shades. Sunglasses. I'm that sure about this deal."

"Sunglasses? Heaven Angels wear sunglasses now?"

"Everybody in heaven wears them. They have to. A little-known bit of trivia, but stop and think about it, Angie. All that shiny stuff there. Streets paved with gold. Pearly gates. Diamonds and sapphires sparkling everywhere. All the while that constant Universal Light floods the place. The glare is awful."

"Lucifer, you're stalling."

"Okay, okay. Here's the deal, Sweetie Pie. Uh-huh. Haven't you noticed that everyone in Mission Control and at Angel U wears a Grace ring on their left ring finger? Everyone, that is, except Gabriel and Raphael?"

"Now that you mention it, yes. Why is that?" Before he could respond, she said, "Hold on a minute. How about all those Grace rings on Gabriel's fingers? Both hands."

"Decorations. He likes their look, that's all. Standard issue trinitarian Grace rings—three carats in one stone. The rest of you are Mission Angels, but Gabriel and Raphael have Heaven Angel status. A continuing resolution passed by Heaven Council named them as liaison officers between what's-his-name's Chief Operating Officer, Malak, and Mission Control."

"Lucifer. We're not allowed to speak M's name." She got so flustered that she didn't notice when her jabbing finger punched the extension phone button and Greg picked up the receiver on his bedroom phone.

"So? I've got something to lose by it?" The devil's cackled a sound somewhere between noise from an irritated chicken and a bleating goat.

"Get to the point, fella," Angie said.

"Point is, nobody in heaven wears a Grace ring. No need or use for one there. You graduate to Heaven Angel status when you hand over your Grace ring."

"That's it? That's all there is to it?" Angela Four was wary. This sounded too simple.

"Surely, you've been to a graduation ceremony."

"No. I haven't been invited to a single graduation." Angie pouted. "Only semi-successful Mission Angels get invited."

"Of course. Should have thought of that. You still haven't reached even pseudo-successful status, have you, Candy Cakes?"

Before Angie could answer, Lucifer said, "Let me fill you in. The high point of the ceremony comes when graduating Mission Angels hand over their Grace rings to Gabriel for deposit in the Mission Control armory."

Lucifer proceeded with his scheme. Its prospects relied on two related steps. First, he had to convince Angie that there was a cause-and-effect connection between handing over her Grace ring (cause) and graduation to Heaven Angel status (effect). He continued harassing her with variations on the same refrain: "They hand over their Grace rings and—poof—next thing you know they're full-fledged Heaven Angels. Just like that. Instant. No strings attached." She heard him snap his fingers near the mouthpiece.

Lucifer knew that the real stretch came next. He had to convince Angela Four to give her Grace ring to him. He knew her weaknesses, although he was unaware how well his strategy dovetailed with the main conclusion of every debriefing team that had analyzed her performance following each of those 249 failed Missions.

The teams found her main reason for failure was Angie's obsession with graduating. In short, her Missions were driven by her own consuming self-centeredness rather than by the best interests of Mission clients. Several teams had insisted she enroll in remedial Total Quality Angelism courses. She had. It made little difference.

"Why should I hand my Grace ring over to you, Lucifer?"

"Do something unselfish for once, will ya? We're talking science here. In the interest of scientific research."

"Whose science? What's science got to do with it?"

Angie could picture him glancing this way and that before responding. Lucifer whispered, "Angie, don't you remember anything from your Celestial Physics courses? Especially the physics principle that Grace, not gravity, is the most powerful force in the universe?"

"Sure. I'm not a total dummy, Slimeball." She smirked at the phone. "Especially because of Grace's capability for keeping the visible and celestial universes in—um—redemptive tension with each other."

"Right." Angie could picture his sneer. "Such a student. Anyway, one of my Administrative Assistants is assembling a crack team of my best scientists, including several Nobel Prize laureates, to examine your Grace ring. They hope to discover how such a small object can exert such overwhelming power over some things." He sounded jubilant. "My AA has even recruited Nigel Braun-Nez for the team."

Angie's photographic memory recalled that Braun-Nez was a two-time Nobel prize winner and pioneer in the interdisciplinary field of bio-physics. His first Nobel was for landmark research into The Bio-Physics of Sexual Revulsion. Unfortunately, Braun-Nez had grossed-out every woman he'd ever met.

His next Nobel prize was for The Bio-Physics of Chronic Loss and Grief: The Case of Chicago Cubs Fans, 1940-*ad infinitum*. His untimely death came from consuming a can of tuna marketed by a notoriously dolphin-insensitive cartel. Angie remembered this scandalized the international Mutual-Back-Scratching academic community.

Actually, Lucifer already knew that his gravest problem with Grace centered in its complex electromagnetism. Specifically, the challenge came from its power to restore a vital polarity or tension between good/righteous and evil/sinner while vaporizing his dualisms of deception.

Lucifer's engineering demons had recently concocted a new substance, apatonium, that resembled vinyl sheeting. The name—apatonium—came from a dead language word meaning "deception." Lucifer's deceptions previously had been limited to removable layers of camouflage that blinded or suffocated individuals, relationships, or groups. Apatonium, however, could be installed in buildings.

His engineers had warned him that this new material's sole defect was its vulnerability to being vaporized via direct contact with Grace's electromagnetism. In the wrong hands, i.e. Mission Control's, Grace was the only thing that could put this newest demonic invention at risk. Grave risk.

Stealing a Grace ring was beyond his celestial prerogatives, of course. The only option open to Lucifer was to entice Angie into voluntarily surrendering her ring. That way his scientists could analyze its capabilities with state-of-the-art instrumentation and figure out how to short circuit Grace's uncanny electromagnetic powers.

> Oh, dear reader, who would have thought a ditzy, proven-failure Mission Angel would hold a key to our cosmic future. Huh? Would she fall for Lucifer's nefarious gambit? Or wouldn't she? *Editor.*

"All we need is your cooperation, Sweet Cakes. To finally graduate and help great science, all at once. Whadya say?"

"I need time to think it over."

"You? Think? Since when have you turned into a thinking machine, Bitsy Brain?"

"And you, Louie? You're nothing less than a perpetual booger in the nasal passages of the universe. We all feel you in there, but there's just no blowing you off."

She took a deep breath. "I'll need three months of Earther time to check things out."

"Too long. Two weeks. Max."

"Four, Lucifer. No less. Raphael won't be back much before that, and I need to verify some of your—um—information with him." She paused. "By the way, how come you, of all people, know so much about heaven stuff?"

"I used to live there, remember? Back when both of us were just kids, kinda?" She heard him clear his throat impatiently. "Gotta run, Toots. Four weeks it is. I have to come down your way anyway to check out an investment of mine. See you then. Bye, baby."

"Bye, Slimeball." ☆ See *Angel Beepsie's End Note.*

There was a click at his end just before she hung up the phone.

An angry Greg returned to the living room. "Angie, the devil is lying. It isn't my style to eavesdrop, but I listened to the conversation. He's lying through his teeth."

"I'm glad you listened, but how can you be so sure he's lying? I so want to believe Lucifer. Maybe just this once he's telling the truth. I mean, Greg, you have no idea how frustrating and shameful it is to fail so many Missions."

"Is it really 249 in a row? Is your record the worst up there?"

"Um, no, actually. Lots have worse records than mine. Angels Lena, Helga, Ole, Sven, and several dozen more. And that's just in our Blondes Division." She noticed his puzzled look. "Every fifty Earther years or so, Mission Control posts our standings. Sort of like Earther major league sports standings in the newspapers."

"Goof-ups galore out there, huh? So, compared to your colleagues' performances, you shouldn't let it get you down."

"Failed Missions? Yes. Major goof-ups? Not very often. Even for me. Most often failures happen because G gives Earthers the freedom to reject our Missions."

"Ah. Free will. Somebody, I think it was Isaac Bashevis Singer, once said: We must believe in free will. We have no other choice."

Angie shook her head. "No. No. That's not the same thing at all. Don't you see? Earthers have free will only to turn down G's offers." She smoothed both hands through her blonde curls and sighed. "His offer to you is through me, through my Mission with you. Otherwise, it messes everything up. Turning the initiative over to Earthers corrupts redemption into a phony transaction, a 'let's-make-a-deal' business where G ends up as your passive partner." Greg hung on her words.

"Anyway, let's get back to Lucifer," she said. "What makes you so sure he's lying to me?"

"Think for a minute. He gave himself away. A major clue was his comment about those graduation ceremonies." Greg scratched his head. "How'd he put it? Oh yeah. 'Poof, and just like that they're Heaven Angels.' Don't you see, Angie? You put your finger on it earlier when you jabbed Lucifer about his kingdom of 'get-it-all-now.' "

"What's the connection with Lucifer's offer? You heard him say there would be no strings attached."

"Sheezz, Angie, there *are*. Big strings."

"Like what?"

Greg counted off on the fingers of his left hand. "First, you exist in G's realm. G, who makes Time connect with right now. If Lucifer has his way, the present would be cut off from Grace and from any accountability to what has gone before or is coming.

"Second, his offer gets down to luring you into his slimy ballpark. You'll go down swinging, three strikes and you're the third out, bottom of the ninth. Sheezz, Angie, isn't it better to live with some failures rather than let Lucifer turn you into a loser in the biggest game of your life?"

"But it could make me a Heaven Angel," she whined.

"Come off it, Angela. Don't you get it yet?" He grasped another finger.

"Then, there's this third part. If you give the devil your Grace ring and his scientists succeed in figuring out how to short circuit Grace's power, where would that leave us Earthers from then on? Huh?" His tone grew harsh, "And where would that leave all the other Mission Angels?" Greg jabbed a finger at her. "I'll tell you where it would leave them—*betrayed*. By you, Angie."

Powerfully conflicting emotions turned on tears. "But G and M and Heaven Council would come up with something. Wouldn't they? Couldn't they?"

"Get this through that angelic skull of yours. One thing's for sure: None of them would roll out a red carpet for your stride into Heaven Angledom. You think any of them would authorize your graduation? Would they?"

Rushing to Greg, Angie sagged and sobbed as he comforted her in his arms. "I'm so confused," she wailed.

Kristin walked in just as Angie cried, "I don't want to be a traitor. I just want to become a Heaven Angel."

Kristin stroked Angie's shoulder. "It's going to be okay, honey. It will. Whatever it is. We're here for you, Greg and me. You know you can count on us." Kristin led her to the sofa and comforted a still-sobbing Angela.

Greg sat in his recliner. While his jaw rested on tented fingers, Greg thought about what had happened to him since Angela came into his life. Helping her sort out things affected him like a boomerang, he realized. His advice to her came back to influence him.

He wasn't surprised by Lucifer's pitch or by how he took an ounce of truth and tried to pass it off as a ton of benefits for Angie. Yeah. The only heavyweight winner in this scheme would be Lucifer, all right.

"Angie is who she says she is," Greg said softly. Kristin seemed puzzled. His chin lightly bumped his tented fingertips. "That actually was Lucifer on the phone, Kristin. He's trying to put Angie between a rock and a hard place. With my own ears, I heard the devil pressuring her big time."

Kristin silently mouthed the words at Greg while gesturing at Angie: "An angel? A real angel?"

He nodded. Kristin's jaw dropped and she gawked at the vulnerable blonde figure huddled beside her, sobs now subsiding to sporadic sharp, shuddering gasps.

☆ *Angel Beepsie's End Note*

Throughout her journal, Angie's epithet "Slimeball" rests on sound scholarly foundations. The term derives from an Old Norse dialect word, "lu," which meant "slime." Hence, "Lucifer" and "lutefisk" derive from "slime."

The other term, "siefer," meant either "ball" or "seeing-eye reindeer." Scholars are divided on the preferred translation. Angie's interpretation leans toward the former, despite her failed Mission experience with Lena, that sex-crazed Viking princess back in the eleventh century.

At six feet five inches and 360 pounds, Lena was a formidable nymphomaniac, even by Viking standards. Her favorite come-on was, "Let's wrestle." Too late would her non-compliant intended discover she wasn't wearing leggings—or anything else—under her bearskin poncho. One,

Ole the Lefty, failed to shove her off. He jammed his thumbs into her eyeballs as a last resort.

So when Angie *Zapped* into Lena's hut on the outskirts of Stavanger, they had to share the premises with Buffy, Lena's seeing-eye reindeer.

TEN

What if Mission Control couldn't find out why her Zapper didn't work at Louie's Place, where she spent most of her waking hours? What would happen to her? Would she have to give up her 250th Mission? G forbid. Angie panicked at the thought. What if her Zapper was permanently dysfunctional? She didn't say anything to Kristin or Greg because she didn't want them to worry. She felt so alone...

Meanwhile, Raphael ordered Engineering to go on Four Halo alert to find out why Angie's Zapper had not been effective on New Year's Eve. Heaven Council was kept informed. Several minutes of thorough testing verified that the fault was not with Angie's *Zap* barrette. So, once again, Zap Central was caught up in what the technical manuals ranked as a Double Doozie crisis. Why couldn't Angie communicate with them on New Year's Eve? Why couldn't she *Zap* away from Denise?

A more thorough investigation was in order. But that could require too much time. Fortunately, within the hour, Mission Control received a pneumatic memo from Heaven Council staff. Central Angelic Intelligence had been tracking an unusual flurry of activity at Sheol Science Synthetics, a wholly-owned subsidiary of Lucifer Unlimited, which operated in one of hell's suburbs. CAI had been alerted several months earlier by an Earther police report of an unusual theft. Several tons of K-Mart shopping baggies had been stolen from that firm's south Texas warehouse without any sign of entry or transport. Those crates had just disappeared.

"Attention! Your Supreme Supervisor has an announcement." The voice of a Heaven Council member's AA boomed over the CRC's loudspeakers. "The mike is yours, Supremacy, Sir."

"Ahem. Yes. Now then." The CRC crowd recognized Gabriel's voice and style. "Now hear this. Cancel all classes at the university for the next hour. All Mission Control personnel will meet in the auditorium. Ahem. The news of Angela Four's whereabouts on New Year's Eve provided us with the missing piece in a heretofore troublesome puzzle. Look for my arrival forthwith. Stat. Over and out. Et cetera."

"Gabriel is a different breed of cat when he's at headquarters," Angel Bert commented to a fellow console nerd. "Not at all like the casual, quirky guy he is around us."

Va-ROOOOM. It took Gabriel only a few minutes to *Zap* in. The sound roared through the open suns-lit windows of *Zap* Central.

Varoom, VRUM.

A flurry of Mission Angels accompanied Raphael to meet the Supreme Supervisor as he idled at the main entry portico in his multi-dented BMW. On the front bumper of Gabriel's car, a sticker declared: ANGELS CARE A LOT. A sticker on the rear promised: WHEN THE RAPTURE COMES, THIS VEHICLE WILL BE THERE.

Varoooommm. The final engine rev-up was almost a purr. A seriously-visaged Gabriel turned off the ignition, hopped out and grabbed his infamous trombone.

"Everything ready?" Gabriel asked. Mission Control staff nodded. As the group headed toward Mission Control's auditorium, a raucous din of voices could be heard. Clusters of Mission Angels were jabbering away in hallways, stairwells, and in the narthex.

Gabriel entered the auditorium, proceeded to the podium, and raised his trombone. "Oh, nooo," Angel Bert said, "he's gonna do it again."

Gabriel's custom and prerogative was to blow his horn preceding an announcement. So, he began to blow that horn—after a fashion. Staff's best guess was that he was attempting "Yankee Doodle Dandy." They cringed at Gabriel's off-pitch tootling.

But Gabriel's miserable music making had the desired effect: Assembly Call. Mission Angels rushed to their seats, knowing that the longer they took, the longer they had to endure this horrid noise. A Heaven Council administrative assistant, who accompanied Gabriel on this trip, asked Raphael, "Where's his trumpet? He's a real pro on that."

"The rings. Notice the Grace ring he wears on each finger, thumbs included. The rings interfere with his valve fingering. He switched to the trombone to keep his lip in shape for Judgment Day."

"To have to listen to Gabriel's new horn borders on doing third-degree Penance, if you ask me."

The angelic host was seated and quiet. Gabriel laid his horn on a nearby table and pulled a gold marker pen from his pocket as he moved to a flip chart. A hush fell over the assembled multitude.

"Hey!" Gabriel shielded his eyes. "Turn off those halos, will you? Too much holy light can blind a guy."

A thousand Mission Angels pinched their noses to extinguish a thousand glowing halos.

"Now then," Gabriel continued. "We now know that Angie was inside Louie's Place when she was cut off from all *Zap* functions. Why? Because the whole place is shrouded by a layer of apatonium."

Questions floated through the crowd.

"Shhhh, if you listen up, I'll explain." Silence prevailed. "Ahem. The name of this substance, apatonium, comes from a dead language word meaning deception. As far as we can tell, Louie's Place and the New York Stock Exchange are the first structures where our Old Foe has actually installed the material. Rumors that he also has shrouded Chicago's Wrigley Field with it have no basis in fact since Cub fans' delusions apparently derive more than early childhood trauma than from demonic causes. Ahem. Yes, Angel Ed?"

"Gabriel, Lucifer has used layers of deception ever since Eden or at least since then. Hasn't he?"

"True enough. And he still does." Gabriel shook his head sadly. "That old Deceiver is as crafty and subtle as ever at it, too. What's new here is that he's managed to fabricate one hundred percent pure deception down there at his Triple-S complex." He held up a sheet of ten-gauge clear vinyl. "Apatonium looks like this, except it has a shimmering off-white cast to it. It's difficult to install. But he had it done around Louie's Place much as an Earther building contractor installs a layer of vinyl sheeting to vapor barrier a new house in North Dakota."

"What's all this got to do with us at Zap Central not being able to get through to Angie on New Year's Eve?" Angel Johann called from the enthralled throng.

"As you know, Jack—and some of you might be bored by this—our *Zap* system uses neutrino waves. Earther scientists know very little about neutrinos. They are still building experiments just to prove those little goodies exist."

"Even I know about neutrinos," Angel Charlie yelled. One of Angel U's truly marginal students, Charlie had repeated twice as many courses as Angie. Since an Angel U semester runs nearly two Earther centuries, repeating a course sorely tests vaunted angelic patience. As bright as any other Mission Angel, Charlie's learning disability was rooted in his addiction to computer war games.

"Just yesterday, I took an hour or so off to surf the Interzap, a little sight-seeing excursion, and I kept my *Zap* gear in double-low," Charlie said. "Even though I throttled down to near stall speed so I could enjoy the scenery, that still didn't keep me below a hundred Winks." (One Wink equals the speed of light. *Editor*.)

"Engineering is working on that speed problem, Chuck." Gabriel cleared his throat. "Meanwhile, back to our agenda.

Ahem. Yes. Now then. Earther scientists do know this about neutrinos: they go through anything. Anything at all. Nothing blocks neutrinos and our *Zap* system except one thing: a layer of Lucifer's deceptions. Up till now, of course, if an Earther wanted to remove a layer, Holy Spirit staff would see to it. No problem. But when his deception is in the form of apatonium and gets installed in a building, well, that stuff is a real toughie."

"How about sending in the Grey Berets?" Angel Jacob called from a back row.

"Good thinking, Jake. The same idea occurred to us at HQ, too." Gabriel admired the three carat sapphire ring on each finger of his right hand. "As we speak, a crack Grey Beret battalion is in 'round-the-clock apatonium deconstruction training maneuvers on the backside of planet Fahrt. Ahem. The volcano there is dormant so you needn't worry about any of our Berets suffocating on its fumes. Ahem. They are gaining precious experience in the use of our new Grace laser which vaporizes apatonium on contact."

> Fahrt is Mission Control's "deployment planet." Hence, its name derives—quite suitably—from the German verb for "travel," *fahren.* Its twin hemispheres are, topographically speaking, quite blah. The only vegetation, short hair shrubbery, grows on ridges of numerous hills dating from the Cellulite Age, the planet's continental drift epoch. *Editor.*

Angel Bob called from a middle row. "Are their new flak jackets ready?"

"Indeed. And we've added a double-whammy bonus to them: four-color reproductions on front and back. The timeless masterpiece of Salman's head of Christ on back." He framed both hands. "About yeah-big. What's on the front, you're thinking? A superb portrait, especially commissioned by the Archbishop of Dubuque, of Our Lady of Guadalupe. We want to cover all bases to protect our Grey Berets."

Gabriel returned to the podium. "If and when M gives the deployment signal, they will depart for earth directly from their training base on Fahrt. Ahem. It could get a bit dicey for our Berets down there."

He glanced at his watch. "Oooo. Time for my trombone lesson. So, now you've been briefed on what's blocking our *Zap* system with Angie and on our strategy for overcoming this latest of Lucifer's wily ways. Ahem. Carry on, then. As you were. Et cetera." He picked up the trombone, glanced again at his watch, and hurried from the Mission Control auditorium.

Zap Central went into Stage Two (of four) high-panic mode. They now knew why they couldn't communicate with Angie whenever she was at Louie's Place. But it was critical to warn her about the apatonium shroud.

Angel Bert huddled nervously with Mission Angel Corps managers as they kept checking for Zapfax messages from Angie. But they got nothing—not one word—from her. What on earth was she doing? Why couldn't they contact her?

Bert straightened in his chair at the computer terminal. "I'm worried. She's blanked out on us several times, and this just isn't like her to not communicate. When she worked with George Washington's cousin, she always checked in on schedule. In fact, she called so much about such trivial things that I often took a nap while she communicated. Now we've got this giant crisis on our hands and can't even tell her about it."

"Maybe she's washing her hair again," Angel Mabel said.

"For three hours? I doubt it."

"Where's Raphael?" Angel Abe answered himself with a finger snap. "He's on planet Fahrt checking out our Grey Berets."

"How long is he supposed to be gone?" Mabel asked.

"Bad news," Bert said. "Sending for Raphael so he can go to earth to check on Angie is beyond our authority. On the other hand, we've got to pull out all the stops so Angie's Mission succeeds this time. She has to graduate to Heaven Angel so she won't cause us more headaches. We all need a rest from Angela Four."

"Bert, I'd appreciate it if you didn't remind us of Heaven luxuries right now," Angel Ingeborg snapped. "I just failed another Mission, and I don't want to be hear about how good it feels to walk with bare feet on streets paved with gold. Okay? I have to wait another two hundred years before I get my next Mission."

After hours of debate about what action to take, Angel Jack said, "Let's call Gabriel."

"Good idea. We don't have another option." Bert slapped his forehead. "Why didn't I think of that?"

Immediately he commenced the Call process.

Although Mission Control had the most advanced celestial technology in some areas, others ironically combined the archaic with high tech. Exchanging messages with Heaven was one Zap Central system that was such a case.

Without warning, a pneumatic tube hissed, its flap door opened, and a drive-in bank canister plopped onto Bert's console. The end cap opened with a mechanical "whrrr" sound. Out staggered a carrier pigeon, holding a microfiche tube in her beak, obviously dazed by her latest pneumatic experience. Bert noticed confused expressions on the faces of several angels as he opened the tiny tube and placed two microfiche squares in the viewer.

"Surely, we've got more advanced technology for Heaven communications than a pigeon." It was clear that Angel Mabel disapproved.

"Afraid not."

"But why a pigeon?"

"Well, the carrier pigeons have this union, see? Formed about the time they went extinct on earth. And their contract has a no-layoff clause and bans outsourcing. But hey, it's work."

"Look!" Ingeborg yelled in her out-of-patience mode. "Are we gonna sit around and talk about pigeons or are we gonna send a message to Gabriel?"

Immediately Bert punched in the Call process code. Moments later, Mission Angels at Zap Central heard Gabriel's loud entrance. Varoom, VaROOM.

Zap Central staff scurried outside to watch Gabriel pull up in his Bimmer. When Gabriel saw the angels rushing toward him, he grinned. No doubt about it, he loved this job. Varoom, VaROOM. Gabriel couldn't resist revving up the engine a couple more times before he turned it off. He jumped out.

"We still can't contact Angie," Bert said.

"Have you tried her Zapfax or Zapmike?"

"Yes, but we can't get through to her."

"Hmm. Let's go inside so you can brief me on what's happened the last few hours." Gabriel grabbed his trombone.

"I don't mean to tell you what to do, Your Supremacy, sir, but why not omit the trombone call." Bert tried to speak in a polite voice. "I think we already have everyone's attention here. All of us have been frantic about Angie. The sooner we figure out how to contact her about the apatonium, the better."

Gabriel paused for an instant and said, "Good point. For a minute there, I was afraid you didn't like my trombone playing."

"Gabriel, about that trombone..." Angel Mabel spoke up, but Bert quickly backed up and stomped on her toe. "Ouch!"

"Mabel, you were saying about my trombone..."

Bert turned abruptly and glared at her. Mabel resented the dirty look, but she cleared her throat and said, "Nothing, Your Supremacy, sir."

At the computer console, Bert punched in every standard *Zap* communication code. Still no answer. With his sidekick, Angel Bob, they flipped every button they could get their hands on.

"Not looking good. Not good at all." Gabriel made a quick decision. "Contact Raphael at Maneuvers. Send it *Code Red, Priority Hustle*."

"That's already been suggested," Bert said. "But, Your Supremacy, sir. I'll never hear the end of it if I disrupt his review of Grey Berets' readiness just to check on Angie's situation."

"Contact him anyway," Gabriel demanded. "He's responsible for Angie and is the only one available with sufficient authority to brief her about the apatonium."

"But sir..." Bert protested.

"Just *do* it, Bertie. We don't have time to argue. Trust me." Bert had no choice. He punched in a Zapfax message to Raphael. "Code Red: Go to Angie. Subject: Apatonium briefing."

Raphael responded without delay. He knew that if he could get Angie's complete attention, she's what Intergalactic Press journalists call a quick study. News about the apatonium shroud around Louie's Place would certainly get her attention.

Raphael *Zapped* to the parking lot of Louie's Place and rushed inside to brief her. He brought Angie up to speed on everything they knew about apatonium. But he also had to tell her that when the Solution was discovered, it would have to be implemented in what technicians called the Matzoh (unleavened bread snap-off/breakthrough) rather than Leavened (slow-rising) mode. They agreed that she would Zapmike in at 10 A.M. each day to keep in touch with Mission Control.

Meanwhile, Raphael would head back to Mission Control and work with Engineering on the Matzoh approach. Angie was to "carry on," as Gabriel would say. Once again Angie felt gloom and doom as she thought about the increasing possibility she might fail her Mission because of this terrible apatonium crisis.

Back to the nitty gritty stuff of daily grinds. Angie enjoyed working at Louie's Place, but it presented yet another problem: transportation. Angie hated being dependent on Greg and Kristin to drive her to and from work six days a week. So Monday evening she announced that she was going to learn to drive a car.

"That's a great idea," Kristin said as she sat on the sofa rubbing her legs.

"It's a horrible idea." Greg scowled.

"Y'all taught me to drive, darling, remember?" Kristin cooed.

"That's why I say it's a horrible idea. Those lessons put me on valium till you got your license."

"One of you will teach me to drive, won't you, please? Pretty please?"

"Of course." Kristin smirked. "Greg should be the one."

"Me? No way."

The two women continued talking about it as though Greg weren't in the room. "Would I have to pass a sanity test like the one they require for drivers on planet Bubba?" Angie scratched her head. "Ha. Now I remember. They test only pick-up truck drivers for that."

Angie was relieved. She turned to Greg. "When can we start?"

He tried to refuse.

"Aw come on, darlin', if you really, really, really love me, you'll do it," Kristin said.

Angie wasn't certain exactly how it happened, but ten minutes later Greg sat next to her as she settled behind the steering wheel. Kristin climbed into the back seat. With sweaty palms, Angie grabbed the steering wheel so hard her knuckles turned white. She noticed Greg's hands clutching the dashboard; the blood vessels in his neck protruded.

When Angie turned the key, the engine coughed to life and the red Nissan swirled into traffic. Suddenly, she was terrified. Where on earth had all those cars come from anyway?

"For Pete's sake, watch out for the other cars." Greg yelled as Angie swerved back and forth in the four-lane traffic.

"I am watching, but that doesn't help much."

"Careful, or you'll hit that truck," Kristin screeched from the back seat.

"What truck?"

"The one coming toward us."

☆ *Angel Beepsie's End Note*

First, Gabriel. Now, Angie. What is it about angels that makes them such awful drivers? Is it that their minds are on such lofty concerns they can't be bothered with trivialities such as traffic? Or, could it be that their natural predisposition to fly conflicts with a driving frame of mind?

Lest one be tempted to assume the answer to this paramount mystery will only be revealed sometime after Judgment Day, the results from a series of angelic focus groups conducted by Celestial Body Shop Associates may be helpful in opinion formation. Ranked in this order, the top three angelic driving distractions include:

(1) grieving over the fate of zillions of harmless little polyesters slaughtered to make tire cord for all those other vehicles;

(2) daydreaming about Earther couture fashion trends;

(3) vocalizing for an upcoming *menuddeh* monotone voice lesson.

Numerous individual quirks abound, of course, besides Gabriel's aiming his dashboard plastic Jesus at roadway center lines.

ELEVEN

Angie yanked the wheel. Truck tires squealed. Several drivers honked. A yellow car filled with teenagers swirled by. The driver rolled down the window and gave her a single-digit benediction.

"What's he trying to say?"

"Never mind that now." Greg's voice was strained. "Just stay in your lane."

"You'll live through this. We all will." Angie's confident tone contrasted with her nervous system.

"*You* will live through this," Greg yelled to Angie. "You're an angel. You won't die. But what about Kristin and me?"

Angie didn't say anything, but she knew Greg did have a point.

Angie's driving lessons continued until, one day, it happened. Kristin took Angie to the driver's license bureau where Angie passed the test and got her driver's license.

To celebrate, Angie prepared Greg's favorite gourmet dinner—rump roast marinated in a secret wine sauce, baked potatoes, corn on the cob, and a fresh fruit salad. Her escargot appetizer also drew raves, although she did not reveal her secret extra ingredient for its marinade: peanut butter.

Greg praised Angie's culinary achievement. "This dinner's marvelous. What's the occasion?"

"To tell you the truth, I've been out driving today."

"The only thing I do when you drive is pray."

"Prayer is good. What do you pray about?"

"Every time you're behind the wheel, I pray for everything. I pray for the steering wheel. I pray for the brakes to work. I pray for your hands to be steady. I pray for the traffic. G, I pray for the other drivers."

"About tonight's big occasion. Your praying helped me get my driver's license today. After I almost hit a stop sign, I thought I'd fail for sure."

"You got your driver's license?" Greg dropped his fork. "You're kidding."

"Nope," Kristin said. "It's true, darlin'. Isn't it wonderful?"

"A gen-u-ine miracle."

Kristin laughed. "The next step, Angie, is to buy your own vehicle for getting to work."

"But I don't have money for a car."

"Doesn't matter." Kristin pointed her hand skyward. "You can use credit."

"Use credit? Don't you remember? My card is maxed out."

"That's no problem."

"But if I haven't paid off that credit card, how could I buy a car?"

Credit cards didn't exist during her last visit to America, when George Washington's good-for-nothing cousin still prowled the streets. So Angie continued to be both confused and bemused by credit cards.

"We'll get you a car loan at my bank."

Angie couldn't help but like Kristin. She came up with the best ideas. And Angie learned so much from Kristin's shopping lessons. Of course, the shopping explained why Angie hadn't saved any money for a car. It wasn't that Angie wasn't making good money. She was pulling in about $300 in tips on a good night at Louie's Place. It's just that the next day they would binge shop, and Angie would spend $500. Or more.

"Are you sure I can afford the payments?"

"If things get tight one month, use another card to meet the payment. That's why I've got fourteen cards."

"Wow! Fourteen credit cards?"

"Sure, I'll show you how it's done. I'm an expert on credit card use."

"In Kristin's case, it amounts to abuse." Greg pointed at Kristin. "Babe, you spend like you're still a big bucks senior vice president."

"Men. They just don't understand us women."

That afternoon Kristin took Angie shopping. Angie came back with another charge account and several bags of clothes, a CD player and a laptop computer. She enjoyed acquiring what the Double-E called material possessions. She began to understand how craving such things could amount to idolatry for some Earthers.

But it also bothered Angie that she had another major temptation to overcome besides brandy alexanders: overspending on credit cards. It was as though layers of something were clouding her vision.

Enough heavy stuff. She'd concentrate on more fun things—such as sporting her new clothes and learning how to use the quaintly limited Earther laptop computer.

The counter top at Louie's was polished to a high gloss. Glasses were lined up neatly on shelves and sparkled in the dim red lights. Standing behind the counter, Angie buffed a glass with a white cloth.

Guy, Tex, and Rita were at the bar. Setting the polished glass on the shelf, Angie noticed Guy's Perrier bottle was almost empty.

"Ready for another, Guy?"

"Sure, but you keep mispronouncing my name."

"Sorry about that. I read Guy and forget it should sound like Ghee. No harm done?"

He shrugged and glanced a puzzled look her way. Like other Louie's Place regulars, Guy didn't believe Angie was an angel. On that issue, the jury was still out for Tex.

Rita laughed. "Better get Guy another drink quick, Angie. He's intolerable when he doesn't have a full Perrier bottle to fondle."

"Long as y'all is serving, I'm gonna need another Laht," Tex drawled.

"And a margarita for me, please."

"Better go easy on those margaritas, Rita," PC said. "Last time you had a couple of those, your date never showed up."

"That's nothing new," Tex teased. "Rita's dates rarely show."

As yet, no one else knew Rita's real motive for hanging out at Louie's Place.

Schwartz laughed, his large shoulders bouncing. "Scared off, I bet." He affected a hands up, no offense gesture at her withering glare. "Maybe you should practice up on the sweet l'il ole me routine. Works on lots of guys."

"I am who I am. If a guy doesn't like it, tough turkeys!" Angie noticed Rita's cream-colored face flush red. It was true. Earther males were intimidated by her brains, looks, and assertive personality.

On the other side of the bar, Angie poured a brandy alexander for herself. She didn't want anyone to see her drinking at work, although Nemmy encouraged her to sample the goods. She had fallen into the drinking cycle, but what else was she supposed to do when none of her *Zap* functions worked in Louie's Place? She glanced at her Grace ring, which she usually left at home, and wondered if it, too, was useless here.

Rita sipped her drink. "Tex, you need another beer."

Scooting his Stetson back an inch, Tex smirked. "Well, that's the first thing you ever said that I agree with, Miz Rita."

"Tex, don't you ever think about your body? Drinking all that beer's gotta be hard on a fellow." Guy was sincere, not scolding.

"Man, have y'all ever looked at the back of a beer can? It's breakfast. Wheat, barley, oats."

Peter Chambers strolled in sporting a dark blue pinstripe suit, a starched white shirt, and blue paisley tie. "Ah, great to be back among friends again." He climbed onto his favorite stool. "Angie, how about starting me off right with one of your specialties." He yanked his tie loose, peeled a ten-dollar bill from his money clip and laid it on the counter.

"How's your wife, PC?" Angie placed the drink before him. "Where's she tonight?"

Leaning over the bar, Peter cupped a palm by one side of his mouth. "Angie, that wasn't my wife I had in here last night."

"But you acted like she was your wife."

"Isn't she something?" He tapped the side of his head. "Not much in the noggin. But, from the neck down...Wow!"

"You're in big trouble."

"Not as long as my wife doesn't find out." He winked at Angie. "Wish I could talk you into some action. Or are you going to tell me that angels don't mess around?"

Angie turned and stalked off. It still embarrassed her that she'd babbled on New Year's Eve about being an angel. She didn't enjoy being laughed at.

"I suppose a woman as gorgeous as you has to come up with some crazy line like that or guys would be hitting on you."

From the other end of the bar, she glanced at PC and decided if she couldn't "beat them," she'd "join them." Greg taught her that Earther saying. "What's the matter? You still don't believe I'm an angel who attends Angel U?"

Peter slowly eyeballed Angie's figure. "I believe you're an angel all right, but a student at some university in another galaxy? Nah, never heard of such a thing. Besides, I don't believe there's life in outer space. Most Baptists don't."

"Most Baptists don't believe in drinking and adultery, either. You, however, seem to manage both. Why do you date other women when you're married?"

"Yeah, why are you addicted to one-night stands and avoid lasting relationships?" Guy pressured.

"'Cuz I gotta do what I gotta do." PC lifted his drink, toasted Angie, and said, "Cheers. *Pour moi.*"

Rita interrupted. "Who's the fat guy over there?" Her head gestured in the direction of a short overweight man in a cheap suit who carried an attaché case with him. He made his way to the other side of the bar.

"Noooo!" PC slammed his fist on the bar. "Fat guy is a no-no, Rita. That's a 'weight-enhanced male person.' "

"Sorry, sir." A corner of Rita's mouth turned up. "Still looks like a fat guy to me."

"I don't know who he is either, but I'm about to find out." Schwartz got up from his stool and walked over to the newcomer. He extended his hand. "Hello, I'm Guy Schwartz, prof at the university. And, you're...?"

A limp, clammy hand returned the gesture. "Walter Irs, the Second. I work with numbers."

"Aha. A mathematician. Teach? Research?"

"Financial numbers. The kind that don't add up."

"Oh." This man had the smallest eyes Schwartz had ever seen. "Well, Walter Irs, the Second, we're always glad to see a new face in Louie's Place. A welcome relief from the moldy ones over there. By the way, you have a nickname? Walt, is it? Or, Wally?"

"Walter Irs, the Second."

Schwartz waited. "That's it? Your nickname? So your mother yells, 'Walter Irs, the Second, come here this instant!"

As though jolted by a live electrical wire, his swollen checks glowing beet red, the man blurted, "Who told you? That's a personal matter. Tell me."

"Sorry, pal," was all Schwartz could manage. He glanced down at the open attaché case on a stool next to the newcomer. The signature notation at the bottom of a memo page caught his eye: W-2. He backed away and returned to the others.

"The guy never blinks," Schwartz muttered as he sat down. "Not once. No nickname, either. Does sign his memos with W-2, however."

When the man told Angie he never drinks at work, she offered him a cup of the bar's free coffee. He accepted and sipped some. "Good coffee, Ms. Angela." He'd peered at the name plate on her bar apron. He kept nodding as he gazed at her. "Thank you." No smile, not the slightest change in facial expression.

"He's kinda spooky, if you ask me," Angie whispered as she wiped a spot near Rita's drink.

"Right up your alley, huh angel?" Rita said. She shared the others' skepticism about Angie's angelic status.

After Walter Irs, the Second, drank his free coffee he asked Angie, "Could I get a refill?"

Without thinking, she automatically poured another coffee and handed it to him. He took the cup and went to a booth where he sat alone. As Angie went about her job, the mysterious man tapped the keys on his laptop.

Several times a week, Walter Irs, the Second, entered Louie's Place, sat by himself, drank free coffee, and made quick notes as Angie went about her business. Angie wondered what he wanted. Was he a spy? And, if he was, what or who was he spying on?

"Drinking heavy tonight, aren't you, Guy? Four Perriers—wow!" PC assumed his quirky grin, his lower lip overriding its mate.

"Yep. A bad week."

"What happened?" Angie poured a drink for Rita.

Guy shook his head and sighed as he pushed his glasses up from the tip of his bulbous nose. "I get so ticked off with those mini-minds at the university. They torpedoed another grant proposal of mine."

Pushing his Stetson back, Tex drawled, "What'd y'all want this time?"

"Some funds to do background research for my Unified Standard Significance theory of the universe. Do you suppose those faculty pointy-heads would support it? Nah. I'm telling you, peer reviewers live in la-la land."

"The USS Schwartz gets torpedoed again." PC was sympathetic. "She still afloat, Guy?" Schwartz sighed and shrugged.

Angie piped in. "I can tell you how the universe came to be. It began when time began. 'G' said, 'Let there be light.' " They gave her a blank stare.

After a few moments of silence, Tex drawled, "Rita, I'm beginning to think you have no love life."

"Duuuh!" PC groaned. "Welcome to the third planet from the sun, Tex."

"Let me tell y'all about what happened to me this morning." Tex ignored PC's insult. "Maybe it can help Rita here. I was thinking about how I was channelin' with my future daughter again. I was gonna ask her about some of them stock market figures, but she says she didn't have the time cuz she's got a date with a real nice guy. I ask her, well, is this guy maybe gonna be my son-in-law? Y'all know what I'm saying? And she said, she didn't know. When I asked what his name was, she didn't know that either.

"Well, I got my thinking hat on and I said to myself, not out loud but silent-like? I said, maybe she's too embarrassed to admit to her pa she ain't got no love life at all." He turned his face toward Rita. "Which reminds me of you."

"Really!" Rita's eyes flashed with anger. "My love life's nobody else's business."

"Appears so." Tex smirked.

"Tex, how can we shut you up?" PC was embarrassed for Rita.

"Just say $53,568.32." Angie stared at Tex.

Tex's face reddened as he jumped to his feet. "Angie? We gotta talk. Outside." She told Nemmy she needed a five-minute break and followed Tex.

"Why are you doing this to me?"

"What am I doing to you?"

"Embarrassing me."

"I'm not trying to embarrass you. All I'm trying to do is become a Heaven Angel. That's why I can't restrain myself from helping Earthers like you."

"Well, you're sure as heck not helping me by blasting that figure around in front of my friends."

Angie studied Tex. "Tell me. What will wake you up?"

"Huh? I'm on full alert."

"Only about the things you want to be," Angie said. "I mean, when are you going to take responsibility for your daughter—the one here on earth?"

"I couldn't take responsibility for her even if I wanted to. I don't know where she is." He gazed at his feet. Tears came to his eyes.

Angie's manner softened. "In that case, I'll make arrangements for you to find her. Right now, I've got to get back to our customers."

She went inside and left a puzzled Tex behind. She was pleased. With her contacts, it wouldn't be difficult to arrange for Tex to spend some quality time with his daughter. The rest would be up to him. She'd provide the opportunity, with plenty of help from above. After all, wasn't that also what angels are for?

The next morning Angie prepared a hot breakfast. The three of them reminisced about their disastrous experience at Group.

"Angie, you do need help with that angel fixation of yours. After our Group fiasco, maybe a new approach is called for."

She withdrew a slip of paper from her robe pocket. "Rita gave me the name of a priest she swears by, a Father Gaelic. Irish Catholic. Rita says he's a terrific counselor, brogue and all. Would you like the name of this man of the cloth?" Kristin spoke earnestly.

"A man of the cloth?" Angie chewed a slice of breakfast bratwurst. "I didn't know G made any Earthers from cloth. I thought they were made from dust."

"An Earther clergy person sometimes wears distinctive clothing, Angie."

Greg put down his fork. "This should remind you how really important it is to study your EE."

"A priest or minister. Why didn't I think of that? Surely a minister, called by G, would understand an angel like me."

"Don't be so sure," Greg warned. "There aren't a whole lot of Earthers who would believe you."

"So you think Rita's priest person could help me?"

"It's worth a try."

In Father Gaelic's office, sunlight shone through a small stained-glass window depicting the Immaculate Conception. It was hard to tell what was the focal point on the only wall not covered with bookshelves: the simple crucifix or the multitude of Notre Dame football souvenirs hung around it. A framed photo of this year's team was draped in black satin, mourning the team's sole loss of the season in the Goodrich Annual Tire Sale Starts Tomorrow Bowl.

"Please, make yourself comfortable." Father Gaelic pointed to a large red velvet chair. "How can I help you, Ms. Four?"

"I get into so much trouble on my Missions. I try so hard. But I keep getting myself in such messes."

"What kind of messes?" From a matching red chair, Father Gaelic used his practiced "Going My Way" smile.

Angie blinked her blue eyes, crossed her legs, sighed, and smoothed her red dress. How best to explain? She paused for silent prayer.

The priest leaned forward. "Don't be ashamed to tell me your problem, my child. There's nothing you could say that I haven't heard before."

Shaking her head, tears came to Angie's eyes. She felt like, well, like maybe this priest was her last opportunity for help. "I'm so embarrassed." Pearly angelic tears dribbled down her cheeks.

Father Gaelic stifled an Irish double-take at his first sight of such tears. Pearly tears? Whoa! "When people tell me they are embarrassed, they've usually been involved in some type of illicit sexual activity. Have you had an affair?"

"Course not." Angie dabbed a few pearly tears with a white tissue. "Angels don't have sex."

"Angels?"

"Yes, I'm a Mission Angel."

"An—ahem—ang-ang-angel?"

Angie wailed. "Don't tell me you don't believe in angels, too."

"Of course I believe in angels, my child. All contributing Catholics do. I, uh, never expected one to come to my office."

At last, she'd found someone who could help her. "I'll demonstrate some of my angelic powers, if you'd like." Father Gaelic nodded, somewhat tolerantly.

Angie demonstrated Quickie *Zaps* several times. *ZAP!* Out and into the priestly office, each reappearance featuring her "Ta Da!" vaudeville posture.

Father Gaelic fell to his knees and grabbed a rosary from the coffee table. "Hail Mary..." he started saying over and over.

"Father? Father Gaelic?" Angie tapped his shoulder but got no response. She'd never heard an Earther say a "Hail Mary!" so fast, yet with such fervor. She felt just terrible because she had caused another disturbance. She rushed down the hall to see if she could find help. A nun scurried past.

"Excuse me. Could you help me, please?"

The gray-haired nun smiled and gave Angie an embrace. "I'm always happy to help someone in need, however I can." She, too, had an Irish brogue. "I'm Sister Heidi."

"Aren't you a sweetie, Heidi." Angie beamed. "I'm Angela Four. I do hope you can help. I'm afraid I upset Father Gaelic."

"Upset Father Gaelic?" The nun frowned. "Impossible. The man's unflappable, one of the calmest men on earth. I'm sure it's not that bad."

When Angie escorted Sister Heidi into his office, a traumatized Father Gaelic clasped the rosary in his left hand as his right arm made repeated forward pass gestures. "Hail Mary...!"

"Glory be!" The nun gasped, slapped both palms to her cheeks. "I've never seen Father Gaelic go Catholic catatonic before. What happened?"

"I came here assuming a Catholic priest would help an angel, but I was wrong," Angie said. "That's what I am. When I demonstrated a couple of Quickie *Zaps* to Father Gaelic, it must have pushed him over the corner."

"The edge, my child. Over the *edge*." Sister Heidi blinked several times. The nun bestowed her practiced "Song of Bernadette" smile on Angie and put a comforting arm around her.

"Come. Sit down, my child. How about a glass of iced tea? It's quite warm today. That may be your problem. Heat can do strange things to the mind. Or perhaps you'd like a cool glass of lemonade?"

"No, thank you, but I'd love a brandy frederick."

Sister Heidi frowned. "Brandy frederick? You mean, brandy alexander? No, my dear, we don't keep booze in parish offices, least of all in our 'Take It to the Lord' wing."

"But I'm mad at him." Angie gestured upward.

"Mad at the Heavenly Father? That's permitted. But tell me why."

"I've been wanting to become a Heaven Angel ever since the Fourth Day of creation. I can't take Angel U anymore." She noted the nun's skeptical frown. "Angel U is on planet Oreo. In the Patty-Cakes suns system."

"Sure it is." Sister Heidi slowly moved a finger in front of Angie's face, testing for eye focus. "Would you like us to do inkblots together?"

"I'm not enjoying earth too much these days." Angie pouted. "Maybe a game would help, if you'll teach me. I've never played Ink Blots before. Does it go by another name, by any chance?"

"Rorschach. Exactly what did you tell Father Gaelic?"

"All I did was tell him I'm an angel. Then I demonstrated some Quickie *Zaps*." Angie's fingers went to her barrette. *ZAP! ZAP!* Each time she tapped the Travel bar, she'd flashed out and back into the room. The folds of skin under Sister Heidi's chin quivered. Her complexion—even her ruddy Irish nose—turned white.

"Blessed Mother!" Sister Heidi shrieked and clutched a spare rosary. She scrambled to her knees next to Father Gaelic. Left-handed, her forward pass gestures were no less vigorous than his. "Hail Mary...!"

Angie wailed. "What have I done?"

It took dozens more vigorous Hail Marys to calm Father Gaelic and Sister Heidi. They took turns massaging each other's aching passing arm.

Angie *Zapped* herself back to Greg's apartment.

Angie fidgeted on the sofa while Kristin and Greg relaxed in the two matching recliners.

"Where can I find help now?" Picking up a newspaper, she flipped through the ad section.

"Listen to this. It says here, 'Dial your troubles away. Dial our spiritual experts and get immediate results.' "

"That ad runs every day, hon," Kristin said. "It's by some religious outfit with a telephone hotline for people in trouble."

"I'm in trouble. All I have to do, according to this ad, is just dial for help. I'm going to call them right now." Flipping blonde curls off her forehead, Angie got up from the sofa and hurried to the telephone.

"Thank you for calling Stuart Sweetly Spiritual Ministries," a pleasant voice answered.

"You're welcome," Angie said.

Before Angie could explain her problem, the recorded voice said, "If you wish to get a copy of our absolutely free book, simply press One and give us your credit card number to cover shipping and handling costs of $15.95. If you need prayer, press Two and give us your credit card number. If you want to volunteer for one of our ministry projects, push Three and give us your credit card number. If you need to speak to one of our Sweetly Spiritual staff persons, sorry, our lines are busy. Please wait. You don't have to give your credit card number to wait."

Nearly ten minutes later, a bored voice said, "This is the operator. How may I direct your call?"

"Yes." Angie breathed a sigh of relief. "I'm an angel from Angel U on planet Oreo. I came here to help an Earther named Greg Matthews get his act together so I can graduate to Heaven Angel status."

"Of course, of course, so does a horse." The operator laughed. "This is a new one on me. Go on."

"Greg's a nice Mission Guy. They don't come any nicer. And he's been making progress on our Mission agenda. He's even stopped boozing it up. But while he's stopped, I've started. Drinking, that is. Brandy alexanders. Instead of working my way up to Heaven Angel, I keep getting into more trouble."

"Lady, you can't work your way to heaven."

"What can I do?"

"Read your Bible, pray, and send us your credit card number. I've got another call. Bye." Click.

Angie hung up the phone, staring at it.

"Not all ministry groups minister," she muttered.

"How'd it go?" After Angie told Greg what happened, he frowned. "Yeah, all some of those groups seem to really want is your money." He leaned forward on the edge of his recliner. "I've got an idea."

"I'm striking out so far. What is it?"

"Read the story of Nicodemus."

"I've read it many times," Angie said, "and talked it over with him."

"This time, meditate on it as you read."

Angie went to her room and did just that. She had nothing to lose. But she had no idea of the surprise that lay ahead.

TWELVE

After a half hour of meditation, Angie heard organ music played on an eight-rank Baroque instrument. A brilliant light filled her room immediately before the *ZAP!* crackle.

Raphael stood before her.

"Raphael, so good to see you." Angie exulted.

"Angela, sweetheart, Heaven Council sent me to encourage you in your hour of distress." He handed her a G-O'Gram. She sat on her bed as he watched her read the brief message.

"Hang in there, Angie. We're rootin' for ya, kid!"

There was a tap on the door. Kristin sounded concerned. "Angie? You all right, hon? I heard some talking."

"C'mon in. It's okay."

Kristin walked into Angie's room. One glance at the night visitor and she gasped, "*Raphael!*"

"How did you know?" He stood up.

"From all your paintings. Greg may have the art history degree, but I went to a Lutheran college where they stuff your gut with art stuff, like it or not." She extended her hand. "So good to meet you."

"Likewise. Sorry about the lateness of this hour. I was misled by my errant timepiece." Raphael glared at his Rolex.

"Should have parted with a few more shekels and gotten me a Timex."

Greg came in just as Kristin exclaimed, "This makes it a certainty for me. I believe that you really are an angel."

"Praise G for consciousness raising." Greg gave his squeeze a hug.

Kristin said, "The nicest part is, I am beginning to feel that my road less traveled isn't a Dead End, after all."

Weeks passed. Louie's Place was crowded and noisy almost every night. One Friday, Nemmy swaggered through the kitchen's swinging doors and approached Angie.

"Angie, I've been wanting to talk to you."

"Everything okay, Nemmy, sir?"

"Couldn't be better, especially since you've come on board. We don't give bonuses, but we are so pleased with your performance that we're going to make an exception. It should help solve one of your problems. It will be delivered later this evening."

She wondered what it could be. She'd had so many problems with this Mission that maybe good luck was headed her way for a change.

"All our regulars enjoy you, Angie. So much so that business has tripled since you started with us. The most noticeable change has been the jump in our percentage of women customers. Several have commented on how good you are at helping them feel at ease here." He grinned. "And the more gals, the more guys."

"I'm so happy you're pleased with my work," Angie said, as she kept polishing glasses.

"Ah, look who's here."

Angie waved to Greg and Kristin as they headed toward their usual table.

"Hey, Nemmy, how's business?" Greg inquired.

"That's what Angie and I were discussing. I'm so pleased with her work. Just look around. See how busy we are now on Friday nights? She's the reason."

"Plus, her drinks. Louie's is becoming famous for them." Kristin flashed the OK gesture her way.

Angie enjoyed getting this big hike in her satisfaction wages. Who wouldn't? Her initiative was paying off. She'd designed a TGIF Happy Hour featuring her original recipe for brandy alexanders. As Angie brought the two of them their usual, it dawned on her that she should be helping Greg to avoid more alcohol. But how could she? She was downing more than her share.

Later that night, the bar telephone rang and Angie answered it. She screamed as sparks flew from the phone's earpiece. Customers were startled.

"What happened?" Guy's eyes widened.

"Is someone in this room channeling?" Tex, as usual, only added to whatever confusion was going on.

Kristin and Greg ran to Angie.

"Oh Angie," Rita whispered as she stared at the still-sparking phone.

"By the looks of it, that must be the devil again," Greg said. "Are you hurt, Angie?" He examined her hand.

"Huh? The devil you say?" PC shook his head. "Never mind." He studied the tumbler in his hand. "This drink must've hit me harder than usual. I'm going to the men's room. If I'm there too long, someone call an ambulance."

"I'm staying right here," Tex pointed emphatically at the counter. "Someone's picking up some channeling vibes from somewhere, I'm telling y'all."

Nemmy hurried from the kitchen. "Angie, what's wrong?"

"I burned my hand. Please get me a pot holder."

"A pot holder? My first-aid kit is right here." Nemmy quickly treated her reddened palm.

With a bandaged hand and a pot holder, Angie returned to the phone. "Just where did you get this number?"

"Angie, baby, it's in our yellow pages. Just got into town to check on that investment I mentioned. Thought I'd phone ahead, though, to make sure you're at work." Lucifer chuckled. "Been hearing good things about you, sweetheart, about how good you are for business at Louie's Place. The really good news is that little drinking problem you've developed. Sneaking some at the bar, are we? And all that credit card debt—oooh, yummy." His cackle-laugh echoed over the phone. "Looks like Mission 250 is gonna join its predecessors in the garbage dump, huh, Sweet Cakes?"

"You're wrong, Lucifer. Dead wrong." But, he'd sent a jolt through her. Could he be right? She was so caught up in spending money, making money, piling up debt, and drinking. Greg had said just last night, "I get the feeling I think more often about your Mission than you do."

"Sweetie Pie, when I get there I'm expecting to pick up your Grace ring. Four weeks are gone. Remember our deal?"

"What deal?"

"Angie, Angie. Tsk-tsk-tsk! Even Earther memories are not that short." She racked her brain trying to remember those three points Greg had made. With her photographic memory, how could she forget something like that? Talking with the devil always stressed her out.

"See you soon, my little chickadee."

"He's so rotten." Angie stared at the phone after slamming down the receiver.

PC waggled his finger at her. "Ta-ta-ta, Angie; not rotten, but rather 'kindness impaired.'"

Angie was absent-mindedly doing her job when she heard a strange noise on the hardwood floor. There were rapid pitty-pat sounds.

"Will you look at that?" Schwartz stared wide-eyed at the floor.

Angie peeked over the bar. "A pig? In here?" Her voice was a decibel or two below screech level. The animal gazed up at her. The way its skin hung in folds, coupled with white hair and a beard, showed the pig's considerable age. The seeing-eye harness, however, seemed quite new.

Turning its head to look at Peter Chambers, the pig rumbled a resonant "Oink." Its snout twitched as this porker studied PC.

Pointing at it, PC glanced around with an incredulous look on his face. "A seeing-eye pig? Doesn't that take all!"

"Oink! Actually, dear fellow, the harness merely is a cover in the event a Health Department functionary shows up while we're here." The pig spoke with an Oxfordian accent, delivered with a certain haughty pitch of its head. "My name is Belly, and I'm a long-time companion of Lucifer's. In fact, I have been ever since I kept getting cast out some time back."

"Lucifer's here?" Angie was astounded that she was talking to a pig.

"Indeed so, m'lady. He's scanning this establishment's ledgers back there in the office." Belly jerked his head. He looked at each stunned face. "I believe I shall join them. Tally-ho, all." He trotted off toward the kitchen, his large butt clumsily swinging from one side to the other.

Absolute silence was broken when PC said, "Now that's a pig who has embraced his swinehood."

So many confusing things were happening. Most important, for now, Kristin had Angie's Grace ring in her purse. Meanwhile, she had beverage orders to fill and serve. But how would she cope with Lucifer here at Louie's Place?

The Old Foe strutted into the bar room. He was decked out in a blue blazer, khaki slacks, an unbleached cotton collarless shirt, hand-tooled leather loafers, and no socks. A very in-fashion look.

When Angie saw him, she quickly took another sip of her under-the-counter drink. She always felt nauseated when facing Lucifer. He'd shown up to torment her on every Mission. But now, Angie hoped a drink might help get rid of the knot in her stomach and steady her trembling hands. She felt half way ready to meet the Old Foe, but only because of the dimming affect of alcohol.

"Good evening," she called to Lucifer quite politely, hoping that if she talked first she might feel more in control. Lucifer approached the bar. He grinned, showing too-perfect white teeth. His large black pupils gleamed at her with a menace belying his *bon vivant* manner.

"Must we be so formal? Come here, Cup Cake. Don't act like we've never met." Lucifer grabbed Angie's hand and held it firmly.

Angie had to admire Lucifer's mastery of disguises, how he managed to fit right in with whatever setting he entered to accomplish his dastardly deeds. Here at Louie's Place, he was handsome and superbly garbed. Indeed, Angie noticed several women customers giving him the eye.

If the situation wouldn't have been so critical, Angie could have laughed at the ironic presence of the devil himself. Forget the horns and other goat-like features. He *never* uses those. They were medieval notions predicated upon the premise that foul odor marked the presence of evil. And what smelled worse to peasants in the Middle Ages than goats?

It was moments like this when Angie wished she had her *Zap* functions available at work. Before, whenever Lucifer made a pass, Angie just *Zapped* out of his reach by touching her barrette. Now she was stuck. As a matter of fact, since she'd been informed about the apatonium at Louie's, she stopped wearing the barrette to work.

With the counter between them, Angie felt Lucifer's hot breath on her. Her angelic nasal passages detected his body odor. It reminded her of Greg's toilet before she began cleaning his apartment.

"Let go of me. You promised to behave yourself."

"Since when have I told the truth?" Lucifer leered at her, making mock kissing motions. Lucifer was so focused on Angie that he didn't notice Greg's approach until his hand closed around Lucifer's wrist.

"Nobody messes with our Angie, fella. Hands off!"

"Ahhh. Greg Matthews is it? Case Number 6497102 Dash Three." Lucifer released Angie's hand and smiled pleasantly. "No offense intended, my man." His manner was mocking. "So you're all set to become the latest mishap in Angie's unbroken string of no wins, all losses, Mr. Matthews."

Greg studied Lucifer. "The game to which you refer isn't over. Not by a long shot."

Angie was surprised. This wasn't the burned-out Greg she was used to. His resolve contrasted with her own lack of confidence in dealings with the fiend who stared at her. Greg faced down Lucifer.

"We have some business here, Mr. Matthews. If you don't mind?"

Greg jabbed a finger at him. "I know all about that shady business of yours."

Lucifer's eyes squinted as they moved down to Angie's left hand. "Where is it?" He lifted her wrist to study her empty ring finger. "Where is that measly Grace ring of yours?"

"Don't have it, Slimeball." She wiggled her hand at him. "See? All gone. Bye-bye."

"We'll see about that!" Lucifer raised and shook his left arm, exposing what appeared to be two wrist watches.

"Wrong arm," he muttered and repeated the motion with the other arm. "Here's what I want." He brought the wrist up to his face and grasped one of the three watches on his arm between his left thumb and forefinger.

"That's his Grace ring detector," Angie whispered to Greg. Lucifer sighted over the top of the now-glowing wrist instrument, slowly scanning the room. Nearly a minute passed. Angie held her breath when the scanner passed Kristin.

Angie thanked G that Lucifer couldn't trace her Grace ring with his instrument since it was in Kristin's purse. Lucifer turned his wrist to stare at the watch-like thing. He shook it and brought it to his ear, as if to listen for some sound.

"Going tock-tick, Lucifer?" Greg said.

"Drat!" The cords in Lucifer's neck visibly tightened with frustration. "It's working. Double drat!"

"Even if I had it on me, Lucifer, no way I'm going to hand over my Grace ring to the likes of you. No way!" Angela Four was surprised at her resolve.

"What? I don't believe it. You? Angela Four? Mission Control's guaranteed goof-up, *par excellence*? Not putting your own self-interest first?" Lucifer's tone grew harsher with each word. His right fist hit the bar top. "Curses. Foiled again!"

Lucifer glowered at them; his nostrils flared. Abruptly, he turned on the bar stool and mingled with the crowd.

Neither Greg nor Angie paid any heed to the pitter-patter of a pig's feet until they heard, "Oink!" They looked down. Belly gazed up at them, slowly shaking his head. "I say, you two have caused my boon companion sore distress."

Angie noticed that two buzzing flies had forsaken the counter for a cozier venue behind Belly's right ear.

"In a fortnight, we shall return and, I do hope, enjoy better success. Tah, tah." Belly turned to pitter-patter away, but stopped. "Oink. I say, Mr. Nemmy asked me to fetch you, Miss Angela, to receive the bonus of which he spoke. It is outside the rear entry. Your friends are welcome to join you. If you would follow me?" Greg beckoned to Kristin and the three of them followed Belly toward the kitchen.

Lucifer got the brush-off from Rita. Noticing two hungry-eyed women at a nearby table, he decided to use his ageless technique to hit on them. They looked him over as he approached and liked what they saw. He squeezed between the two women as he glanced at the lighter circles of skin color on fingers where they usually wore their wedding bands.

It went well. Too well, in Lucifer's opinion. They were too eager. No contest. After all, the quest was half the fun.

Before splitting for more interesting challenges, he smiled. "A bit of friendly advice." He gestured at their thighs. "With that much cellulite, longer skirts would be prudent."

Nemmy led Angie, Greg, and Kristin out the back door to show Angie her bonus. There stood a shiny new Harley-Davidson. Perched on the seat was a gleaming gold metallic helmet. A flashy pair of goggles hung from the handlebar. Its customized windscreen was shaped like stylized angel wings. A black leather jacket with silver studs down each arm was thrown across the back fender.

Angie squealed with delight. "Nemmy, is this for me? Really? My very own *Hog?*"

"Oink!" Belly snorted. "I beg your pardon."

Angie laughed. "Oh Belly. That's a biker's term of endearment for their Harley."

"It's all yours, Angie," Nemmy said. "Given with appreciation and best wishes for safe travel."

"Thank you, thank you," Angie gushed. "I love it!"

"This couldn't have happened to a nicer person, Angie." Kristin placed her hand on Nemmy's shoulder. "Such a thoughtful bonus."

"I'll say amen to that. But I do worry, Angie, given your swerving impulse when you drive." Greg pointed at the Harley.

Angie snapped her fingers. "Not to worry."

He wanted to show Angie the motorcycle's features. "Let me explain how these beasts run."

"I already know from the Double-E. It's all in there about Harleys. I'll show you." With that, she swung her right leg over the seat, slipped on the jacket and helmet, turned the key, jammed down on the kick starter. Varrooom! VROOM! VaaROOOM! Three times she circled the full parking lot's outer perimeter. Each time she approached Nemmy, Greg, and Kristin, she squealed with glee while Belly scampered behind a battered pickup truck, ever watchful as she headed out again, exclaiming, "Oink! I say!"

Angie stopped and revved the engine several times, listening to its deep-throated growl. "Sounds even better than Gabriel's Bimmer. More guts."

After the others went inside, Belly resolutely approached the Harley. He lifted a rear leg and, in a dog-like manner, registered his liquid disdain on the front tire of this uncouth machine. "Oink! I say!" His pitty-patty feet carried this ageless porker through the open back door into the establishment.

After closing, Angie polished the last few glasses. She reached for hand lotion as the hot, sudsy water in the bar sink drained. She thought of her waiting Harley. But her smile faded. Angie thought of Mission Control, Angel U, her long-time colleagues—nerds and nice, alike—and, suddenly, she felt so lonely. Tears slowly traced down her cheeks. Quiet sobs began as she massaged her lotioned hands.

Pitter-patter. From the kitchen waddled a concerned Belly. "Oink! I say, Miss Angela, art thou—darn. Update it, Belly. Try again. Oink. I say, are you grieving, Miss Angela?"

She sobbed. She came from behind the bar and sat on the floor. "I'm so lonely."

Belly approached, got a load off his pig's feet, and rested a grey-bearded chin on her right knee.

"Oink. I know the feeling, Miss Angela. Being apart from your own kind. My breed went extinct, except for me. Two thousand years ago, they say. I survived only because my boss put me into rehab after being cast out several times too many. Not all that bad, being cast out. But it can get quite rocky in Galilee, treacherous under foot. I've had back trouble every now and then since that time. Nonetheless, I am the last of my breed. Alone. Unlike you, however, I have no one to go home to."

"What about Lucifer?"

"Indeed, what about him?" Belly oinked. "Heavy duty, that one. Down there, I do enjoy air-conditioned quarters. Excellent library too. Traveling's my thing, as today's Yanks like to say. Last year, for example, I was able to check out rumors that a small herd of my breed was somewhere in Namibia. My Swahili was quite useful, by the way."

Belly paused, remembering. "This was in an area where Norwegian missionaries had vigorously propagated their faith. Unfortunately, for me, the Namibian slang word for aberrant swine sounds too much like the Norwegian word for troll. Lucifer, however, wants to co-opt some Norwegian trolls for his minions since they so resemble his true appearance."

Angie shooed away several flies and stroked the back of Belly's neck. "Ahh, Miss Angela, yours is the first tender touch I have felt in four centuries. Thank you, dear angel."

Back in her room at Greg's, Angie brushed her hair without enthusiasm. She thought of her friends at Angel U—especially Angels Lena, Sophia, and Peggy Sue. She hadn't seen them for weeks now. Oh, how she missed them. Recalling her conversation with Belly, she was impressed with that piggy's empathy.

Angie laid the hair brush back on the vanity and opened her small jewelry box. She took out her Zapper. Studying the double-bar gold barrette, she turned it over and over in her hands.

Maybe she should check her Z-mail again for possible messages. Angie clicked the barrette in her hair. She always wore the barrette on the left side, over the neurons governing her angelic psycho-emotional systems.

No sooner had Angie snapped the barrette in place than red letters on her right palm flashed: "Urgent!" Her heart pounded. It was obvious that Mission Control had been trying to contact her.

She pinched the tip of her right pinkie to switch her Zapfax to Receiving. Her eyes widened as she read Raphael's message recounting their earlier conversation about Gabriel's briefing, apatonium, its installation at the New York Stock Exchange and at Louie's Place.

Then a new message flashed: Go to 3X E-power. To get Triple Eyeball Power, Angie blinked three times while squeezing her nose. Immediately she began to study detailed diagrams transmitted to her palm while listening to Raphael's descriptions coming from her left hand. She cupped her hand over her ear to keep the volume low so she wouldn't wake Greg.

Angie got an update on the Grey Berets' training by watching on the ball of her middle finger a high-definition 3-D video clip of their maneuvers on planet Fahrt. Gasping, she saw the devastating power of a Grace laser vaporizing a sheet of apatonium.

"Yuck!" She regretted that she hadn't disengaged the smell-o-vision feature. Deconstructing apatonium smells like a combination of goat cheese, used sweat socks, and a serving of rancid lutefisk.

For the next half-hour, Angie teamed with Raphael, via Zapfax, to explore every possibility short of deploying the Grey Berets—the final option—and the awful carnage that would result.

Engineering had worked out an alternative Matzoh strategy. But more data was needed.

"Tell me this. Is there anything different at Louie's Place?" When Angie started telling him about the increase in business, Raphael interrupted. "No, no, Angie. I mean is there any difference in the structure, the facility itself? Any changes of any kind?"

Bingo! "They started the ladies' room expansion yesterday to add some stalls because of the increased number of women customers." When Raphael heard the project involved tearing out one wall, he started giving an excited Angie instructions. The Matzoh strategy had come together.

"So it gets down to this, Angela Four. It's either you...or the Grey Berets."

After a night of carousing and naughty behavior, Lucifer returned to a depressed Belly, who longed to return to his quarters so he could finish reading the screenplay for *Hellzapoppin,* the Olsen-and-Johnson comedy film classic. "Time to head back to home sweet home, Belly, my boy. Ah, what a night. Nice that I can't catch any of those things Earthers get from staying out late."

"Oink. Like what?" Belly's swinehood swung from side to side while strolling with Lucifer.

"Venereal disease, my boon companion. Other than that, if Earthers stay out too late, they can be really irritable in the mornings."

"Oink. Lucifer, you're already irritable in the morning. And in the afternoon. And evening."

"Hey," Lucifer snapped at the venerable porker, "do you wanna go back home or not?"

"Oink. Not necessarily."

A tirade of naughty words from various dead languages flew from Lucifer's mouth. "Don't get cute with me, Beelzebub. You're going back to hell with me whether you want to or not." Lucifer raised his left arm and spoke into one of his wrist watch-like instruments.

"Lucifer, here, for the travel office. Who's on duty now? Dorothy? Good." He and Belly waited. Lucifer cracked his knuckles impatiently until a tiny beep sounded. "Ready? Beam us down, Dottie."

After her *Zap* conference with Raphael, an impatient Angie slipped out of her pajamas and into a blouse and designer jeans. She quietly slipped out of Greg's apartment and hogged over to Louie's Place. She was about to tool her Harley into the parking lot when she saw several unmarked panel trucks being loaded with debris by a succession of faceless workpersons in red coveralls. She watched and listened for almost an hour, unnoticed. Angie's observations led to one conclusion: their project's demolition phase was almost complete. She would have to begin her project the next morning. She prayed it wouldn't be too late.

THIRTEEN

Angie usually started work at 11 A.M., before the liquid-lunch crowd arrived. Today, however, she unlocked Louie's Place shortly after 8:00 to begin her project before anyone else arrived. Oh, how she hoped it would work.

She went to the storeroom, grabbed a floor fan and rolled it into the ladies' room. She returned and found a small stepladder, propped it on her hip, and headed back to the rest room. As she positioned the ladder, Angie noticed that last night's faceless workpersons had cleaned up carefully. They'd hung a fresh piece of fabric over the opening where the wall had been torn down.

Angie turned the fan on low so air would blow toward the vacant space beyond the now-billowing curtain. She moved to the recently cut edges of the opening. With normal vision, she couldn't see the thin layer of apatonium between the lathing and plaster, where Raphael said it should be. So she blinked both eyelids twice to gain 2X E-Power.

"Yes," Angie whispered to herself. There it was—she could see it. A thin off-whitish vinyl-looking layer of apatonium was right where Raphael had predicted. No wonder her Zapper didn't work at Louie's Place. *Zap* neutrinos could not penetrate a shroud of apatonium.

Her heart pounded as Angie climbed the ladder to begin at the top opening. She gazed at her Grace ring and took a deep breath.

"Please, please, make this work," she prayed. She brought her Grace ring up to the top edge and began to draw the ring slowly down the opening. Immediately, she smelled it: vaporizing apatonium. It was working. Even so, Angie knew she had to be careful. If her Grace ring traced the opening at the right pace, it would vaporize the deceiving apatonium shroud to a depth of four feet into the fixed wall.

She repeated her task on the other wall edge, top to bottom. Last, she moved her ring along the top edge. After Angie stepped off the ladder, she dashed to the door and peered into the bar area. It was still empty.

Angie put the stepladder away and returned to the ladies' room. She traced a message on her palm with a fingernail: Phase one done. Okay?

She waited a few seconds. Would it work? Or, would M have to send in the Grey Berets? Raphael said the Mission Control engineers speculated that an outer apatonium shroud also could have been installed. If so, there was little chance for Angie to succeed at her project.

But Angie didn't have to worry long. There it came—Zapfax confirmation on her palm. The message read simply: Congratulations! R.

Angie pumped her right arm and exclaimed, "*Yes!*" The odor was almost gone when she heard a knock on the ladies' room door. She panicked. Had someone seen her doing this ultra-secret project? She opened the door. Nemmy was standing there.

"Everything all right, Angie? You're here earlier than usual," Nemmy glanced at his watch.

She nodded and noticed Nemmy's eyes move past her to the floor fan. "Sure—um—sure, everything's okay," she blushed slightly. "I've just got some catching up to do. That's all."

"But why the fan?" Nemmy seemed suspicious.

"Oh, that. One of the exhaust fans isn't working. I'll turn it off in a bit. Will that be all right?"

"Sure." Nemmy seemed a bit embarrassed at his intrusion. Angie realized she'd just told a little white lie. She begged G's forgiveness.

At 9:30 Nemmy left on an errand. Angie quickly went to the main panel of light switches and unscrewed its face plate. Her fingers trembled as she remembered Raphael's warning to be careful of the electrical contacts. She curled her fingers into a fist as her Grace ring slowly traced each edge of the rectangular opening. Again, Angie smelled the odor of vaporizing apatonium. Phew. It's a dirty job all right, but some angel has to do it.

She replaced the face plate and retrieved the floor fan from the ladies' room as she directed air flow toward the kitchen door and rear entry. She opened the heavy back door and studied the empty parking lot. The smell of sixteen square feet of vaporized apatonium around the lighting panel worked its way out the door.

By the time Nemmy returned, everything was back in place, and Angie was rearranging bottles on the center bar shelf. Her heartbeat returned to normal, but Angie was worried. She still had a lot of apatonium to deconstruct.

Angie showed up at Louie's Place by eight o'clock the next three mornings. That way, she got in at least an hour of uninterrupted apatonium deconstruction work with her Grace ring. Every light switch opening, base plug, fan and lighting fixture got the treatment, as a four-foot radius of apatonium vaporized from each opening.

The final morning Angie turned on her *Zap* barrette and slowly walked over every square foot of floor space while *Zap* Central probed and mapped the remaining apatonium. Their probe scanned the entire floor space, except for one area. And she had no intention of checking that zone.

After Angie's inspection, she wrote a message for Raphael on her palm: How does it look from there?

The answer came immediately. "Seventy percent deconstruction, Angie." Raphael's voice sounded pleased. "Excellent work."

But Angie overheard someone from Engineering say: "But what about the men's room? Its apatonium shroud is still intact."

"Tell your engineers I can't go into the men's room. My reputation would be ruined if word got around at Angel U that I'm hanging out in men's rooms."

"But there's apatonium in there that has to be vaporized. If you go in there, we could hike the apatonium deconstruction rate to at least eighty percent of the total cubic footage in Louie's."

"No way am I going in that men's room."

After arguing with Angie, Raphael put Bert and Gabriel on-line to see if they could talk her into it.

"Stop and think, Angie. Who will deconstruct the men's room apatonium shroud if you don't?"

"Send one of our Grace Guy angels down here to do that job."

"I sent the only available Guy to work on the men's rooms at the New York Stock Exchange," Raphael said.

Raphael, Gabriel, and Bert prodded, but to no avail. They couldn't get Angie to change her mind. So, the men's room would remain a graceless place, a room harboring deceptions. (Dear Reader: So what else is new? *Editor*.)

Angie decided her Unintelligible Topics (UT) list had grown much too long. She needed to *Zap* up to Angel U for a few days to check out her UT items in the EE volumes and class notes from relevant Earther Experience courses. When she told Greg and Kristin of her *Zap* travel plans, Greg posed a question baffling many astronomers: "Are there really black holes in outer space?"

"Lots and lots. But stay away from those suckers. Once, I made the mistake of daydreaming on a *Zap* trip and got pulled into a black hole. Whew!" She smoothed a hand through her curls, remembering the experience. "I had over a week of bad hair days afterward." Angie shook her head. "Even the cosmetology staff at Angel U isn't much help after a black hole encounter."

"I realize this is changing the subject, Angie, but there's something else Kristin and I have been wanting to pick your brain on," Greg said.

"Pick my brain? Why...when you have your own?"

"You're a hoot, Angie. Anyway, why has there been a noticeable change in some people's attitudes at Louie's Place the past few days?"

"Such as?" Angie frowned, concerned that she might unintentionally violate the Celestial Secrets Act. She dared not give even the slightest hint of Heaven Council's and Mission Control's knowledge of Lucifer's apatonium. Nor about its inability to survive the focused power of Grace. Her new friends must not learn about her deconstruction project. She would never graduate to Heaven Angel status by giving away a Celestial Secret.

"Such as last night. I actually had a lucid conversation with Tex and, come to think of it, he hardly drawled at all," Greg said.

Kristin leaned toward him. "And did you notice Kashi and Rita flirting with each other? Not only that, but never once did Kashi mess up his R's while they talked."

Greg continued. "Then, there was general schmoozing about the Belly business when Schwartz said, 'That porker stinks.' PC corrected him, as usual, with 'No, no, he's odor-enhanced, Schwartz.' For the first time I can recall, PC quickly changed his mind and agreed with Schwartz. 'Yeah, you're right, Guy, Belly does stink.'"

Angie was impressed with the changes happening among Louie's customers. But she had to quickly move to another subject to avoid revealing Celestial Secrets. "Let me ask you two something. What is that Irs guy up to? He comes in a couple times a week. Drinks only the free coffee. Sticks to himself."

"Weasel Eyes?" Greg exchanged glances with Kristin and shrugged. "Dunno. Not a clue. Maybe he's a Commie spy or something."

After that, no more questions were posed concerning the change in some of Louie's customers. Angie thanked G for that as they headed for Louie's Place.

Later that night, Angie asked her boss for three days off. She didn't give the real reason for her request—to research her Unintelligible Topics list. Nemmy welcomed it.

"You've been putting in so much time without a break that you could get a bad case of burnout, and that's not good for business."

Nemmy's comments reminded Angie of another item for her Unintelligible Topics list: what is this Earther jargon about burnout? Just before this Mission, she'd read articles on characterological depression, avoidance mechanisms, and related topics. One EE study noted that many Earthers prefer to use euphemisms to avoid coping with something seriously wrong.

"Angie, I do have to check with someone on your request, however. Won't take long." Nemmy headed toward the kitchen's locked wall telephone that no one else was allowed to use.

Curious, Angie tiptoed to the kitchen door and peeked through the narrow window. Nemmy punched the same button three times on the wall phone: 666. Then he curled his right arm around the back of his head until several fingertips stuck in his left ear. His head cocked downward.

Angie wondered why he was talking into his armpit. She noticed the phone's handset was still on the hook. She pinched her right earlobe twice and placed it against the gap between the swinging doors. Her now double-powered hearing caught the rest of the conversation—his end of it, that is.

"Yes, Your Badness...I understand what you're asking....Which six regulars? Uh, huh. What evidence can you share, O Evility, that they may be slipping from your grasp? Really? I hadn't noticed that. Didn't our engineers guarantee that apatonium would prevent this sort of thing? Yes, Your Lowness, Sir."

Angie noticed two tiny points of high intensity red light moving on the polished stainless steel wall panel whenever Nemmy raised his head. She was startled to realize the red lights came from his eyes. She suspected why. The more Nemmy focused on evil, the more intense those eyeball beams became. Not even Visine could get that red out.

Angie retreated to her place behind the bar before Nemmy hung up. A moment later Nemmy emerged from the kitchen. He grinned and flashed the thumbs-up signal. "My colleague says it's fine, Angie, and have a good trip."

After quitting time, Greg and Kristin walked with Angie to the parking lot as she put on her studded black leather biker jacket. They laughed and high-fived her when she said the Harley was *Zapping* with her. Both were amused by her determined look as she arched her eyebrows and squinted while putting on the helmet.

"How long will this trip take?" Greg steadied the motorcycle as Angie swung onto the seat.

"With the Hog along, I'm not going to risk pitting its paint job with star dust. So, instead of cruising at my usual seventy thousand winks, this time I'll throttle her down to fifty-five. That should take—um—about nine Earther minutes from this spot to the front portico at Mission Control."

Angie adjusted the gleaming gold biker helmet. "I suppose Safety is going to try ticketing me for not having an inspection sticker on this vehicle. But, hey, if Gabriel's beat-up Bimmer can pass inspection, it'll be a breeze for this baby." She patted the gas tank between her legs affectionately. "Okay, guys. Back in three days. Right here in my parking spot. Meet me then." She reached out her arms and said, "Huggy time." Angie embraced both of them.

Kristin and Greg stepped back. Angie gave her finger wave with one hand as the other reached up inside her helmet to tap her *Zap* barrette's Travel bar. Ten seconds later, her friends heard the sound: *"ZAP!"*

Angie and her beloved Harley disappeared from their sight in the proverbial blink of an eye.

When Angie paraded into the library at Angel U, several angel friends dropped their books and rushed to her.

"Thank G, you're back," Angel Sophie exulted.

"Amen!" Angel Lena shouted.

"Hallelujah!" Angel Peggy Sue chirped.

Everyone in the library began clapping hands, stomping feet and making joyful noises unto the Lord. Even the staid, fussy staff librarian, Angel Helga, hiked her voluminous skirts and did a little jig behind the counter.

Angie's biker jacket drew oooh's and ahhh's aplenty. Then she led the angelic entourage out to see her Harley. Gabriel was already there, admiring the gleaming machine, his multi-ringed fingers obviously itching to take it for a spin.

But before he could ask, Angie inquired, "What's the Grey Berets' status on planet Fahrt?"

"Standing down." Gabriel couldn't take his eyes off her Harley. "I understand Earther bikers call these beauties Hogs. Is that true?"

"It's true."

"Ooooh, I'd love to hog the road with this thing."

"Sorry, but you can't, Gabriel."

He appeared startled by her refusal. "Why not?"

"It doesn't have an Oreo inspection sticker yet. And you know how tough Safety can get about things like that, even with an archangel such as yourself."

"Don't I know it. When your Hog passes inspection, could I..."

Angie wavered one hand in an "iffy" gesture. "Not enough time this trip. Maybe next time." She almost gagged at the thought, given Gabriel's notorious driving record.

As Gabriel led Angie by the elbow toward Project Debriefing at Mission Control, where Raphael and the others waited, he peppered Angie with questions about her new Harley's performance stats, questions Angie couldn't answer.

Cheers and applause greeted their entry into Command Central at Mission Control. Angel Bert gave her such an enthusiastic hug that his glasses fell off his prominent nose and ears. Things soon settled down to the business at hand as everyone took their places around the Project Debriefing Pit.

"Our Research and Analysis people were fairly sure a Grace ring would eliminate apatonium. But, as we say around here, 'the proof is in the pudding,' " Raphael beamed.

"Earthers say that, too. About the pudding."

"They do?" Raphael seemed shocked. "But in the Celestial Secrets Act, it's listed under part three, section seven of Unrevealed Truths." He glanced around the PDP (Project Debriefing Pit). "We'll have to launch an investigation on that saying."

"No need for that, Raphael." Angie shrugged. "The explanation is simple. Back in the Earthers' thirteenth century, a Norwegian queen dropped her glass eyeball into a bowl of tapioca pudding. She needed it to prove she could see and, hence, was competent to rule. That's why she said, as her grubby hand swished around the bowl, 'the proof is in the pudding.' "

"Oh."

The discussion and inquiries continued around The Pit for some time and were quite productive, a fine example of Celestial focus grouping principles in action. Angie found out a few things, too; it wasn't all about pumping her for information. She learned that the Grey Berets were "standing down" on planet Fahrt rather than returning to their base on planet VFW. Why? Because Heaven Council had not yet reached a decision on whether or not to deploy them to deconstruct Lucifer's apatonium shroud around the New York Stock Exchange.

The meeting adjourned for supper. Angie sat with a cluster of her best angel buddies as they asked her questions about the apatonium deconstruction project, her Harley, how many shekels her biker jacket cost, brandy alexanders, and such. Angie was appalled by the cuisine they were eating. Descriptions of bland and tasteless would be exaggerations.

"How can our organization be so technologically advanced, way beyond where Earthers are, and be so positively primeval when it comes to the food we have to eat around here?" Angie slapped her palm on the table. "Why, even Earther cave persons ate better than this." She looked down at her plate. "Look at this, will you? White stuff over everything."

Angel Helga tried to explain. "That's because everything here is fat-free, calorie-free, sugar-free, salt-free, artificial coloring-free."

"And taste-free," Angie said. "No spices. No taste. What's going on here? Are we being catered by a Norwegian restaurant or something?"

"I've gone strictly vegetarian for weight control," Angel Peggy Sue said.

"Earther hippopotamuses are strictly vegetarian, too, Peggy Sue. What does that tell you?"

No one said anything.

"You angels who haven't been to earth for centuries really need to go just for the food, if nothing else. You should taste pepperoni pizza. It's delicious. Spicy. Wonderful." Angie went on to describe the glories of Earther food to her enraptured table companions. "I would, however, caution those of you going on your next Mission to avoid Tex-Mex food."

"Why?" Peggy Sue asked.

"It's the reason why Mexico is in such trouble."

It was so good to be back with her own kind. Everyone was listening to her, intent on what she was saying. Then a Safety angel came to their table and placed his hand firmly on Angie's shoulder. "Angela Four?"

Angie nodded.

"You're to come with me. Raphael has asked to see you immediately."

Now what, Angie wondered. Was she in trouble?

FOURTEEN

Angel Isaac from Mission Control's OSHA (Office of Safety, Hygiene, and Awry) escorted Angie to Raphael's office. As they waited for him to get off the phone, she whispered, "Thanks, Izzy. I'll take it from here." She had the awful feeling she was about to face yet another embarrassing issue. Her life was so complicated since going to earth.

"As you wish. I must locate another Mission Angel who was recalled."

"Is someone else in as much trouble as I am?"

Isaac gave Angie a weak smile. "Not *that* much trouble." He hurried out the door.

Raphael hung up the phone. His manner was grave as he gestured for Angie to be seated in the red chair opposite his desk.

"Trouble, Raphael?"

"Potentially serious trouble." He handed her a sheet of stationery with red print. "From Lucifer's attorney general."

Angie took the paper and read the top line: NOTICE OF INTENT TO INDICT. The rest of it read like legalese jargon. "What does this mean?"

"The bottom line is that Lucifer is a sore loser as well as the original chronic Accuser. For one thing, he's probably figured out that you messed up his apatonium installation, although he probably doesn't know how extensive the damage is." Raphael settled on the edge of his desk. "If your case does come to trial, you can count on all of us here at Mission Control backing you one hundred percent."

Angie studied the paragraph listing the charges Lucifer intended to file against her:

1. Willful destruction of demonic property
2. Interference with a demonic deputy in the performance of his duties
3. General dereliction of duty in her employment
4. Persistent insubordination toward her employer
5. Alienation of affection (six individuals)

"I'm afraid he has a case with number one," Angie said.

"Not at all. Destruction of demonic property is the weakest of the five. Angie, a jurisdiction superior to his fully authorized you to destroy an illegal substance."

"Illegal? I know apatonium's big trouble for Our Side, but is it illegal too?"

"Yes, contrary to the Natural Law of Physics, which holds that neutrinos go through anything." Raphael frowned. "We're pushing the envelope on the illegal angle, but it should stand up in Celestial Court." He led her through a thorough discussion of their strategic and tactical options as well as possible risks.

"Angie, we think it's safer for you to remain here on Oreo until this dastardly scenario runs full course to its desired outcome."

"You mean, throw in the dishrag on my Mission?"

"*Towel,* not dishrag."

"Whatever. So I should throw in the towel before my Mission is accom-plish-shed?"

Raphael shook his head. "Accomplished, Angie. Not accom-plish-shed."

"But George Friedrich Handel…"

"Earthers talk that way only in oratorios."

She tried to find a slot in her now-disheveled memory for those two new EE inputs. "I must go back. In three days, I have to *Zap* back to my Earthers."

"That's too risky."

"Maybe so. But, I've got to go. I can't stay here."

"Why not?"

"Well, first of all, I have to earn enough money to pay off my credit cards so Kristin doesn't end up holding the marbles."

"Bag, you mean. The *bag*."

"Whatever. I've got to earn money so Kristin doesn't get into trouble because of me. She co-signed for my cards."

"How many shekels—dollars, I mean—do you owe?"

"Six thousand, three hundred forty-three dollars." She stared down at her hands. "Plus a late fee charge or two. Maybe—um—four."

"At your current Earther level of income, less fixed costs, that means you'd have to work at Louie's Place nearly seven more months." Raphael shook his head. "We simply can't have that. Too risky."

"Um. Where were we? Oh yes. Second, I cannot break a promise. I promised Nemmy, Greg, Kristin, and everyone else that I'd be back in three days."

Raphael nodded.

"Third, I'd be letting down Greg Matthews right when he needs me most. He's been making such good progress, you know. Come to think of it, so has Kristin, although she's not part of my Mission Package." Angie took a deep breath and awaited her ultimate coordinator's response.

Raphael studied Angie, his folded hands on the desk top. "Angela Four, this is the first time since the Fourth Day of creation that I've heard you put others' needs ahead of your own self-interest. You're even risking your own safety for the sake of your Earther friends."

"What else can I do?"

"What you've done so many times before—look out for Number One." He pointed at her.

"But, but this is different. I really care about these Earthers. I want to help them."

"Go back to earth then, Angie; go with our blessing." Raphael paused, then frowned. "Do you want back-up? Angels Greta and Tanya have finished their kikwanlo courses. *Summa cum laude,* too. Earned their pink belts. They can accompany you just in case you get into a fix like you did with Denise. Rita may not be around as much now, what with her new love interest."

> Few Earthers know that kikwanlo is karate's most advanced discipline, more focused and less acrobatic than other forms. When used by an expert, furthermore, it is most effective yet entails less risk of serious permanent injury. Especially effective against testosterone-aggressive Earther males, it rarely causes major aftereffects other than a permanently higher pitch in the assailant's voice. *Editor.*

"Thanks for the offer, Your Ultimacy, Sir. Trouble is, back-up would complicate this Mission. Besides, there's old reliable here," she said as she tapped her barrette. "Even at Louie's Place, now." Both laughed.

"As long as you stay out of the men's room." An amused Raphael escorted her to the door.

Angie finished every item on her UT list. She also refreshed her memory on practical information such as how to balance a checkbook. A review of her notes from a seminar on the "Secrets of Systematic Debt Reduction and Other Earther Myths" also proved useful. She even managed to spend some quality time with several angelic buddies.

Angel Bert was in a snit. He said, "Michael is pulling another of his surprise inspections at Zap Central tomorrow."

"If you know when he's coming, how can it be a surprise?" Angie said.

"I know. I know. Although there are no surprises here, he still insists on calling it that. Sometimes Michael can be such a *nebbish.*"

"Bert? Do me a favor, will you? One of Michael's jobs is to preside at Celestial Court proceedings. Something's just come up. And," she trailed a fingertip over the side of his neck, "and a moody Michael just might make things a little stickier. Know what I mean?"

"Angie, you're not indulging in affection unbecoming to an angel, are you? The sort of thing Cleopatra liked to do? You failed that Mission, too, remember?"

"I know, I know." Bert squirmed his shoulder. "How about rubbing a little to the left. Oh, that feels so good."

"Not affectionately good, though. Right?"

"Right. Oooo."

An hour before *Zap* time, Angie finished tidying her dorm room. She investigated a lump under her mattress and found an overdue library book: *The Secret Romances of Several Saints.*

The checkout date was two Earther centuries ago. "Am I ever in trouble." She headed to the waiting Harley, shoved the book in her biker's helmet, and detoured to the library.

She'd known Angel Prunella, the head Angel U librarian, from the Fourth Day of creation. Angie had a lot in common with her. Pruney got her *menuddeh* demotion for botching her creation assignment: design ducks—which resulted in the duck-billed platypus.

In the library, Pruney examined the book. "Angela, Angela. My dear, my dear. This book is two centuries overdue. Why?"

"It's a very interesting book."

"That's why we need it. I've been looking for this for a hundred years. There are hosts of angels on its waiting list."

"I'm sorry, Pruney. I promise to return books on time from now on."

Pruney gave her a fond hug. Angie hurried to her Hog.

Kristin and Greg were at Angie's parking spot a half hour early to make sure it was clear. There was a traffic jam on

Intergalactic 35, so there was a brief delay on her take-off while traffic was rerouted to the leeward side of the Cheerios galaxy.

The same cracking *ZAP!* sound preceded Angie's reappearance. After a joyful reunion, Kristin and Greg followed Angie and her Harley back to Greg's place.

"We have a lot to talk about," she said. After filling them in on Lucifer's litigious threat, it was Angie's turn to listen.

First, there was Kristin's news. At her uncle Billy Bob's request, she would be flying home to Lubbock for the weekend.

"A slow-growing brain tumor the size of a pecan was found on the part of the brain that keeps Rotten Person functions under control, the sort of behaviors that issue from the Hitler lobe. The apparently successful surgery took place last week."

"Maybe the tumor was the cause for his shabby treatment of you," Angie said.

"Could be. His phone call seemed to bear that out. He cried while we talked. He pleaded with me to come home so he could apologize in person and work on a reconciliation." Kristin was understandably skeptical, but hopeful.

Greg brought the next bit of news. "Last night, we asked PC how forgiveness works. Know what he said? 'Don't ask me. I'm among the Doctrinally Impaired.' "

"PC admitted that?"

"Amazing, isn't it? There's more. When we asked Schwartz the same question, he said, 'I only deal in concepts, not in how or whether they actually work. But maybe it's time I start figuring that out.' "

"Both conversations happened at Louie's Place?"

"Right at the bar," Kristin said.

Angie couldn't hide her pleasure. Lucifer was boiling mad about what she had done to his apatonium shroud. Thus far, at least, it was clear he hadn't been able to fix it. Good things can happen when Earthers don't trap themselves inside shrouds of deception.

"Weasel Eyes came in night before last," Greg said, "but left as soon as he heard you weren't working." He laughed. "I still think Irs is a spy."

Kristin cleared her throat. "I don't know if I can forgive Billy Bob Goldfarb after all the rotten things he's done, tumor or no tumor. I mean, to really, really forgive him." Clasped hands pulled her knee up slightly, "Can you help me, Angie?"

Her Mission Strategies courses had stressed the importance of watching and waiting for an opening, even if it took several Earther months. Now, Angie's pulse raced. The first real opening had finally come.

Angel Abelard, one of her professors, had said that the biggest obstacle to Earther's spiritual maturity is an inability to connect their theology with how they live and treat each other. Angie remembered the words he spoke in Latin, her favorite language because it had such a zingy cadence to it. "Everyone's got a theology, whether they'll admit it or not." Now, Angie finally had her opening to help them start making those connections.

Angie knew that Greg and Kristin both are well above average in faith literacy. But the trouble is, they were taught to connect doctrines with other doctrines, rather than with everyday life. That directly contradicted their catechisms' emphasis, of course. Spiritually, they were afflicted with cerebral constipation.

Theirs had become a quadriplegic faith, no legs or arms—and on life support. On the other hand, their religious training meant that Angie wouldn't have to keep going back to square one to explain everything.

"Most Earthers' notions about forgiveness are counterfeit, even when they're whitewashed with Bible Speak," Angie said. "Kristin, there are five words that can help genuine forgiveness work with you and your uncle.

"*Relationship.* Focusing on what you and Billy Bob think each of you needs is negotiation, not forgiveness. Forgiveness asks: what does our relationship need? Hurt and sin and offense are infections in the living body of your relationship. Forgiving is about diagnosing and healing those infections."

"Diagnosing?" Kristin asked. "No need for a CAT scan or MRI there. I know what he did to me."

"But that's not the point, Kristin. You get to Lubbock reeking of entitlement and there's no way healing can happen. We're not talking Kristin and Billy Bob; we're talking family. The Goldfarb family to which both of you are bonded."

"You mean his seven kids, too?"

"Partly." Angie stared at her hands as she counted. "Let's see now. Four of those kids are pastors. One's a missionary in Papua, New Guinea, two are on staff with Lutheran Social Services. A real selfish and greedy bunch, huh? Carbon copies of where their parents' hearts were during those children's formative years." Angie arched her eyebrows. "Kristin, all of them have a stake in this, too. The trouble between Billy Bob and Kristin Goldfarb is bigger than both of you."

"That's heavy going for me, Angie. Like, it puts this weekend on overload."

Angie gestured to Kristin, palms outward. "A family in the Lord is actually a living person. Rabbis before Paul also knew this. An 'Us that is more than the sum of its parts.' As though G brings two Earther dimes together to create a quarter. Only, it's even more than that. It's a living, breathing person."

"I don't know. I just don't know." Kristin wrung her hands. "I don't know if what's best for our family person can override how I feel."

"This is Tuesday. Three days from your flight. Before you get on that plane, write a Dear Lord letter."

"Excuse me?"

"Something like, 'Dear Lord, the matter is this.' Here comes the part you'll keep revising as you peel away the camouflages, layers of deception that have piled up since your dad died. 'Lord, this is what really happened.' Next, 'This is what it has done to our Goldfarb family person.' And then, 'This is what must happen for healing that person you created for us.'"

"But Angie, what about me? The Goldfarb family person is alive, sort of," Greg said. "My marriage to Marge is dead.

Dead as a doornail. Infections don't make much difference to a corpse."

"Dead. How tragic. But what you must ask yourself is whether its death was a case of murder." Angie shrugged at him. "You harp on what she did to your BMW. But wasn't that Bimmer episode an accessory to murder after the fact, as Earther legal beagles like to say? After her affair with Ralph, her diving coach—you called him 'that swimming rodent'—you convinced yourself that your marriage wasn't fulfilling your needs."

"How do you know all this?"

"It's in your files, Greg."

"Sheeezzz."

"Your marriage may be dead and buried, but there are other one new persons at risk for you and Marge. Your vocations, for example. Why do you stick with your current job when you have no sense of calling in it? What are you doing with your expertise in art history? Zippo! Besides, in the past six months, your commissions have been considerably less than you'd earn working through most charitable agencies.

"And, then there's Marge. She's had one job after another since the divorce. Flying off the handle, short-fuse explosions, all those Earther euphemisms for deep trouble trying to survive the state of nonforgiveness."

Silence followed. Angie glanced at her watch. "Gotta go to work. You, too, Kristin."

"But what about those other four words?" Greg remained seated as the two got ready to leave.

"We've got three more days to talk about them before Kristin's trip. I can list them for now. *Imitation.* Next is *Hostages.* Fourth is *Discern* what G is doing in all this. Last, but not least, is to *Forget* it. For genuine forgiveness that means relinquishing and handing over your control of what's been forgiven."

Angie put on her jacket. "By the way, there's much more at stake than your personal relationships, important as they are. The Scriptures make it clear that forgiveness has to work between you and others in daily life or it stops working between the Lord and you."

"Forgive us as we forgive those.... Uh-huh. The Lord's Prayer." Kristin buttoned her trench coat.

"Parable of the Unmerciful Servant." Greg aimed a pull-the-trigger gesture at Angie. "See? I know that stuff."

"Connect what you know to where you hurt, to the mess you and Marge are in." Angie opened the door for Kristin and they left for work.

Kashi had met Rita for lunch. One of her clients was an observant Jew who not only referred to rabbinic law but deferred to it as well, clearly preferring it to American contract law. She turned to Kashi, the only rabbi she knew, for the expert advice she needed and invited him to lunch. That evening at Louie's Place, Rita and Kashi resumed their conversation, which moved from the bar to a relatively quiet table. The next evening, the same thing happened.

They were drawn together through a mutual interest in rabbinic law, but that interest receded in favor of other facts of life. One evening when the faint sounds of one of her favorite tunes drifted in from the ballroom, Rita said, "Hey, Kashi, let's go dance to that." They did. And, to another classic. After half a dozen more, they returned to their table.

"We do really well together, don't we, Kashi?" Her bare elbow brushed the back of his hand, and Kashi felt goose bumps all over.

Normally shy and stressed in dating situations, Kashi admitted to himself that Rita had, indeed, become such a situation, rabbinic law interests notwithstanding. So why didn't he stress-out around her?

Angie teased him when he came to the bar for another Sunrise and margarita. "Something going on between you and Rita?"

Kashi quipped, "Thank the Lord for feminists."

Rita made the first moves because she was liberated from old taboos. She began telephoning boys when she was in eighth grade. Her parents insisted that only sluts did such a thing. Didn't bother Rita. She was as strong-willed then as she is now. This attractive and desirable woman so wise in the ways of the world was determined she'd be a virgin on her wedding night.

Long walks in the park on Sunday afternoons followed for Rita and Kashi. Several evenings a week they satisfied their mutual passion for Rook. Usually they played with a retired Lutheran pastor and his wife who were delightfully compulsive cheaters at the game. After repeatedly losing, Rita realized that both wore shirts and blouses which were patterned with all four trump colors. During bidding, each could finger a color at the other: right index finger on that color signaled a strong suit. Next game, Rita and Kashi wore *their* Rook shirts, which they used to more advanced cheating advantage by adding a left forefinger signal—for short suit.

Kashi and Rita were becoming an item at *Chabad ha-Tulseh*, too. Anticipating her first visit to Kashi's shul, Rita worried whether she could pass for Jewish. "What shall I wear? Kashi, all the ministers' wives I've seen wear frumpy clothes. Should I do that too?"

"Frumpy clothes? Never! Not on Kashi's woman. A class act should dress accordingly."

She did, and his flock of oil-field, roustabout Hasidim admired their rabbi's taste in women. A few of their wives did too.

Kashi was perplexed, torn between his heart and his career-driven brain. He had fallen in love with a woman who could never pass for a blonde, even out of a bottle. If he married Rita, he could kiss those rich suburban congregations bye-bye. Then there was the problem of her compulsive treatment of him as "so cute." She loved to twirl her fingertips in his forelocks, for example, as they sat in their now-favorite corner table at Louie's Place making goo-goo eyes at each other.

As much as Rita toyed with Kashi and teased him, she adored her rabbi guy. And he knew it. Honesty time came.

"Sweetie, remember that bit about my momma being a gypsy fortune-teller?" Kashi nodded. A tear or two welled up and rolled down Rita's flawless cheek. "Actually, she's an impoverished widowed Contessa trying to make ends meet. She works as the night shift concierge at a Super-8 motel in Firenze (the way Italians say 'Florence'). Our family's fortune went belly-up when its plastic religious figurines empire was bought out by a Romanian conglomerate, which got control but never paid up in convertible currency. Only in *schlotzkys*, worthless in the West."

Then, one Friday evening at *Chabad ha-Tulseh* Shabbat services, Rita fidgeted in her seat among other women in the balcony. She couldn't concentrate on Kashi's long, learned discourse on a minuscule Talmudic issue: something or other about whether a house was still kosher if a *goy's* dog lifted its leg on the garage door during Shabbat. "No problem if it's a *detached* garage," Kashi had pronounced, drawing appreciative nods from the more learned Hasidim seated toward the front.

Rita was impatient. She had big news for her beloved rabbi guy. It had come in that day's mail from the Italian Genealogical Service. News that would trigger Rabbi Toshio Kashihara's proposal of marriage to Miss Rita Tortellini, Jur. D.

During the covered-dish smorgasbord following services, Rita thrust the report's summary into Kashi's hand. There was the proof. On her mother's side, her ancestors were Spanish Jews who fled to Florence during Ferdinand and Isabella's final expulsion of the Jews from the Iberian peninsula in 1492 rather than become *conversos*. (The word refers to forced conversions to Christian baptism vs. execution. Either way, the government got your cash. *Editor.*) In 1848, the family voluntarily became Catholic. Rita finally understood why she kept thinking of chicken soup while saying the rosary.

What the report's genealogical charts clearly showed was that every mother on the maternal side of her family tree was a direct descendant of those Spanish Jewish forebears. Since Jewishness to this very day gets passed on through mothers, the conclusion was obvious. "Kashi, boobala, I'm true blue Jewish. *Yes!*"

Thus deprived of their favorite epithet for this stylish presence in their midst—*goyische schiksa* (gentile floozy)—the frumpier wives at *Chabad ha-Tulseh* groused: "but can she make a good *ladtke*?"

Meanwhile, business steadily declined at Louie's Place after Angie deconstructed most of the apatonium. Angie's tips also fell to barely a hundred bucks a day. Angie hadn't anticipated this secondary effect of her project. What was she going to do about her bills? No matter how often she stroked her "Trust in the Lord" rabbit's foot, prospects were dimming that she could pay off her credit cards any time soon.

On the other hand, the downturn meant that forgiveness conversations with Kristin and Greg didn't have to wait until the trio could meet at his apartment. When things got slow around the bar, Angie could take breaks to join them at their favorite table, now in an apatonium-free zone. Of course, Kristin and Greg didn't know that. Because it was a Celestial Secret, Angie could not mention apatonium around an Earther.

The trio scheduled some talk time at Louie's Place that night. Soon after Kristin and Greg strolled in, Angie joined them at their table.

"Kristin and I've been thinking about your forgiveness teaching."

"Yes, Angie," Kristin said as she played with her red earring, "let's cut to the chase. Last time we left off at relationships. What did you say the second word is?"

FIFTEEN

"The second word about forgiveness is *imitation*. Imitating the way G treats you rather than the way Earthers treat you. Otherwise, it's not G—ly forgiveness."

"Jeely?" Greg asked.

Kristin patted his hand and smiled apologetically at Angie. "This poor man's neurons stop connecting when something reminds him of Marge and his Bimmer." She turned to Greg and whispered, "G as in God."

Angie cringed. "His name's too sacred to say out loud."

"I thought it might be okay if I just whispered it."

Earthers. Would she ever figure them out? Angie shuddered.

"Angie, two days back home isn't much time to forgive my uncle who so wronged me."

"But it's plenty of time to get started peeling off layers of camouflage that have piled up over the years. Don't you see, Kristin? Full forgiveness rarely happens overnight. Expect some surprises. You peel off one of those layers, and you may find another you thought you'd forgotten."

"Are you saying we Earthers build up camouflage layers to survive what's too hard to face?" Greg said.

"Exactly. And left in place, those layers will eventually suffocate the relationship underneath them."

That's when Tex drifted in and Angie went to serve him. Angie noticed W-2 watching her every move with his beady eyes. He was at his usual place, laptop on the counter. He adjusted his wire-rimmed glasses to watch closely each time Angie pocketed a tip. Then his fingers clickety-clacked on the laptop's keyboard as a faint smirk creased his chubby face.

"Want your regular, Tex?"

"Yeah, my Laht," Tex cleared his throat. When Angie handed him the beer, he leaned across the counter and asked, "You been doin' any channeling lately?"

Angie laughed. "If you only knew."

"Listen, Angie, I've been wanting to talk to you about something really bothering my soul."

At the mention of soul, Angie jerked back into angelic ministry-mode. "I'm always willing to listen."

"Y'all remember about Tamara? I want to do something about that mess in my life, Angie. I really do." Tex pulled his Stetson forward a couple inches. "I've been doing lots of soul searching, Angie. Just between us, do you suppose the Lord can ever forgive someone like me?"

"For what specifically?"

Tex took a deep breath. "For my failure to be a real daddy."

"Tex, the Lord's in the forgiving business for those who know how badly they need it."

"I've been thinking about you, Angie. I figure anyone who could quote that child support figure has spiritual connections that could help me." Tex continued to whisper. "I decided I want to get in touch with Tamara and somehow find a way to pay her child support. And maybe even start being a daddy in her life." Tex wrung his hands. "If she wants me. Do y'all think that's a crazy notion?"

"It's not crazy, Tex. That's wonderful."

"Shhhhh!" Tex warned, as several customers glanced at them. "Only thing is, Angie, I'm not sure how to go about finding Tamara and her mommy. I mean, where do I start? Last the judge told me they'd moved to Arizona, but the number I tried was disconnected. It's gonna take some real spiritual connections to find them. To tell the truth, I've tried and tried channeling, but I ain't getting connections of any kind."

Angie realized Tex wasn't getting any phony connections at Louie's Place because of the apatonium deconstruction. "How about leaving that part to me?"

Tears came to Tex's eyes. "Any help you can give me I'd much appreciate, Angie."

Nearby customers were obviously curious, including W-2. At the end of the bar, PC raised his hand trying to get her attention. "Are you on task at the moment, Angie?"

"Be right there." She whispered a quick blessing, "G be with you, Tex." Tex managed a smile and sipped his beer as she went to PC.

"Angie, have I gotten ugly all of a sudden? Bad breath?" PC exhaled. She giggled. "Have I lost my touch or something? Can't figure it."

"Can't figure what, PC?"

"I'm batting zero lately. First, there was Anna, the gal I was with the other night. She's called off our relationship. Just like that."

"Your affair?"

"Yes." Since the apatonium deconstruction project, PC wasn't flaunting his conquests, as was his gross custom. "Then, there was Mona. That brunette with a body that just won't stop? The one with four divorces, and she's only 32? Well, she's been coming on to me ever since she came to Abacus Technologies, where we both work. So, I met her here one night while you were away."

"What happened?"

"I was so sure I'd score with her, big time, but it didn't happen. We were sitting at my usual table over there. I've lined up more than a few scores there." That table was now in an apatonium-free zone. "And, well, uh, no fires got going for either of us. She wanted to talk about what a failure she was at marriage. As for me, I was just sitting there feeling really guilty about Louella, my wife, the mother of our seven children."

"Seven kids?"

"Nine years from start to finish. Oldest one's fifteen and youngest is six. After our last baby was born, Louella told me to get myself fixed. Can you imagine? She just comes out and tells me enough is enough."

PC placed his hand over Angie's hand. His eyes widened with a semi-terrified look as he leaned across the bar and whispered, "Angie, she insisted on me being surgically separated from my manhood. Permanently. So I couldn't make any more babies."

"Is that when the business with the other women started?"

His eyes got misty and he bit his lower lip. "Soon afterward. But can you blame me, Angie? Louella cut me off, just like that unless I had it done."

Angie patted his hand. "You're a good man, PC. You just don't know it yet."

"That's crazy. Downright crazy." He said in a quiet voice, "Louella told me the same thing you just said, that I'm a good man and don't know it."

"So why don't you believe her?"

PC stared at his hands. "I don't know. Do you suppose that woman still loves me?"

"Sounds like it." Angie wiped the counter top. "Tell me more about that Mona episode. You started to see things in a different light, more clearly?"

"Yeah. I've been so blind."

Angie leaned toward him. "PC, it's not the usual blind. You've been blinded by deception. The good news is that now you can see what's real, what's been there for you all along."

Shortly after their conversation, PC went home to his wife. For a change.

Could this be a sign that Angie's Mission tide was turning? Don't jump to conclusions, Dear Reader, lest you assume a neat and tidy ending to her Mission lies dead ahead. Neat and tidy just isn't like her. As the world turns, we can count on more potholes and detours along Angie's Mission road.

Later, Guy swung onto his favorite bar stool. "A bottle of your usual white lightning, Schwartz?" Angie had resorted to using his surname since she kept mispronouncing the first one.

"Yeah, I'm craving that Perrier."

She set the cold plastic bottle before him. "How're you doing? Haven't seen you for a couple days."

Guy sipped some Perrier in a manner some people use with fine wine. "I'm back working on my project. Could really be big too. You know, my Unified Standard Significance theory."

"Man, y'all been working on that for five years," Tex said.

"But I may be onto something, finally. I just feel it. If it works, my theory would show other philosophers and physicists how to figure out the universe."

Wow, could Angie ever identify with that. "Big job, isn't it, Schwartz?"

"Sure is, but it would become an enduring footnote, right up there with the biggies. I can picture it: USS Schwartz."

"How much longer will it take you to finish?" Tex asked.

"After I get to Madrid, five, maybe six months."

"Madrid? Y'all going there?"

"Got to. There are some medieval Arabic archives I need to consult." He spoke earnestly. "Some of their philosophers did top notch work that should help immensely on a keystone issue in my project."

"Which is?" Angie stopped polishing a glass.

Schwartz leaned forward, lowering his voice. He looked first at Angie, then Tex, then back to Angie. "The significance of the year zero. It should gain quite an audience among scholars who are trying to figure out how to handle the year 2000." He stared at his Perrier bottle. "All I need is sabbatical funding approval by the peer review committee." Schwartz sighed. "There are times when I think the only thing growing in the groves of academe is Bureaucracy Weed. Worse than the government."

At the word "government," W-2 glared at them, fingertips poised above the laptop's keyboard.

"Keep your voices down," Angie said. "Can't trust Weasel Eyes over there. That's what Greg calls him." Angie enjoyed her new role as confidante to these regulars.

Schwartz changed the subject. He realized that someone as sneaky-looking as W-2 could steal his USS brainstorm. "Angie, how come you're a female type? I thought all angels are men."

"Only while we pose for paintings," Angie said. She knew he didn't believe she was an angel. "Hang in there, Schwartz."

After Schwartz and Tex left Louie's, Angie settled in a chair at Greg and Kristin's table to pick up on their forgiveness conversations. For the first time since coming to earth, she felt that she was making important contributions to Earther lives.

"*Hostage* is the third key word in the forgiveness package. Hostages destroy forgiveness."

"I don't understand." Kristin took a handful of popcorn from a bowl on the table.

"Me either." Greg went for the peanuts.

"Feelings can be the hardest to deal with. Sometimes we hold forgiveness hostage to how we feel. Kristin, you may wonder if you feel *ready* to forgive your uncle, yet."

"I've been struggling with that."

"We can't hold forgiveness hostage to such preconditions."

"Preconditions?"

"You know how some Earthers try to bargain with persons they need to forgive: if you do this or don't do that, I'll forgive you. So, if Billy Bob offers you your job back at Luigi's, fine, as long as that doesn't become a precondition for your forgiving him."

Angie could tell from the way Kristin swept her long red hair back from her face that she understood.

After that, Greg and Kristin said nothing. Both had a lot to think over. She went back to the bar to polish glasses.

After work, Angie hogged straight home to check in with Zap Central. She could hardly wait to tell Bert about her night of positive Mission trends. But when she entered Greg's apartment, Kristin was crying and Greg was trying to console her.

"What's the matter?"

Was something going to ruin her good day after all?

"Oh, Angie," Kristin sobbed. "I'm so very, very afraid of my trip. What if things don't work out?"

Suddenly, Angie wasn't so pleased with the day's Mission trends.

"All you can do is to work on forgiving your uncle, baby. Do you think I'm looking forward to confronting Marge?"

"Of course not." Kristin dabbed tears with a handkerchief. "But what can I do?"

"At times like this there's only one thing to do," Angie said. "Call Zap Central."

Greg made herbal tea for Kristin while Angie called Zap Central. Greg and Kristin were drinking more tea and less alcohol these days. She had been so busy in ministry this evening, she drank only two bottles of Perrier.

In her room, Angie settled on the purple fake fur bedspread she'd bought at K-Mart. She tapped her *Zap* barrette and spoke into her thumbnail Zapmike, "Calling Zap Central. Angel Bert, come in, please."

"Zap Central on planet Oreo, located in a galaxy in Heaven's neighborhood. Angel Bert speaking."

"Hi…" Angie began, only to be interrupted by Bert.

"A jazz concert featuring archangel Gabriel and his trombone is being held tonight at McAngel's." Now and then, Mission Angels got such commercials while checking in with Zap Central.

"Bert, I'm not going to McAngel's tonight for that racket, thank G! But I need some advice."

"Pronto. Your wish is my command, Angie."

"Could you patch me through to Raphael, please?"

"Of course. This is Angel Bert patching Angela Four through to our very own Ultimate Coordinator."

Angie smiled. She was never quite sure whether Bert's remarks were intended as satire or whether he was taking his job too seriously.

Raphael's voice boomed over the *Zap* phone, Angie filled him in and asked for advice. Raphael complimented her on the good night of ministry. The best thing she could do at this point was to pray for: (a) the gift of discernment, and (b) for Greg and Kristin to be open to the Spirit's work of enlightenment.

After Angie signed off, she prayed to G.

SIXTEEN

The next day, Kristin alternated between apprehension and excitement about her trip. By evening, eagerness began to edge out dread. She had a hunch that her waitressing days were numbered at Giorgio's J & G (Japanese and German cuisine).

Giorgio's innovative crossovers had gained regional fame for this trendy restaurant, especially a spectacular sushi-schnitzel, with its superb presentation on ecumenically-matched Noritake and Rosenthal bone china. Luncheon offerings were a business crowd hit with two options: the German power lunch menu, or the samurai offerings with saki-based sauces.

As she packed, Kristin recalled the way Daddy Goldfarb had drilled the need for forgiveness into Jimmy and her. She could still hear him yell: "You risk going to hell if you don't truly forgive somebody who's wronged you, the way God forgives you."

Kristin's struggle was over how to muster up *real* forgiveness with Uncle Billy Bob. She'd always been a profoundly honest person. For her, phony forgiveness was not an option. And, even if she forgave her uncle, how could she forget all the bad things he'd done to her? Go for hypnosis? Put on less painful camouflages, as Greg had done since he was ten? Kristin had lots of questions. This forgiveness business gnawed at her. It had turned into an audit that revealed how near bankruptcy her spiritual treasury actually was.

Meanwhile, Greg hadn't looked at a *Playboy* for some time. His interests began to return to art history volumes he hadn't touched in years, reconnecting with his past while considering his future.

He thought of his marriage to Marge and knew he had to deal with his anger. He finally understood he'd been deceived by Marge's beauty and her Houston family's wealth. He'd thought their marriage would guarantee security for an art history and computer science double major like himself.

Marge's parents had taught her that a woman's purpose was to look pretty, please her man, and keep busy in Junior League. Greg bought into that scene, despite being raised in a family tradition that expected its women to be high achievers.

What did the trashing of his Bimmer really have to do with their breakup? He realized that the accident represented the destruction of his delusions about their life together, its sandy foundations and vacuous destiny.

As her husband, Greg had been the perfect escort at endless Houston society galas where, he suspected, many of the attendees matched that half of the original Salomon Brothers partners who barely finished high school. Bubbas in cummerbunds and cowboy boots—Lucchese, of course. They trashed New York City even as their women flew there on monthly shopping sprees and binged on Broadway shows.

Greg found himself analyzing the clutter that had smothered his life since the divorce. It was as though Angie's cleaning up his apartment was a symbolic tie-in with an emerging sense of order and purpose for him. Marge and his marriage was dead and buried, beyond resuscitation, murdered. Greg realized for the first time that he was at least an accessory to the crime.

Forgive Marge? Twice, he'd started The Letter only to tear it up. Greg realized The Letter would only be the half of it. Maybe easier than the other side of the forgiveness agenda he faced: to forgive himself.

Greg and Kristin decided to invite Rita and Kashi over to Greg's for supper before Kristin left on her trip. They still had questions on forgiveness, and Angie hoped Kashi could prove helpful. Angie volunteered to prepare the meal, partly because she loved to cook and partly because she'd tasted Kristin's cooking.

Later that evening at dinner, when Kashi pulled out a chair for Rita, she leaned over, kissed Kashi on the cheek, and tilted his chin while her other hand swept aside one of his forelocks. "Isn't my rabbi guy the cutest thing you ever saw?"

Kashi blushed. "Oy! We're becoming a spectacle."

Greg pointed to the family-style array of carefully prepared kosher foods. "Doesn't Angie's meal look great?"

As they began to serve, Greg asked, "Kashi, tell me. How'd you know Rita's the one for you?"

"As soon as I realized she's the first woman who doesn't make me ruin my R's."

"You gonna ask Rita to turn herself into a blonde? So you'll have yourself a bottle-blonde *rebbitzin*?" Greg passed a platter.

"I wouldn't dare."

"Better not even think of asking, boobula." Rita stroked his cheek. "What you see is what you get."

Angie, Kristin, and Greg thoroughly enjoyed watching the interaction between this Japanese bachelor Hasidic rabbi and his strong-willed, stylish, streetwise, attorney girlfriend.

During the main course, bantering centered on the misfortunes of the Chicago Cubs. By the time everyone was ready for dessert, a perfectly chilled chocolate mousse, the conversation turned toward forgiveness. With their permission, Angie had told Kashi earlier about Greg and Kristin's forgiveness problems.

"Kashi, would you tell us about the teaching background on what the Bible means by forget and how it works?"

"Certainly." Kashi licked a dab of mousse from his finger. "It's based on the Hebrew word for remember and means to prohibit remembering. So, when the Psalmist says 'Remember not the sins of my youth, O Lord,' he's asking the Lord—your G—to prohibit those forgiven sins' participation in the present, right now."

"Because they haven't been forgiven?" Greg asked.

Kashi wiped his mouth with a white napkin, reached in his pocket and took out a half-dollar. "Forgive is one side of the coin." He turned it over. "If it's on this side, too, the whole coin is counterfeit." His index finger tapped it. "No, this side has to be 'forget' if the coin is to have valid currency."

"I just don't know if I can purge my memory of all those negative things, even if I can forgive my uncle for them." Kristin was struggling.

"You won't have to. In Tanach—excuse me, I should say in Scriptures—forgetting a forgiven transgression means to block its power to destroy your life now or in the future." He placed both palms on the table and added, "So, that's okay if it lingers in your memory. Just so it doesn't become a factor in your relationships or gets used as a weapon."

"By me?" Kristin placed a hand on her chest.

Kashi nodded. "Or, by the Evil One. That's why the Scriptures also give him the name 'Accuser.' "

Angie gulped. She realized this was what Lucifer was trying to do with his Indictment ploy against her. She tried to put that worry in the back of her mind so she could concentrate on the conversation. "The biggest issue in forgetting is about who controls their remembering. You? Or the Lord?"

"Couldn't have said it better myself."

"I have to let go of whatever grievances I'm forgiving?" Kristin raised her reddish-brown eyebrows.

Kashi shook his head vigorously, his curled forelocks tossing. "No, no, no. Not just let go. Hand it over, deliberately, to the Lord."

There was more conversation on forgiveness before talk drifted back to the Chicago Cubs. Throughout the thirty minutes spent on the hapless Cubbies, Angie was bored.

(Given her own track record, Dear Reader, you'd think she'd feel empathy toward other hopeless causes. *Editor*.)

Angie thought this would be as a good time as any to ask Rita what to do about a most awkward situation. "Rita, could I speak with you for a moment in private, please? There are some legal things on my mind that I really need to talk over with you."

"Sure." Rita laid her napkin on the table. "Sweety, be back soon." She kissed Kashi's cheek.

Angie shut her bedroom door and said, "Rita, I'm desperate for legal advice. You don't mind?" Angie motioned for Rita to sit.

"Of course not. We're friends."

"Good. Um, I don't know how to begin. I've never been in such a mess."

"Believe me, I've heard just about every mess there is. Nothing would surprise me."

"Better not say that quite so quickly, Rita. I have a feeling this could be quite a shocker to an Earther.

"Earther?"

Angie didn't bother to answer. "I'm being accused of illegal activities."

"What are the charges?" Rita's tone was compassionate.

"Well, um, charges that Lucifer has filed against me."

"Unusual name in today's society."

"Not for the devil."

"Angie, you're not making any sense." Rita switched to her lawyer mode. "Now then, what are the specific charges?"

"Well—um—let's see. There's willful destruction of demonic property, interference with a demonic deputy in the performance of his duties…"

"Hold it. Are you trying to tell me that you've gotten into some kind of Satanic cult?"

"Of course not." Angie cringed at the thought. "I'm just trying to answer your question."

Rita's creamy-skinned face worked into a smile that Angie read as pity. "Okay, go ahead. I'm listening."

"And the other charges are: general dereliction of duty in my employment, and persistent insubordination toward my employer, and alienation of affection."

"Angie, you're still not making any sense. I need all the facts. In what court have these charges been filed?"

"The Celestial Court of No Appeals."

"Right, and I'm little Red Riding Hood. Where is this court?"

"On planet Oreo."

"Angie, what's the matter with you?"

"Perhaps it would help if—um—you knew—um—that I really am an angel."

Getting up from her chair, Rita scooted by Angela Four. She gently placed her arm around Angie's shoulder. "Have you been drinking again?"

"No, no."

"But this is the same story you told everyone on New Year's Eve. I'm supposed to think you're an angel. Just like that!" Rita snapped her fingers.

Angie jumped off the bed. "Okay. I'll prove it." She did a Quickie *ZAP!* Gone. Then back. Rita gasped in horror.

"Now do you believe I'm an angel?"

"I must've had too much wine at dinner."

"Rita, we didn't serve wine."

"Oh, right. Right." Rita nodded numbly.

Angie knew she had to do something else to convince Rita. "Greg and Kristin know that I'm an angel. They'll tell you."

"Right." Rita laughed, but the color was drifting from her face. "I really need to get back to Kashi."

Angie followed Rita back to the kitchen. When Kashi saw Rita, he jumped to his feet. "What has happened to Kashi's woman?"

Faintly, Rita sat in her chair. "I'm not feeling too well."

"She will be fine as soon as she believes I'm an angel."

Kashi put his arm around Rita. "Angie, now is not the time to tease."

"Greg, tell Rita that I'm really an angel. She'll believe you."

"It's true. Angie really is an angel."

"Ha." Kashi gave a disgusted laugh. "That's not hard to believe. That's *impossible* to believe."

"But, rabbi, don't you believe in angels?" Angie was puzzled.

Kashi rubbed Rita's shoulder. "Of course, I believe in them. I just don't think you're one of them."

"Let me prove it then." Angie did another Quickie *ZAP!* Kashi's face turned white.

"Now, do you believe me?"

"No, no. Oy, no. I do not."

"But Kashi, you're a rabbi."

"And Greg's an expert in the security alarm business."

"Meaning?" Greg asked, arching his eyebrows.

"Meaning you know a lot about electricity and lighting." The rabbi's voice shook. "Please, Greg, the joke is over now. Okay?"

"It took me awhile to believe too," Greg said.

"What did it for you?" Rita asked.

"The extinct saber-tooth tiger."

Kashi and Rita looked at each other.

"Go ahead, Angie," Greg said. "Show them."

"Good idea," Kristin agreed.

Angie brought her thumbnail to her lips.

"Oy! You're sucking your thumb?"

"Calling Angel Bert. It's Angie. I need you."

"Zap Central here." Bert's voice boomed from Angie's CD palm speaker. "What can I do for you?"

"Could you—um—send Evelyn?"

"Sure. But do you really want her? You know what happened last time."

"I think it'll be okay."

ZAP! Suddenly the extinct but every alive tiger joined the diners. Angie patted her and announced, "This is Evelyn. She's been around for a long, long time."

"Oy! I believe. I believe. I do. I do."

"There's got to be a logical explanation for this." Rita's lawyer mode was getting mighty muddy. "There always is."

Just then they heard loud, screeching, off-key trombone blasts coming from Angie's left palm. Rita's eyes widened. "What's that?"

"Gabriel, practicing his trombone," Angie said.

"The archangel Gabriel? Oy. But why does he play trombone—and so badly?"

"It's a long story," Greg said.

Rita challenged Angie. "If you're really an angel, why don't you get Gabriel to come down here?"

"Very well." Angie spoke into her thumbnail. "Bert, could you take Evelyn back and ask Gabriel to come on down. We're trying to turn two skeptics into believers."

Five diners heard the sound: *ZAP!*

A grinning Gabriel stood in their midst, replacing Evelyn. Rita screamed. Kashi gasped. Greg groaned. Kristin was in shock. Now Angie realized how frightened Greg must have been when she *Zapped* into his apartment New Year's Eve afternoon. Nothing can disrupt a dinner party, or anything else for that matter, more than a *Zapping* angel.

Dressed in Earther garb of blue jeans and running shoes, Gabriel wore a blue sweater with yellow letters that read: Go ahead. Ask me about Judgment Day.

"Greetings, everyone," Gabriel said. He clutched his trombone.

"Gabriel? Archangel Gabriel?" Kashi whispered.

"Gabriel!" Greg said, "or, are we suppose to call you G too?"

Gabriel held up his palm. "No G for me. There's only one G."

"G?" Rita was confused.

"Yes, you know—God," Kristin whispered.

"Kristin, you should not even whisper his name," Angie said. "Remember?"

"I've come to bring good tidings." Gabriel started to raise his trombone.

Angie waved frantically. "No, no, Gabriel. Not that. No official announcement this time. Just give it to us straight."

A disappointed Gabriel lowered his horn and shrugged. "Okay." He coughed and lightly tapped his chest. "*Zap* traffic was diverted through the Gobbledygook Belt today and encountered unexpected stardust." He swallowed some water from a glass Kristin offered.

"When Heaven Council went into its Foreknowledge mode at today's meeting, it became apparent that Rita Tortellini and Toshio Kashihara, here present, have to be brought into the loop."

Angie knew better than to question a Heaven Council decision even when its full reasons were not yet revealed. But the term stumped her. "Loop? That's—um—in Chicago, isn't it?"

"A figure of speech, Angie. What it means for now is that I'm here under two Heaven Council directives. First, to extend their encouragement to you. They are quite pleased with your Mission's progress. But also, their Foreknowledge mode discerned the necessity that your angelic nature be revealed to Kashi and Rita."

Arms outstretched, Gabriel grinned. "To get both birds with one stone: that's my agenda on this *Zap*." When Angie's mouth opened to ask what birds have to do with it, she stifled her impulse.

"Angel?" Rita was stunned.

"Righto." Gabriel put his arm around Angie's shoulder. "Both of us. Different status but 100 percent angels, nonetheless."

"Now, do you believe Gabriel and I are angels?"

"I d-d-don't know," Rita stammered. Kashi gently placed an arm around her as though she were a fragile piece of crystal.

It took a while. They were bombarded for over an hour by Rita's lawyer-mode questions. Angie and Gabriel *Zapped* in a Dodo bird and several other extinct animals. Finally Rita and Kashi both acknowledged what Kristin and Greg already believed. Angie and Gabriel were, indeed, angels.

Gabriel sighed. "Actually, Angie, I'm glad you called me here. I need an audience." He picked up his trombone as his sapphire-ringed fingers sparkled. "I've got a jazz concert role called 'Up Yonder' to do tonight at McAngel's. I'm not sure I'm quite ready. I hope you don't mind."

"I love jazz." Kristin said.

That was a big mistake. There was nothing anyone could do but to endure Gabriel's trombone trauma for an excruciating four minutes. After just thirty seconds of it, both of Kashi's forelocks lost their curl.

After he'd *Zapped,* the quintet agreed that Gabriel was a very nice archangel. But, oh my, oh mercy, did he have a lot to learn about the trombone.

After work the next day, Angie explained *discernment,* another key forgiveness word, as she relaxed with Greg and Kristin in his living room. Kristin had been pumping her for more advice on what she should do about this and that with Uncle Billy Bob.

"I've noticed that when you Earthers are conflicted, it's as though you've put on cow blinders and..."

"Horse, Angie. It's *horse* blinders," Greg said.

"Of course, horse." She shrugged. "Me and my thing about cows." Angie gestured with her palms moving out from each side of her head, wiggled her fingers, and then let her arms drop by her sides as she resumed.

"It's as though a conflicted Earther focuses only on what he or she has to do, or what the other person might do or has done. The really important thing is to discover what G is doing in the situation."

"What's G got to do with it when it's between Marge and me? Or between Billy Bob and her?" Greg nodded at Kristin.

"All through the Scriptures, G's favorite way to reveal his ways and purposes to his people has been in conflicted situations."

Greg dismissed the thought with a flick of his wrist. "Nah. Conflict is bad news. Everybody knows that."

"Is that so? Then, why do most miracles in the Scriptures happen amidst conflict? Think about that. Tell me, huh?" Angie's voice softened. "One of the reasons you fled Houston and went into exile here in Tulsa may be because you weren't trying to see what the Lord was doing for you—and for Marge—in the mess you two were in."

"I take it that this word is 'discern' then?" Kristin's eyes were fixed on Angie. "*Discern* what G is doing, or trying to do?"

"Right." The trio was quiet for awhile, thinking.

When the discussion ended, Kristin finished packing and snapped her suitcase shut. "Angie, how about giving me a dollar? I'll add another, and while I'm in Lubbock, I'll buy each of us a ticket in the Texas Lottery."

"Gambling?"

"Angie, the jackpot is up to twelve *million* for Saturday night's drawing. Besides, I've heard the profits go for education."

"If it helps schools, then, okay." Angie took a dollar from her day's tips and handed it to Kristin rather absent-mindedly. She was still preoccupied with the forgiveness struggles both of her Earther friends were having.

The next morning, Angie roared into the parking lot. She was enjoying the last deep-throated VAROOM of her Harley. Her *Zap* barrette buzzed. That could only mean one thing—Urgent message. Angie's fingers tweaked her pinkie to switch on Receiving. Her Zapfax printed out the dreaded message Angie had hoped she'd never see.

SEVENTEEN

The message read: "Lucifer has moved to indict. Preliminary hearing in Celestial Courthouse tomorrow at 10 A.M. Don't *Zap* in late. Love, Raphael."

Angie knew nothing about court proceedings or how serious her legal problems might be. It's not that she didn't have law books available. The EE had huge sections on Celestial Court and Earther's law. Angie had gone to Angel U's library numerous times to study the law material, but clothing fashion sections kept sidetracking her.

When Greg stopped by Louie's Place shortly after Angie started her shift, she told him that the matter had moved from the "Intent" filing to an actual "Indictment" hearing.

"What should I do?"

"If it's this slow in here this afternoon, talk it over with Rita when she comes in. She's really sharp. Knows her way around the courtroom."

"Now that she accepts my angelic nature, that should help."

When Rita strolled in, Angie had already served the only two customers at the bar. She invited Rita to join her at a small table in an apatonium-free area. Apatonium was the last thing she needed to confuse things right now.

To Angie's surprise, Rita agreed to represent her in Celestial Court. "I've never had a case like this before. Finally, I can argue a case on the merits of justice instead of technicalities. That's why I went to law school in the first place. To make a difference, not just to make a living."

If Rita had not agreed to defend her, Angie would have had to take her chances on a court-appointed angelic defender. And, as every angel knows, they are so enamored of the Gospel that most of them are inept around the Law. Angie knew plea-bargaining would not be an option against the lies of Lucifer.

It was Friday afternoon, so Kashi was busy with Shabbas preparations at *Chabad ha-Tulseh.* Rita had time to ask Angie some necessary questions. Angie adjusted to her defender's jaw-dropping gasps over tidbits about Mission Control, Angel U, EE books, and her 249 failed missions.

Rita already was moving into the religion bit, big time because of her interest in Kashi. The information she obtained from Angie, however, whirled her mind into overload.

Rita phoned Kashi so he could tell his Hadassah ladies that his Intended wouldn't be at Shabbas that evening because of an emergency charity case.

Sadie and Sophie, nitpickers both, hurried from the kitchen to ask Old Herschel whether Rita's skipping Shabbas services could be tolerated. Although Old Herschel's senility was quite advanced, when it comes to *mishnah* matters, his mind is marvelous.

"Stop davening long enough to listen, Hershey." Sophie tugged one of his forelocks. Hershey fully believed he stood at the Wailing Wall in Jerusalem. In fact, the stones before him were cinder blocks in *Chabad ha-Tulseh's* bingo hall. True, this is the hall's *west* wall...

Sadie posed the question to Herschel, the Scholar. An emigre from Odessa more than seventy years before, he responded in Russian. Both Hadassah ladies understood only the last two words, "classy chick."

"In Yiddish. In English even, Herschel. Please. So we can understand." Sadie pleaded with the old saint, yanking his other forelock.

"Ow. Oy veh, already." He solaced both forelocks and began muttering to himself. Cocking his head this way, then that, his computer-like brain scanned all relevant *midrashim* and obscure *responsa* for the opinion these Hadassah ladies craved.

"Nu." Old Herschel's jaw set. The printout was on its way. "*Rahamim* overrides all technicalities."

"That's it?" Sophia shrieked.

"No, 'on the one hand, on the other hand'?" Sadie said.

"Ladies, please. You asked. You got. *Tanach* and Talmud speak to us with one voice. Godly compassion overrides legalistic mumbo-jumbo. Even on Shabbas."

Old Herschel's heavy-lidded eyes began to sag, no longer seeing the women as he turned to the wall. "Baruch atah..." Sophie and Sadie hurried back to the kitchen to inform the others.

Raphael, although he was Angie's Ultimate Coordinator, had to consult with Heaven Council on her extraordinary request: could an Earther attorney represent a Mission Angel in Celestial Court on charges filed by the wily, slimy, devious, and just-plain-rotten Lucifer?

Fortunately, Heaven Council was in its Quickie Decision mode when Raphael's query Zapfaxed into chambers. It arrived while the council debated whether the pope could say mass in Norwegian. The council's definitive decision: "iffy." It would be okay, however, if the pope ever showed up in Oslo.

Raphael's inquiry took far less debate in Heaven Council. Not only were its *sephirotic* members, G's closet pals, fully conversant in rabbinic law and the Lutheran Confessions, they were also up to speed on the latest CNN polls. "Yup" got Zapfaxed back to Raphael, then to a very relieved Angie, who passed the news to an understandably apprehensive Rita.

"What should I wear when we *Zap* there?" As soon as the words left Rita's mouth, she realized what an apostate to the feminist credo she'd become: We are womyn. We are strong. We wear power suits.

"How about makeup? Where I come from, religious girls don't dance and don't wear lipstick." Such questions poured from Rita's painted lips.

"Rita, Rita, Rita." Angie touched her defense attorney's forearm. "Be yourself. Come as you would in Earther court."

"The power suit okay then?"

"Sure."

"Maybe we should bring Kashi, too? In case the other side brings up rabbinic law?"

"Everything follows the Celestial Justice Code, Rita, so that won't be necessary. Besides, I have every confidence in you."

Saturday morning, the two of them rode Angie's Harley to the nearest K-Mart. In the Jaclyn Olson section, they picked out what Rita called "credibility clothes" for Angie—a suit that had less power than Rita's. Then they hogged to the parking lot at Louie's Place where Greg, Kashi, and Kristin waited to bid the two protagonists *bon voyage*.

"*Zap* safe, my beloved," Kashi murmured after kissing Rita.

"Give him hell, Angie. That's where Lucifer belongs, right?" Greg gave Angie a spirited slap on the back.

Angie slid an arm around Rita's waist. Rita's left hand found hers and, as instructed, grasped it in the secret Lutheran hand grip.

"All set?" Angie glanced at Rita, who nodded, her nervous eyes on a bravely smiling Kashi. He was blowing kisses to Rita just as Angie's other hand tapped her barrette's Travel bar. "Countdown. Twenty seconds."

ZAP. The cosmic duo was off as Rabbi Toshio Kashihara shook his head in amazement. "Gollee" was all he could utter as his wide eyes stared at the spot where Angie and Rita had been standing.

"Hear ye. Hear ye. This Celestial Circuit Court is now in session. His Honor, Archangel Michael, presiding," Angel Joe intoned.

Angie and Rita had *Zapped* there barely in time for Rita to open her attaché case and arrange documents on the Defense table.

Lucifer smirked as he acknowledged their presence, while his Accusatory Assistant, Hermes, shuffled papers.

Everyone stood as Michael entered.

"Polyester?" Rita whispered to Angie. "He's an archangel and wears a *polyester* robe?"

"Heaven angels keep complaining about having to wear that stuff. They say it's so hot. But so far, all Heaven Council has said is they can't afford silk for all 144,000 of them. They keep a tight snow on costs, that bunch does."

"Rein, Angie. Not snow—*rein*," Rita whispered as they sat down.

The preliminaries were perfunctory. Trivial motions granted. Other equally trivial motions were denied. Motions to strike this and that. Then came Hermes' motion to Ball.

"What's that?" Rita whispered to Angie before standing at the defense table. "If it please your honor, might I have an explanation?"

Hermes rose at the prosecutor's table. "If the court pleases, permit me, Your Honor."

"You may proceed, Mister Assistant Demonic Accusator." Michael nodded.

"Ball is a motion which is out of the Strike Zone, Miss Tortellini. It's in the ball park, but not serious enough to make the defendant go down swinging." Hermes reached for a document. "Such as these two addenda to the original Indictment, which we offer for this court's consideration."

The bailiff distributed copies of the document.

"An overdue library book?" Rita snorted. "You've got to be kidding, Mister Assistant Accusator." Her right hand slapped the paper. "And this other addendum is *prima facie* out of order, improperly drawn. Your honor, I move to strike both addenda."

"Your honor," Hermes spoke quickly, "the Accusators are prepared to present evidence that the defendant has, indeed, repeatedly violated the King's English."

"Objection, Your Honor." Rita jumped up.

"On what grounds?" Hermes snarled.

Michael banged his gavel. Then, he nodded at Rita.

"On grounds that a *queen* reigns in England now, not a king."

"Motion to strike granted. On the first addendum because its triviality insults this Court. On the second addendum because, as Miss Tortillini has pointed out, it's improperly drawn and no less trivial than the first." Michael waggled his finger at Lucifer and Hermes. "Careless, careless, guys. How sloppy of you."

As the hearing proceeded, Angie's admiration for Rita's courtroom prowess increased tremendously, especially when Rita had Lucifer on the witness stand. His anger escalated with each successful legal gambit she pulled off, including getting the court to stipulate his status as a False Witness on the grounds that, otherwise, it would be a betrayal of his demonic nature.

Rita put him on the defensive so much that he ventured his favorite non-verbal courtroom ploy. When Angie saw his eyeballs start to glow red, she picked up a Bible and rushed to Rita. She reached her just as his glowing escalated to full laser power. Lucifer's eyes focused on Rita's lapels. Oh no. He's going to ruin her power suit. Just then, she thrust the Bible in front of Rita. The burning twin red laser dots reflected back from the Bible and hit Lucifer's right ear.

"Ow. That hurts," he howled, rubbing his ear as the red glow faded from his eyeballs. He reached into a pocket and withdrew what Hermes knew was Lucifer's worry ball. Seeing Lucifer roll the steel ball bearing vigorously in his right palm, Hermes surmised that his boss knew they were in deep do-do.

Rita followed that episode with a motion to cite for contempt of court. Michael ruled quickly in the defense's favor. Lucifer's hand massaged the ball bearing furiously now.

"Is that your bearing, False Witness?"

"Y-y-yes. From a propeller shaft on the *Hindenburg*."

"So, that inferno was your work, eh, False Witness?"

Hermes jumped up. "Objection, Your Honor. My superior declines to answer on the grounds that it could incriminate him."

"Sustained."

"Your Honor, since he's taking the Fifth, we have no further questions of this False Witness." Lucifer glared, baring his teeth at Rita.

"They turn into fangs when he's this mad," Angie said as Rita sat down. At the Accusator's table, Hermes' hand covered Lucifer's mouth as he urged his boss to calm down, take deep breaths, and so forth. Lucifer did so, dissipating his anger and, with that, the size of his canines. It had been a rarely seen demonstration of this demonic defect.

The preliminary hearing verified that sufficient cause has been shown to justify trial on each charge cited in the original indictment. Angie was released on her own recognizance until the trial convened ten days hence.

"Good. Maybe I can earn enough tips to pay off at least a thousand shekels—um—dollars on my credit cards," Angie said as they stood by the Mission Control portico, waiting for their *Zap* slot.

Rita flipped the last page of a legal brief and tapped it with one elegantly manicured fingernail. "Why would the devil use the word 'Sheol' instead of just plain 'hell,' Angie?"

Angie shrugged, "That's his way, I guess. Earther churchy types do it, too: use Bible Speak words for credibility when they're out to get their own way." She glanced at her watch and tapped her barrette's Travel bar.

"Twenty seconds, Rita. Traffic's moving well on Intergalactic-35 so there shouldn't be any delays." Her arm went around Rita, who again grasped Angie's hand in the secret Lutheran grip. *ZAP*. They were off.

After a smooth flight free of pulsar bumps, they stood in the parking lot they had left a few hours earlier. It was an hour till sunset, so it would be awhile before Kashi could pick up Rita.

"I've got lots more questions about your case," Rita said. "Let's leave a note for Kashi to join us at Giorgio's J and G. My treat. They've added a kosher section to their German menu." She winked. "Another of Kashi's sideline business deals. We can talk over our case until he gets there."

"But your car isn't here."

"Car. Schmarr," Rita laughed. "Let's just hog ourselves over there."

Angie plopped her gold helmet on her head. Since Rita didn't have a helmet, Angie drove more cautiously than usual. She was relieved when they wheeled into Giorgio's parking lot without incident.

A gorgeous waiter with a lisp took their appetizer order. Iced tea and sushi wings. Rita leaned across the table toward Angie. "Kashi's trying to make a similar kosher deal with the Japanese menu chef here." She got the giggles. "He can be so funny, telling stories on himself." She cleared her throat. "Although Kashi and the chef get along pretty well—Kashi's quite the gourmet, you know—it seems that when he showed the chef his list of kosher regulations, the chef screamed at him. "I kamikaze you, you Osaka fleak." Angie burst into laughter.

Several days later, however, out of loyalty to Kashi, Rita and Angie had to stop having power lunches there. Why? Because members of *Chabad ha-Tulseh* were exercising a long-repressed flair for protest marching.

Round and round they moved on the sidewalk outside the main entry to Giorgio's J and G. But only during (formerly) peak business hours. Why? The placards they carried explain the issue: the Japanese cuisine chef's refusal to add a kosher section to his menu.

One placard was yellowed with age and had several bullet holes in it: Down with Tyranny. Seems that Old Herschel's father had fought with the Lincoln Brigade in the Spanish civil war back in the thirties. Dad was in the habit of standing up in his foxhole to wave this very same placard at fascist troops across the way who would fire away at the sign. Another fascist bullet also claimed Dad's right forelock and earlobe. Well, his name *was* Vincent.

The campaign placed considerable strain on Kashi's friendship with the chef. The latter questioned Kashi's family values. Kashi responded by quoting the great medieval philosopher, Maimonides (Rambam): "Friendship is good. Business is better."

Meanwhile, Hasidic women hurled peeled soft-boiled eggs at wannabe customers trying to cross the moving picket line.

Driven to restore their friendship, the chef proposed a compromise. He would inaugurate a kosher sub-section to his menu following all regulations to the letter, only he'd name it: Tibetan. "Only the Dalai Lama would know the difference. And he ain't here," the Japanese chef said. The two friends shook hands on it. They announced the deal. The picket line high-fived for a while and went home in time for the Shabbas meal.

In most *Chabad ha-Tulseh* homes that evening, the incumbent Queens of the Household served up many varieties of egg dishes from a secret menu ("Nine Ways to...") distributed by one of them in anticipation of victory, and boogles of unhurled peeled eggs.

For much of Sunday, Kashi joined Rita and Angie as they discussed the trial. He excelled at playing the role of devil's advocate. But he also brought a wealth of rabbinic logic and scholarship to bear on their strategizing. Unlike most American rabbis, he was learned in medieval Jewish piety—sometimes misleadingly called "mysticism"—and its insights into struggles with the Evil One and against the Other Side.
☆ See *Angel Beepsie's End Note*

Monday morning, Kristin's Vomit-Comet commuter flight from Lubbock to Tulsa was delayed twenty minutes, so she picked up a Sunday newspaper left on a nearby seat.

She pulled out the two Texas lottery tickets she'd bought for herself and Angie. She'd mistakenly put the same numbers on both tickets. She'd also been so preoccupied with thoughts of her weekend with Uncle Billy Bob that she hadn't bothered to read the lottery listing. Fumbling through the pages, she finally spotted the right page: Twelve million...two winners.

Kristin's green eyes widened as she compared the winning numbers with their tickets. For a moment, Kristin sat, stunned. She wouldn't have believed it, but there it was right before her eyes. All the numbers matched. The realization was like a surge of magma building up pressure against the cap of Mount St. Helen's. Until she erupted from her seat.

"We won. We won. Angie and me. We've won the Texas lottery," she shouted. She ran in circles, jumping, laughing, screaming, crying. Before she boarded the plane, Kristin dashed to the ladies' room and tucked the winning tickets in her pink bra for safekeeping.

Airport security debated whether to let Kristin board the Metro, fearful of her effect on other passengers in the small plane's confined space. But, after giving Kristin's carry-ons a thorough inspection, they concluded she had a valid ticket, wasn't a terrorist, had bathed within the past month, and wasn't foaming at the mouth. In Texas, that makes you a qualified air traveler.

After her flight, Kristin had an exuberant reunion with Greg at Tulsa's airport. Greg had good news too: he'd mailed The Letter to Marge, and he'd finally sent off his résumé. Those two accomplishments, Greg knew, were but footnotes to the lottery news. They hurried to Greg's apartment. Kristin ran into the living room where Angie was polishing furniture.

"Angie, we won!" Kristin screamed. She thrust the tickets into Angie's face. "We won, Angie! We won the Texas lottery! You and me, twelve million." Kristin grasped Angie's shoulders as she jumped up and down. Tears of joy abounded, and other celebratory behaviors were immediately forthcoming.

Angie couldn't wait to inform Zap Central of her good fortune. She dashed to her bedroom, settled on the purple bedspread, and Zapfaxed a message that read: Angel Bert, get Raphael immediately. I've got great news for the gang, and I want him to hear it, too.

In less than a second, Raphael Zapfaxed to Angie: Tell us.

Angie Zapfaxed: I won the Texas lottery. Six million dollars is my share. Kristin gets the other six.

Raphael immediately sent another message: Have you been drinking again?

Angie sighed in disgust, jammed her thumb into her mouth and shouted, "No, I haven't been drinking."

"How many shekels is that?" Angel Nebbie whispered in the background.

"A lot," another angel said.

Raphael's voice betrayed no emotion. "We appreciate your keeping us informed."

"Aren't you excited? Raphael, this means Kristin won't be liable for my bills." Angie was puzzled.

There was a long pause. Then Raphael said, "I am, Angie. It's just that so much money can be a real problem for someone who's not used to it."

Later that morning, Kristin and Angie hogged over to the Tulsa branch office of the Texas Football Coaches Scouting Federation, a state agency, to receive their lottery checks.

The first item Kristin bought was a sparkling purple biker helmet, which was essential, of course. Angie's top priority was to clean up her credit card mess before her Mission was completed so Kristin wouldn't be responsible for her debts. Kristin also had come to grips with her spending binge. She realized her excessive use of credit was an expression of frustration and loss after Billy Bob had fired her. Now that she was returning to a management position, she needed to put her own fiscal responsibility back on track—now. So, they hogged around Tulsa, paying off credit cards.

The next day, Kristin gave her two week's notice to Giorgio's J and G, and Angie told Nemmy that she would be quitting her job at Louie's Place. She needed time to strategize with Rita before the trial date.

Nemmy looked glum as he responded. "Actually, the way business keeps going down, there isn't much reason for you to keep working here. But let me check it out with my colleague anyway."

Nemmy went to the locked wall phone in the kitchen and punched in 666. Angie peeked through the door crack as she had once before. She blinked to Double-E power and tapped her ear lobes to triple-H power. Nemmy raised his right arm, as before, and spoke into his armpit.

"Boss? It's me, Nemesis. Need to run something by you." He spoke softly, but it didn't take much discussion. An ominous uneasiness rose in her angelic gut when she heard him utter two words: "Greg Matthews." All Nemmy said for the next several minutes was an occasional "uh-huh" and "atta way, boss." Nemmy was not an imaginative sort and possessed the vocabulary range of many football scholarship recipients.

Angie noticed the red glow begin to build in Nemmy's eyeballs. She had no way of knowing, of course, but this ocular phenomenon occurs when Lucifer and/or his demons are occupied with one of two activities: scheming to place some soul at risk or planning a ploy to impose eternal embarrassment on an Earther or Mission Angel. In demonic circles, it is called the Ruby Whammy.

As the glow reached full laser power, Nemmy was careful to turn his head a bit so the two laser dots reflected off the stainless steel panel, away from himself. Angie heard a sizzling sound. She changed position at the door crack so she could see what was happening. Nemmy's eyeball laser's deflection was giving a mound of uncooked french fries the

Ruby Whammy, frying them to a crisp. Angie hoped those twin lasers wouldn't move around the kitchen and cause a massive meltdown.

Normally, Lucifer wouldn't use up so much precious time laying out this particular evil plot. Usually, he would bring a plot to Nemmy or Hermes in an ostrich egg-like container. The two would take turns sitting on the egg for a while until one felt a butt-tingling sensation happening inside the spheroid and got off. Both would watch the plot peck its way out of the shell. As the plot staggered to its feet to take on legs of its own, it would chirp, "Cheap. Cheap." Freshly hatched demonic plots, after all, are cheap—for demons, that is.

Since Angie could hear only Nemmy's end of the conversation, she had no clue to what this demonic pair planned to pull on her Mission Guy, Greg Matthews, Case Number 6497102 Dash Three.

☆ *Angel Beepsie's End Note*
During their conversations with Kashi, Angie and Rita first learned that Freud's childhood nanny was steeped in that Jewish mystical tradition, and that the debate continues over what influence this nanny had on Freud's psychoanalytic theory. While its parallels with medieval Jewish mysticism are often uncanny, a primary scholarly principle applies: The significance of finding two parallels is that you've found two parallels.

EIGHTEEN

In the adrenaline rush of becoming an instant multimillionaire, Kristin's important trip to Lubbock had taken a back seat. But not for long. After work, the three got together to talk about her weekend with Billy Bob. Kristin slipped off her Air Jordanians and began.

"I could hardly believe it. Uncle Billy Bob sobbed uncontrollably when he told me how he held my father in his arms, out there on the 14th hole's rough, when Daddy Goldfarb gasped his last breath on that Fateful Day. Would you believe it was the first game in years that Billy Bob hadn't used illegal golf balls?"

"He admitted that?"

Kristin nodded. "My uncle was curious to find out if he could actually beat Daddy fair and square. He had already figured out a great recovery shot when that pit bull burst onto the scene. When Billy Bob saw how furious Daddy was, he ran after his older brother. But he got to Daddy too late. My father breathed his last in his kid brother's arms."

"That must have been tough for Billy Bob." Greg touched her arm.

"Know what? That wouldn't have crossed my mind until this weekend. I guess our talks on forgiveness had a lot to do with it."

Angie was pleased. She'd done something right. She hoped Heaven Council noticed.

Later in her account of the profoundly moving weekend, Kristin said, "Billy Bob mentioned that when it came to taking responsibility for things he's done to Daddy and me, he hasn't yet sorted it all out. He's relied on terminology from the old Missouri Synod hymnal of his childhood: 'By my fault, by my own most grievous fault.'"

"We sometimes use those words in dorm devotions on my floor at Angel U. Setting Two—gangsta' rap—really moves them along."

Kristin laughed, then pensively smoothed her skirt. "We came a long way, Billy Bob and me. He shared family secrets. Angie, you'll never know how much what you told Greg and me helped." Kristin rubbed her hands together. "But doctrine and life don't always connect so neatly right away. Not when you find out your grandfather turned into a drunk after Daddy went off to college. Uncle Billy Bob, as the eldest child still at home, had to scramble to keep their household in some semblance of order."

"Big job," Angie said.

"Apparently so. I didn't know Billy Bob had all that responsibility growing up." Kristin stared at her hands. "He said that grandfather drank himself into an early grave. Screwdrivers nailed his coffin. Now I understand much better."

"Of course. Billy Bob had to program himself to bring things under control," Greg said.

"Exactly. And he knows that. He's struggling to shake himself free of these control habits. Boy, do I ever see that man in a different light! I still remember the horrible things he did to me, but I think G is carrying us through this."

Angie smiled. "Sounds like the forgiveness process has already begun."

"How about that?" Kristin turned her palms out to Angie. "You were so right. For Bible teaching to connect with everyday living, thick walls often have to be broken down or overridden."

"Professor Abelard never said anything about that."

"Unless he spent time in medieval Russia or Florida, ol' Abelard probably never heard of screwdrivers either," Greg said.

"I also didn't know about Aunt Martha, who ran off with hippies back in the sixties. She was just sixteen when she had a son by some druggie. Angie, I've got a cousin out there somewhere, and nobody knows who or where he is."

That reminded Angie of an important favor she promised Tex. She had to get Zap Central working on Tamara's whereabouts. She meant to do that before they told her about the lottery, but it was lost in the commotion. Raphael's warning rushed in her mind: be on guard about so much money.

Kristin continued. "Billy Bob helped Daddy shield the family's reputation by covering up for Martha. They sent her to stay with relatives in Minneapolis until the baby was born. Can't get over it. My Aunt Martha, now a missionary in Cameroon, was a hippie! When grandfather became an abusive drunk, she ran away from the pain of it all while Billy Bob hung in there."

"Uncle Billy Bob offered me a new position as Chief Operating Officer at Luigi's Pasta Specialties, Inc. Greg, there's no easy way to tell you, but I've accepted his offer, conditional on our working together to sort out our family's clutter. I've given Giorgio's my two-week notice."

"Oh boy," Greg said.

"You're going to leave Tulsa? I guess what's most important is that reconciliation is happening." Angie was hopeful for this unplanned Mission dividend.

"Yes. Seems so. But we have a long way to go. More is involved than his Hitler tumor surgery and just the two of us. Whooo, it does get complicated, family biography. In our family, at least."

The three chatted about pleasant trivia for a while. Then Angie asked Greg if he had a good weekend.

"Let me show you." Greg went to his room and returned with a letter, his long-delayed communication with Marge.

He gave each of them a copy. "Here, take a look at this. See what you think." Back on the sofa, Greg rested his chin lightly on tented fingers as he watched Kristin and Angie read.

"This is wonderful!" Angie said, tapping her four sheets of paper.

"You really think so?"

"Yes," Kristin and Angie answered in unison.

"My brother Jimmy should read this." Kristin gestured at the papers. "It could help him cope with his confusion about Denise and their failed marriage."

Angie enjoyed a new sensation. It felt so good to see positive results happening from her efforts. Quite a new experience for her after her 249 botched Missions. She was most favorably impressed with The Letter's candor and lack of self-justification. Greg also had shunned the generic and general; his confessions were as specific as the stipulation of offenses for which he must forgive Marge. No transaction was implied, yet it was clear that he craved her forgiveness as well as declaring his own.

"What about your résumé, Greg?" Kristin was understandably curious about Greg's future plans. "Where did you send it?"

"To a museum in Texas," was all he would say.

With her job at Giorgio's winding down, Kristin divided her time between preparing for her move to Lubbock and boning up on Luigi's corporate condition and direction. She was on the phone with Billy Bob several times a day and poured over reports and sales data he'd provided her.

Wednesday evening, Rita and Kashi were dinner guests again at Greg's apartment. Angie knew Kashi's perspective would be invaluable while she and Rita prepared for the trial.

She prepared a kosher batch of pasta. She'd poured wine into the sauce just before serving it. Motivated by her need to keep a clear head during pre-trial preparations, this was the only alcohol she'd had since her return. No more brandy alexanders.

During dinner, Kashi offered a suggestion. "Angie, it could strengthen your case considerably if a credible witness were to testify on your behalf in Celestial Court."

"You have someone in mind?" Rita asked.

"Yes." Kashi pointed at Greg. "You would make an excellent character witness."

"Great concept," Angie said. "But I don't know if he can. I've never heard of an Earther testifying in Celestial Court proceedings."

"Anyone you can ask for a ruling about Greg?" Rita asked.

Angie thought. Suddenly her eyes brightened. "Raphael! He'll know." She reached up and tapped the Talk bar of her barrette. Nothing happened. Her fingers felt around the gold piece. "Uh-oh. Clasp isn't engaged." It took but a few seconds before the group heard Angie's Zapper click into place. Shifting in her chair, Angie brought the thumbnail to her lips. "Bert, this is Angela Four. Come in, Angel Bert." Angie's right palm faced her friends so they could see when the Zapfax letters appeared. Angie wrote: Let's go audio so my attorney and friends can listen in.

"Am I coming through?"

"Loud and clear. Bert, can you patch me through to Raphael? It's urgent."

"No sooner said than done."

Angie switched from Zapmike to speaker phone so the others could join the conversation. When Raphael came on Zap circuit, there was a slight echo from their end. Angie informed Raphael that Kashi, Rita, Greg, and Kristin were present. She turned it over to Rita.

After explaining their reasons for Greg's testimony, Rita posed the issue. "Do either Mission Control or Celestial Circuit Court regulations prohibit earther testimony?"

"Miss Rita, if the Earther sincerely believes that Angie is an angel, then his presence here for that purpose would be permitted." The diners breathed a collective sigh of relief over this good news.

Rita and Raphael conferred until Raphael said, "I'd better patch in Angel Tort. He heads our Legal Department." His voice lowered. "However, I must advise you that his English isn't very good."

"Oy?" A nasal voice was the next sound from Angie's palm. "For what can I do you?"

Kashi sat upright and ventured a response in Hebrew. Tort sounded surprised, "Hebrew you know already, Earther? Would you by chance any Yiddish speak? That's better even."

For as long as Rita had questions, Kashi was their English and Yiddish translator. Rita took copious notes. Angie observed, left elbow on the table, palm up. They went for nearly an hour until Angel Tort's flow of Yiddish included the words "Dr. Pepper." Kashi shrugged and grinned. "He suggests we take a short break while he gets a Dr. Pepper from the cooler."

"Dr. Pepper? But, Angel U only serves Coca-Salsa."

"Private stock. Tort tips a *Zap* courier to bring him a case from Waco every fortnight," Raphael said.

"Fortnight?"

"Every two weeks." Rita looked up from her notes. She jabbed her pencil eraser end at them. "This guy really knows his stuff."

"Of course!" the voice roared from Angie's palm. They heard the snap of a soda pop can being opened. "I taught the law at what became Oxford till 1290, when that schiksa queen got her schmuck of a husband, the king, to toss all us yehudim from England out." They heard Angel Tort guzzle his beverage. "The ship I was on? Sank. Me, too."

"Jews. *Yehudim* means Jews, Angie." Kashi leaned toward her.

"Angie? Angela the Four, is it there with you?" Tort's voice seemed excited. "The word is going Oreo around that Angela the Four just might a winner have, this time. Und, that you just might the whole enchilada get, when it's all over."

There was a brief pause and Tort continued. "Kashihara, tell me. You think my Cubbies are to the World Series this year going?"

"Doesn't look too promising, Angel Tort."

"Just once already, in person I want my Cubbies to see."

Angie entered the banter. "We win this case, and maybe I can make that my graduation present to you."

"Ah, Angela the Four, for that I would of you a statue make, with mine own hands."

All three of them would *Zap* to the trial—Angie, Rita, and Greg. They were ready. Rita had thoroughly prepared Angie's defense, aided by Kashi and numerous consultations with a Cubs-motivated Angel Tort.

Rita's preparations also included the purchase of two ultra-thin Bibles that fit into pockets of a blouse she would wear under her power suit in Celestial Court of No Appeals, just in case Lucifer's eyeballing went laser-critical again.

They were in the Hog's parking spot well before the scheduled *Zap* slot would open. This time they would arrive at Mission Control at least an hour early. Or, so they thought.

Bert had advised several rehearsals of the proper *Zap* stance, since they would be traveling as a trio. Or, so they thought.

Bert advised a longer neutrino-compression countdown because of the extra *Zap* travel bulk. They needed more than the usual ten seconds for solo travel, since there would be three of them. Or, so they thought.

"Just to be on the safe side, set it for forty-five seconds, Angie." Bert's voice spoke calmly from her left hand. Rita was positioned between Angie and Greg, Angie on the left so her hand could be free. They had their trio stance down pat, almost old pros at using the secret Lutheran hand grip. Kashi was there to see them off. The four of them chatted, with five minutes to go before countdown.

Suddenly, Walter Irs, the Second, pushed open the back door to the kitchen of Louie's Place. "Aha! There you are!" His short stubby legs tried to carry his short weight-enhanced body with an aura of authority. But, as always, they weren't up to it.

W-2 braced his tiny feet as he faced Angie. "Angela Fore." His voice was stern. Angie rolled her eyes instead of correcting his misspelling. "I'm a fully authorized field agent of the IRS."

"IRS?"

He shook a finger at Angie. "Oooo, don't play dumb blonde with this guy," his thumb jerked toward his chest, "Internal Revenue Service. The outfit that serves the God-fearing taxpayers of the good old U.S. of A."

"Never heard of it," Angie said. She glanced at the others. "Have you?" They all stared in disbelief.

"Angela Fore, I have proof in here that you're guilty on at least two counts of criminal fraud against my government." He tapped his attaché case. His weasel eyes gleamed at her. "First, you have never, ever, filed a federal income tax return."

Angie tried to speak, but he raised a hand and shook his head. "And second, you have never reported your tips as income, as required by IRS. My conservative estimate, based on direct field investigation over the past three weeks, is that retroactively over the past twelve months, you owe the tax man $11,250.53. Plus penalty. Plus interest."

"You've got it all wrong." Kashi tried to intervene. "After all, Angie has been on earth less than two of those months."

"Back off. This is about this criminal." W-2 gestured to her. "Come with me."

"I can't. Not now."

"This is an order! You are to accompany me down to our field office. Immediately!"

Greg gestured at his watch and mouthed the word "fifty" at her. Angie slid her left hand up to her *Zap* barrette and casually tapped the Travel bar. The three of them assumed *Zap* travel stance and joined in the secret Lutheran hand grip.

"You refuse my authorized order?"

She nodded. W-2 snarled as he reached into a coat pocket and pulled out handcuffs. "I'm authorized to take you into custody, Angela Fore." He snapped one cuff on his right wrist and reached for her left hand. "You have the right to remain silent, et cetera. You know the rest from TV."

Angie jumped up and down with impatience for the *Zap!*

"Five seconds," Greg counted. "Four...three... "

Snap! The other cuff locked around her wrist and Walter Irs, the Second, picked up his attaché case with his other hand.

ZAP! The crisp sound caused Kashi to wince. Then he stood alone and waved, vaguely, skyward. The rabbi shook his head as he wondered how it would go for them since Walter Irs, the Second, had apparently been *Zapped*, too.

NINETEEN

With the extra baggage of W-2 and his not assuming the proper *Zap* stance and secret Lutheran hand grip, it was almost half an hour before the unplanned quartet stood on Mission Control's portico. A visibly concerned Angel Isaac hurried toward them.

"This isn't my federal building." W-2 screeched, glancing around frantically. He glared at Angie. "Aha. Now we add the charge of kidnapping a federal government official."

Angie pointed to the handcuff as Angel Isaac reached them. "Izzy, could you get this thing off me?"

"Is that unlawful?" he asked her.

She nodded. He grazed the metal with his Grace ring and the shackle snapped open. Angie smiled at Irs, who was totally confused.

"Grace ring," she said. "Mighty handy. Never know when you need one. They're not only effective against apatonium, but against unlawful bondage and other stuff."

"Apatonium," he gasped. "What's that?"

No one bothered to answer.

As Isaac gently rubbed Angie's wrist, he told her, "The three of you are authorized, but he's not."

"I am too," W-2 yelled, "by the federal government."

"Who is this guy?"

Looking up from the open cuff that wouldn't snap shut ever again, W-2 waggled his index finger at Angel Isaac. "And I've got you on another charge: willful destruction of government property."

"What?" Isaac wrinkled his forehead.

"I'll explain as we walk." Angie and her friends followed Isaac as he guided them to Celestial Court chambers. Walter Irs, the Second, trailed.

"Hey!" W-2 yelled from fifty feet behind them in a corridor. "If this is Mission Control, how come it doesn't look like Houston?" The dangling handcuff jingled as his right hand gestured. "I don't see it out there, and I don't see Houston in here."

"That's because this isn't Houston," Angie called back over her shoulder without breaking stride.

W-2 found his way to the courtroom while principals and court staff drifted in, chatting as they set up for the trial. Lucifer and his Demonic Accusatory assistant, Hermes, conferred in whispers at the Accusator's table. The observers gallery was nearly full, mostly with Angie's angelic cohorts. W-2 found a small table off to one side. He claimed a spare chair, opened his attaché case, and scurried about trying to discover the name and location of this facility. Before long, he was back at the table clicking the keys of his laptop, the defunct handcuff dangling from his right wrist.

There wasn't time for the familiarization tour Angie planned for Greg. Despite the unique surroundings, he was able to stay focused as the three of them went over last-minute preparations at the defense table.

Two bailiffs entered. Standard procedure called for just one. Raphael, however, had advised Michael that two bailiffs might be prudent, given the potential for an unruly courtroom with the big crowd of Angie's buddies and the unexpected presence of W-2.

Each bailiff took position on either side of the ornate, imposing, exquisitely hand-carved alabaster judge's bench.

As on earth, the bench is more like an imperial throne. Only, this one glowed slightly throughout the courtroom. Other furnishings were in Scandinavian modern design, fashioned from finely-grained live oak finished with hand-rubbed ears wax.

Shortly before Michael's entrance, the senior bailiff announced, "Haloes off, please." Four hundred Mission Angels in the observers' gallery tweaked their noses. Lighting conditions in the courtroom returned to normal.

Rich hues from the stained glass windows were supplemented by full spectrum illumination from the Patty sun through skylights overhead. The windows were made by twelfth-century craftspersons who had brought with them the secret of medieval red glass. On the front wall, a terrific golden mosaic spelled out: *Ad verum et soli G gloria* (For truth and the glory of G).

"Impressive," Greg whispered to Rita and Angie. "A setting like this can't help but intimidate Lucifer."

"Let's hope so. Even that simpler preliminary hearing room seemed to unnerve him." Rita took a deep breath. "We're ready."

"How are our chances, Rita?" Angie had not dared to pose the question earlier.

"At least even, maybe better," her defense attorney nodded as she reached for Angie's hand and squeezed it reassuringly.

"Oyez, Oyez. All rise." Everyone in the crowded courtroom stood after the senior bailiff intoned the traditional order, including that strange first word.

> A little-known fact: "Oyez" originated in a fifteenth-century English courtroom when a large chip from the bailiff's ill-fitting wooden false teeth dislodged just as he was to announce: "Get off thy butts." "Oyez" was all that came out as the wood chip tried to invade his throat. A really dumb tradition had begun. *Editor.*

"This Celestial Court of No Appeals is now in session, the honorable Archangel Michael presiding," the senior bailiff announced. Michael, in his non-flowing polyester judicial robes entered. Magisterially, of course. When he reached his ecologically correct Naugahyde-upholstered golden chair, Michael declared, "Let us pray."

The prayer was in German, since that's been G's preferred non-Hebraic tongue since Eden.

As Michael prayed on, Angie felt relief at understanding every word this time. A century of taking tutorials in German had finally corrected her persistent confusion of Old Norse with *auf deutsch,* an essential achievement if she was to graduate to Heaven Angel status.

"Amen. Please be seated." Michael gestured and sat down. As the prayer had proceeded, Lucifer fumed until his eyeballs glowed red. Noticing this, Michael snapped the fingers of his left hand and presto!—the red glow switched off. Only archangels have that power, you know.

"Case Number DA Two Thousand and One: The People of Demonic Ilk versus Angela Four, Mission Angel, Your Honor." After bellowing the announcement, the senior bailiff handed an official-looking document written on Nile papyrus to Michael.

"Papyrus, Lucifer?" Michael raised one eyebrow. "In this day and age?"

"Strictly business, Your Honor," he choked on the word. "One of my subsidiary firms has been producing that material for nearly three millennia. Don't try to run it through a laser printer, though. Doesn't work. My staff's working on the problem."

Michael acknowledged Lucifer's response with a faint nod and reviewed the Indictment document and several appendices. "Very well. This seems in order. You may proceed. I remind the court that this Indictment lists five charges facing the defendant, Mission Angel Angela Four. They are: willful destruction of demonic property, interference with a demonic deputy in the performance of his duties, general dereliction of duty in her employment, persistent insubordination toward her employer, and alienation of affection."

Hermes rose and strode to the accusators' lectern. "If it please the court..." And, for the next twenty minutes, Hermes introduced their case with numerous attempts to use the phrase: "The People intend to show...." Each time, Rita immediately objected and was sustained. "I stand corrected, Your Honor. The People of *Demonic Ilk* intend to show...."

As Hermes finished, Rita whispered to Angie and Greg. "He's good. Very good."

"Maybe. But he won't get away with using technicalities to make Lucifer's case." Greg's fingertip tapped their table. "Not in this court, Rita, as long as you and Michael force Hermes to proceed under the principles of Celestial Justice. They'll be kept on the defensive, all the way."

"I'm not used to that in Earther courts, but I'll try my best."

"Do it, Rita. Hammer away at him every time he tries to override Justice with some legalese technicality."

"You're right, Greg." Rita gathered up some notes and went to the defense lectern. "Your Honor, it is indeed a privilege, a very rare privilege, for an Earther such as myself to represent an angelic defendant in this court. I wish to thank the court for this privilege and," she gestured around the room, "for the gracious hospitality given us by almost everyone here."

"Objection!" Hermes jumped to his feet. "We object to the use of language associated with Grace insofar as it injects sectarian jargon into these proceedings."

"Overruled. Grace is a fundamental force in the universe and supersedes any limits sectarian bias might try to impose on it, whether you and your colleague like it or not."

Hermes sat down with a sense of dread that such ploys would be foiled too often unless that Earther, Rita Tortellini, slipped up. Oooo, he hoped she would do just that.

Rita's opening presentation was shorter than Hermes' was, barely ten minutes by the large Alpha-and-Omega wall clock. By contrast with the innuendo and other slimy stuff sprinkled throughout Hermes' introduction, Rita was focused, well-reasoned, succinct, fair minded, avoided exaggerations, etc. In short, she did a really neat job.

"She's good. Very good," Hermes whispered to Lucifer. "Scares me. This is gonna be tougher than you thought."

"Nah." Lucifer leered at Rita. "She's only a woman. Just another courtroom skirt, Hermes. We've got it made in the shade."

Michael banged his gavel. "There will be no leering in this court. By you, Mr. Lucifer, or anyone else. Does the Bench make itself clear?"

With the faintest of reluctant nods, Lucifer slouched in his ecologically correct Naugahyde-padded chair. He resented that, too, since Lucifer saw to it that all his minions got to sit, recline on, and wear swine leather goods. It's also why he resents Earther football—especially punters—because of its brutal treatment of pigskin.

"The Accusators call as our first witness, demon Nemesis." The trio hadn't noticed this demon's presence in the courtroom. Why not? Because Celestial Law required true appearances of all witnesses and principals in Celestial Court proceedings. Instead of the suave, slick-looking, with-it Earther he appeared to be at Louie's Place, Nemmy's true appearance shocked our trio as he got on the witness stand. Large ears, almost in the Dumbo class, were pointed at both extremities. His bulbous nose put W.C. Fields in the bush leagues. Shiny black hair was stylishly slicked back on either side, but the top of his head was completely bald. Two eyes were set so close together that they almost rubbed. Nemmy's complexion also showed the aftermath of a really bad case of acne long ago.

"Whew! Not a pleasant sight," Greg whispered.

"Yuck," Angie said.

Rita's objections were delivered with surgical precision throughout Nemmy's banal testimony. All but one objection were sustained.

It soon became apparent to our heroes that the Other Side's strategy was to use Nemmy as primary witness on charges two through four and as secondary witness, if at all, on charges one and five.

For readers and the authors alike, whose minds are showing initial symptoms of senility, the five charges listed in the Indictment are repeated here with parenthetical reminders.

1. Willful destruction of demonic property (the apatonium shroud at Louie's Place)
2. Interference with a demonic deputy in the performance of his duties (that must mean Nemmy, they figured)
3. General dereliction of duty in her employment (Aw, c'mon! Or, could this have to do with her hitting the sauce behind the counter?)
4. Persistent insubordination toward her employer (Was it because she'd eavesdropped on Nemmy's kitchen phone calls? Or, because of Lucifer's failed Grace ring gambit?)
5. Alienation of affection (who were those six individuals? And, did they have Louie's Place in common?)

Serious unanswered questions remained for our team. The defense was ready, but unfortunately true to form, Lucifer lied through his capped teeth during the pre-trial evidentiary discovery phase. "Liar, Liar! Pants on fire." ☆ See *Angel Beepsie's End Note*

On counter-examination, Rita tore Nemmy's testimony to shreds. (Cross-examination is deemed sacrilegious in Celestial Court, non-denominationally speaking. Hence, the alternative phrase is used. *Editor.*)

"Had you identified yourself to the defendant as a demonic deputy? Did you show proper identification such as your Hell's Demons membership card? Your photo ID Social Insecurity card?"

"No, I did not, because it wasn't necessary." His weird ears started twitching. "Look, that broad isn't the dumb blonde she plays she is. She knew my true nature all along."

"Can you offer evidence to this court that will substantiate your claim of the defendant's foreknowledge?"

"Well, not exactly."

"Yes or no, Mr. Nemesis?" Nemmy had to cave in on that one. Rita pressed the rest of charge two. "Now then, what does the Demonic Ilk allege is interference by the defendant?"

A visibly unsettled Nemmy was still coherent. "My chief duty as Manager of Louie's Place is to encourage customers to pile more layers of deception over their lives and eyes."

"What purpose could that possibly serve?"

"Ours. But why do you bother asking? You know that one name for my Boss is the Deceiver. Anyone who's read the S-S-S-S." Nemmy never stuttered, except on sacred words.

"Are you trying to say the *Scriptures*?"

Nemmy nodded furiously. "Yeah-yeah-yeah. Anyone who's read that thing knows that."

"Hmmm." Rita moved to the other side of the witness stand. "And with more layers of deception, what happens?"

Nemmy had his answer down pat. "First, the thicker the layers of deception, the harder it is for G's Grace to get through to Earthers' lives. Second, therefore, Grace can't change their eyes—how they regard themselves and other Earthers. And, this…"

Rita interrupted. "Eyes? I thought Grace effects a change of heart."

Nemmy grinned. "Hey, if our Other Side retains control of how Earthers see their lives, no way can a change of heart stick. No way!"

"This court is fully aware of such matters. But the witness may proceed to his third point, for your edification, Miss Tortellini. But," Michael looked sternly at her, "without further interruption until he has stated it. We must move on. It's getting close to lunch break."

Rita nodded at Nemmy, who resumed his testimony. "Third, that's when we get Earthers trapped in the ultimate idolatry: themselves. That's when they become all ours. Even notions about G become cogs in their self-fulfillment machine. Marriage? They'll stick with it so long as it fulfills their imagined needs. Family and all the rest? The same. Yeah, that's when we've really got 'em!" He exchanged smirks with Hermes and Lucifer.

Glancing at Michael, who gave her a go-ahead nod, Rita drew him out a bit further. "Does your third point relate to Demonic Ilk's project with the NYSE?"

While the three demonic partners exchanged shocked glances, Michael asked for a clarification: "NYSE?"

"The New York Stock Exchange, Your Honor. Pardon me, sir. I assumed that since so many Earthers watch CNN..." She shifted gears when she observed that CNN drew a blank with other angels.

Nemmy didn't notice Lucifer and Hermes' vigorous negative shut up gestures because he was caught up in savoring his next managerial position at the new Louie's Place under the NYSE. He leaned back in the witness chair, gazed at the ceiling, and smiled. "Ah, yes. There is our side's consummate altar to Me First. To Me First and Damn the Future!" He placed bunched fingertips to his pursed lips and blew a kiss at the ceiling. "Mmmm-yah! Beautiful!"

"Looking forward to it, huh?"

"Yeahhhh." He bolted upright. "Only this time, we're not gonna make the same renovations mistake." He stared down at his shifting feet. "Unless they move the place to Jersey."

Rita paced slowly. "Now, Mr. Nemesis, about charge three, general dereliction."

"Angie's been hittin' the sauce a lot. Right there on the job."

"Is that a violation of the job description you gave her?" Rita's voice rose and took on an accusatory tone. "Did you not encourage the defendant to sample the goods? Weren't those your exact words?"

Nemmy squired in the witness chair. "Yeah, yeah. You're right." ✹ See *Angel Nebbie's End Note*.

Rita proceeded with a craftily sequenced setup. "Mr. Nemesis, after Angela Four began working at Louie's Place, what other changes were made?"

"Facilities-wise, we expanded the number of stalls in the ladies' room."

"So, we note the Potty Factor. What else? Say in operations? Personnel? Any significant changes since Angela came aboard at the establishment?"

Nemmy thought, pondered, and racked his demonic brain. "None, I guess."

"But how about this Potty Factor? Did it increase business, or was it to accommodate an increase in customers that had already occurred?"

Nemmy squirmed as he muttered, "The latter."

"Louder, please."

"The latter. We had seen a significant gain in the number of women customers."

Rita went to the defense table and brought back two folders. Removing several papers from one, she handed them to Nemmy. "Please examine these, Mr. Nemesis. Are these accurate copies of the financial statements Louie's Place submitted for defense examination during the evidentiary discovery process?"

"They are."

"Prepared by," she turned to the final sheet, "the HH&S accounting firm?" When he nodded, she continued. "And what do those initials stand for? Remember, you're under oath, Mr. Nemesis."

He cleared his throat, then looked at Michael. "I've still got a chance? Eventually?" Michael nodded. Lucifer and Hermes frantically tried to wave Nemmy off, to no avail. "Hellish, Hellish and Sheol."

"And, the initials following: C.P.A.?"

"Certified Phony Accountants."

"Thank you for clarifying these matters for the court, Mr. Nemesis. She opened the other folder and showed its contents to him. "Your Honor, this is defense Exhibit A." She handed Michael a notarized copy. "It is the financial statement submitted to the state of Oklahoma and prepared for Louie's Place by the highly reputable Earther accounting firm of

Delight & Touchy. "Have you seen this before, Mr. Nemesis?"

"Yes."

"I call your attention to the last half of page nine in this report." Flipping pages till he found the section, Nemmy studied the figure for a moment. "By comparing this reputable analysis with that of the HH&S firm, what reasonable conclusions might any impartial Earther draw?" she asked. "For example, would it be reasonable to conclude from the Delight & Touchy report that business and profits for Louie's Place more than tripled during the time of Angela's employment there?"

"It would seem so."

"Would it also be quite possible that, while personnel from Hellish, Hellish and Sheol were going over fiscal data in Louie's kitchen, they were in fact cooking the books to deceive the defense and this court?"

"More than possible, Miss Tortellini." Rita was taken back by his volunteered candor. Nemmy continued, "They kept calling me back there to answer what they referred to as feasibility questions."

Michael called Rita's attention to the Alpha-and-Omega wall clock, pointed to his stomach, and mouthed "lunch!" at her.

"To sum up charge three: Could a reasonable witness such as yourself conclude from the hard data that there is in fact no evidence to support the accusation that the defendant was derelict in her duty while in your employment?"

A tear came to Nemmy's eye. "Not only that but, but she's been such a diligent and fun worker." He pulled out a hankie and dabbed away.

"The defense concludes with this witness, Your Honor."

Michael rolled his eyes and sighed in relief. With a bang of his gavel—hand tooled Navaho silver overlaid on hardened steel salvaged from the camshaft of a '57 Chevy—he boomed, "Lunch! this court is in recess for seventy-five minutes."

☆ *Angel Beepsie's End Notes*—Liar, Liar, Pants on Fire

During the diligent research that so obviously permeates this book, the authors uncovered the true origin of this poesy epithet. While omitted from later Genesis manuscript copies, the saying does occur in the recently discovered but really, really old, *codex Osloensis* fragments.

Right after the forbidden fruit scene and Eve's explanation that "the serpent deceived me," G convened a special meeting of Heaven Council and patched through an audio-video connection with Lucifer. That smirking fiend had returned to his toasty denizen when M demanded an explanation.

"Who? Me? Had nothing to do with it." That's when somebody on Heaven Council yelled at the big screen image of Lucifer lounging in his flaming nest—you guessed it—"Liar! Liar! Pants on Fire!" This was a true and accurate statement, literally.

Nitpicking quibbles posed by envious scholars questioning the *codex's* authenticity, citing the phrase—I Love NY—on Fragment 28, are beneath contempt.

✺ *Angel Nebbie's End Note*

Nemesis isn't very adept at lying. That posed real problems for the Accusators.

Hermes was moonlighting as Lucifer's Accusatory Assistant in these court proceedings. His first love is enticing Earthers to intrude on mysteries that are nobody's business. When, in the face of suffering children or high death toll natural calamity, Hermes could get Earthers to whine, "How could a loving God let this happen?" it would send him off into paroxysms of sheer demonic delight.

Nemesis' expertise, on the other hand, focused on making bad things happen to otherwise good and decent people. He specialized in the sort of bad things that entice Earthers to doubt G's compassion and mercy.

A great team—Nemesis and Hermes. And Lucifer owns the franchise.

TWENTY

A horde of Mission Angels from the observers gallery drifted into McAngel's, one of Angel U's favorite hangouts. Raphael waited for the trio at a small corner table. A giggly Luther Leaguer angel waitress brought their foreordained vittles shortly after they sat down. Millie was printed on her name tag. When she smiled, her braces flashed. Her eyes sparkled as she scooped up Angie's generous tip. Nothing loosens the purse strings for tips better than having worked as a waitress yourself. "Millie's a summer intern while she's on Earther life-support," Angie explained. "She was thrown from her horse, I understand."

This was Rita and Greg's first taste experience of angelic cowburgers laced with Coca-Salsa, that remarkable concoction which doubles as beverage and condiment. Once you get used to the cloying aftertaste, it's not that bad. Coca-Salsa also is fast becoming the underarm deodorant of choice for Zap Central staff angels.

"Fabulous," Greg said after wolfing down his first bite, "especially after no breakfast." The Norwegian boils were a tasteless disappointment, he admitted, even after generous doses of white ketchup. French fries are not available at McAngel's, only Norwegian boils.

But, there was serious business on Raphael's mind. "I've had our Zap Central staff on overtime ever since Lucifer's indictment was handed down. First, however, gimme five, Rita." He grinned at her as they slapped high-fives. "Spectacular work this morning. Angel Tort was so impressed that he's volunteered to be called as a witness, if needed."

"He's that desperate to watch the Chicago Cubs play?"

Raphael nodded vigorously, then shook his head. "If he was fanatic about the Yankees, I could relate to that. All G's people could. But, those Cubbies of his? Oy."

"Oy, Raphael? Did you say Oy?" Angie gawked at her mentor.

"It slipped out. All those centuries of trying to help out Israelites. You know how that can get to an angel. Plus the fact that I've met Kashi."

"Now about your staff, Raphael." Rita brought them back to focus. "Have they come up with something?"

"Six of our CAI field agents have uncovered major data that should help Angie's case on charges four and five." Raphael reached into the breast pocket of his newest Italian designer-with-only-one-name blazer.

"CAI?" Greg asked. "CIA, you mean, don't you?"

"Central Angelic Intelligence. So it is CAI." Raphael opened certified copies of the deed and certificate of occupancy for Louie's Place. "These prove that the actual owner of Louie's Place—and your real employer, Angie—is Lucifer himself."

"Lucifer? That couldn't be." Greg was shocked.

"Lucifer. Louie's. Of course. It fits. Why, that wily son of a bunny." Rita's mind raced. "So, the real issue in the insubordination business is what, Angie?"

"My Grace ring. That's it." She showed it to Rita and briefed her on Louie's failed scheme to have her give it to him.

"Attempt to defraud. Open and shut." Rita turned to Raphael. "Would Celestial Law have something about that on the books?"

"Certainly. With Lucifer around, we put it in a long time ago." Raphael explained that Mission Control had established a century earlier that the owner listed on both documents of G.P., Inc. was actually a dummy corporation whose shares were wholly held by Lucifer. "And that's a matter of record."

"G.P., Inc.?" Rita frowned.

"*Gemutlichkeit* Properties. Translated, I guess 'Happy Time' comes close." Raphael nodded at each of them. "Our CAI field agents also got a line on charge five."

"Alienation of affection." Rita became more enthused as this new data plugged some defense holes that had worried her.

"It's clear that this particular charge originates from Lucifer's fury over seeing what he had built up so carefully fall apart. Fall off is closer to the truth. Yes," Raphael said, "we're talking layers of deception that worked when these individuals were outside Louie's Place, not just when they were within its apatonium shroud."

Angie gasped. "Your Ultimacy, sir. The Celestial Secrets Act."

Raphael waved a hand reassuringly. "We have special dispensation from Heaven Council to brief Rita and Greg on the matter because it is essential to the interests of Celestial Justice in this case." Angie added comments here and there as Raphael explained the apatonium deconstruction project.

"Have the CAI field agents been able to identify those six unnamed individuals?" Greg already suspected he was on the list.

"Besides you? Kristin, Rita, Peter Chambers, Guy Schwartz, and Stanislaus Roncowiscz."

"Tex? But he still acts weird," Angie said.

"Maybe so. And yet Lucifer must know something we don't, something that makes Slimeball believe he's no longer got Tex in his greedy grasp. We may never find out, nor do we need to, for this case." Rita nodded at Raphael.

"But here's the real kicker." Angie was impressed by Raphael's mastery of Earther slang. "A seventh name almost made the list and just might yet. And that's due, in large part, to your influence, Angie."

The trio waited with baited breath, a remnant from the creamed herring McAngel's used instead of tomatoes—on their Cowburger Deluxes. "Who is it? Kashi?"

"No, not Rabbi Kashihara, Angie. Only the apatonium affected him. His main deception, although minor, was his obsession with finding a blonde *rebbitzin*. That's a rabbi's wife, Angie."

"I know. I know."

"So that's why it took me so long to get his attention." Rita laughed. "Why I couldn't get to first base with my rabbi guy until after our heroine here did her thing with her Grace ring." She punched Angie's biceps playfully.

Greg got them back on track. "Who's that seventh name?"

"I'll give you a clue: A little exchange that few, if any, in that courtroom noticed this morning." He paused, savoring the trio's anticipation. "When he pleaded with Michael, 'Do I still have a chance?'"

"Nemmy?" Angie gasped.

Raphael nodded. "Indeed! Nemesis. Himself. We only know part of the story. But the fact that the Other Side risked putting him on the stand shows how shaky they know their case is against you. Beyond that, however," he took a deep breath and exhaled, "when word gets out that there's still hope of redemption even for one of Lucifer's chief demons, what Earther can drown in despair over eternal life after knowing about Nemmy?"

"Wow, I say. Wow!" Angie was stunned.

Raphael covered her hands with his. "Angela Four, it just might happen that your 250th Mission could be the most successful in Mission Control's history." Angie's jaw fell open as she thought of that possibility.

"It's too soon to tell how it will turn out with Nemmy and the others, except Greg here. But if it happens, you could end up living in one of the grandest mansions of all." He grinned. "Close to my own neighborhood."

"Archangelville?" Angie gasped. "*Jee-ly!*"

He nodded. "As close as non-archangels can get."

When a well-fed Celestial Court reconvened, Rita recalled Nemmy to the witness stand. During lunch, she'd realized he should be upgraded to a quasi-enemy. She knew she had to proceed carefully with him, lest she compromise his larger potential to become an ontological split-infinitive; that is, the first ever known instance of an eternal bad guy defecting to the good guys. Good Lord, she thought, what Angie's done in her ditzy decency could decide Nemmy's declension from the demonic denizens to everlasting decorum. Who would've dreamed this scenario could issue from the likes of Angela Four?

"Mr. Nemesis, charge four of the indictment alleges that the defendant has been insubordinate to her employer. In the discovery phase of this case, an affidavit was submitted by the people of Demonic Ilk identifying you as her employer. You are aware of this?"

"Yes."

"How would you describe to this court your working relationship with the defendant?" Rita noticed he seemed uneasy, as though torn between telling the truth and tough trouble. "In your experience, has she been a consistently cooperative employee?"

"Yes."

"I see." Rita moved to the distant side of the witness stand so Lucifer and Hermes could watch her zero in for the kill. "Has she been kind, loving, sweet, and gentle at all times, no matter what?"

"I'd say so. Yes."

"Strange." Rita tapped her chin. "What are we to make of this? Here we have an employee who's given her best, has an excellent working relationship with you, Mr. Nemesis. Business and profits have more than tripled during her short tenure at the establishment called Louie's Place..." Her voice trailed off, and she paused for effect. "And yet, this court has before it charge four." Rita moved to the defense table and returned with a folder containing the documents Raphael had given her at lunch.

"Boss?" Nemmy sat, palms out, addressing Lucifer. "You know I've never been much good at lying."

"Boss, you said? The affidavit submitted to this court identifies you as the defendant's boss. Perhaps you weren't party to this." She showed him the certificates of occupancy and ownership, then handed notarized copies to Michael and Hermes.

"The dates." Nemesis pointed at the two pages. "These were before I arrived there."

"I see. So, you could have no prior knowledge of the data in these documents?"

"Hardly." Nemesis cleared his throat. "I got there the day after I caused that earthquake in Chile. The one he," Nemmy gestured at Lucifer, "ordered me to do."

"We remember. The one where many children died? The atheist press had a field day with that one. Your work, huh?"

Nemmy stared down at both hands, a tear trailing down his left cheek. "I'm too good at what I do. I, uh, was the most creative of the angels. So, I was told to care for the Tree of the Knowledge of Good and Evil in Eden. Ever since, I've known what it was like for Adam, what it was like for Ahab. Y'know, in *Moby Dick*? For creators of the atom bomb? We're all alike. Seduced by our creativity, until it destroys us."

"*Moby Dick*. Yes, I spent an afternoon in the Melville collection at the Newberry in Chicago. I read his notes on medieval Jewish stories about the golem. About how even the most altruistic creation can destroy its creator. The white whale was Ahab's *golem*. Of course, it destroyed him." Rita paused for a long, thoughtful comment. "Thank you, Mr. Nemesis. I understand your torment a lot better now. Back to less important matters."

"Objection!" Hermes jumped to his feet. "Defense is attempting to trivialize a genuine big time indictment."

"Sit down, Hermes." Michael banged his gavel. "Overruled. Matters the defense attorney has so knowledgeably elicited from this witness are more important than charge four." Michael glared at the Assistant Accusator. "Pseudo, just like the rest of your kind. Hyping mere charades as grand mysteries."

"I asked you, Mr. Nemesis, to read aloud to this court the name on line eighteen of the occupancy document, and lines two, nine, fourteen, and twenty of the ownership certificate. Both documents are on file with the Recorders Office in Tulsa, Oklahoma."

"G.P., Inc."

"Who owns G.P., Inc.? The sole owner, that is."

Nemesis pointed. "He does. Lucifer." A buzz went through the Celestial Court.

"In fact, then Lucifer, not you, was the defendant's actual employer. Is that not so? The defense can offer additional documentation to substantiate this point, Your Honor."

"Yes! I can save you the trouble." Nemmy glowered at the Accusators.

"And, since that is the case, Your Honor, the defense moves to have this court cite the Accusators for contempt of court. Clearly, they have attempted to defraud these proceedings."

Michael, clearly miffed, banged his gavel. "So ordered." He grimaced at the demonic duo. "You guys think we're a bunch of dummies up here?"

"Insubordination against her employer. Hmm. That would be Lucifer. Hmm." Oooo, Rita was playing this to the hilt. "Might you be able to enlighten the court on this matter, Mr. Nemesis?"

For the next five minutes, she led Nemmy through his vivid recollection of Lucifer's failed Grace ring gambit with Angie, including his gesture at Greg. "He was there. Saw it all." Greg nodded.

"Your witness." Rita didn't even glance at Hermes.

"We have no questions of this witness. He's," Hermes cleared his throat, "spilled too many beans already." The Assistant Accusator shuffled papers.

"The Accusators call Lucifer as their next witness."

TWENTY-ONE

As a primary witness, the court's true appearance rule applied to Lucifer. "Homely as a mud fence," Rita whispered to her colleagues.

"A snout like that would do any porker proud." Greg flaunted a barf-inducing gesture Luficer's way.

"This is the first time I've seen his true appearance," Angie said, "but I never expected he'd be so utterly ugly."

Though his lips were large enough to flap in a moderate breeze, they couldn't hide his fangs. Neither eyeball seemed to care much for whatever its mate was doing. But then, given Lucifer's cock-eyed view of things, one shouldn't be surprised. Lest we inadvertently encourage teen readers to identify with Lucifer, we won't say anything about all those zits.

"Please state for the record your name, occupation, and current address." Hermes stood at the Accusators' table.

"Lucifer. Pyromaniac. Condo unit 666 in the Nether Reaches subdivision, Hell." He straightened his swineskin blazer as Hermes approached the witness stand where this False Witness sat.

"You have known the defendant since...?"

"Before the Beginning. Yeah, we go way back, don't we, Angie baby?" To counter his malevolent sneer, Angie's hand went to the oversized pulpit Bible she'd placed on the defense table, handily, lest he tried pulling another Ruby Whammy on any of our terrific trio. Lucifer's snout sniffed up several dribbles of demonic disdain.

"Mr. Lucifer, you have been called to testify on charges one and five of the indictment." Rita grinned. Our Guys had guessed right on the Other Side's strategy.

"Would you describe for this court the circumstances surrounding the alleged willful destruction of demonic property?"

Lucifer did so with surprising clarity and brevity. Greg guessed it was because embarrassment over his true appearance sapped the usual swagger and bravado. After ten minutes, Hermes stepped back. "Your witness."

Confident in her power suit, Rita began counter-examination. "We will stipulate that the defendant did, indeed, deconstruct over seventy percent of the apatonium shroud you had installed around Louie's Place. And we will further stipulate she did so willfully and deliberately with intent to deconstruct this nefarious substance."

Lucifer and Hermes were stunned. An angelic buzz went through the observers' gallery as four hundred Mission Angels tried to divine these stipulations' significance. Michael pounded his gavel.

"However, the defense moves to dismiss this charge."

"On what grounds, Miss Tortellini?" Michael wasn't used to seeing such shrewd law practiced in Celestial Court.

"Two, Your Honor." Rita went to the defense table and brought back two tomes from the Celestial Law Codes. She opened the first to the place marked and handed it to Michael. "According to Part Three, section fourteen, paragraphs nine through twenty-one from the Celestial Criminal Code, this court distinguishes between destruction and deconstruction." Michael's finger traced lightly over the facing pages. "That ruling issued from the case of the People of Demonic Ilk versus Gunga Din."

Michael nodded and Hermes approached the Bench to see for himself. He read silently as Rita waited. With a we-lost-that-one shrug at Lucifer, Hermes returned to his seat.

"In this," she pointed at the open book, "Your Honor's landmark 'All's Fair in Love and War' ruling, willful destruction terminology cannot be applied to actions in a state of declared war. And so, Gunga Din was let off scot free."

> The Reader may recall that episode. Gunga Din made such horrible faces at Lucifer's favorite stallion that the terrified steed galloped off into the brush and into the clutches of a prowling tigress. Her feline family thoroughly enjoyed their fresh horsemeat dinner. Lucifer was livid over the loss of his Lippizaner. *Editor.*

Michael waited on Hermes. The Assistant Accusator again shrugged at Lucifer, rising half way. "The Accusators concede the point, Your Honor."

Rita opened the other tome. "The second point of Celestial Law addresses the indictment's use of the term property. Defense challenges the propriety of property on two grounds, Your Honor."

She retrieved a document from the defense table. "First, we challenge the term's implication of legitimate ownership of this substance."

Lucifer's hand dug his favorite ball bearing out of a swineskin pocket and gave the sphere his stressed-out massage. Bad habit. Dead giveaway, and Rita spotted it. She knew she had him on the ropes, if not yet on the run.

"Mr. Lucifer, apatonium is manufactured from what raw material?"

Lucifer shifted uneasily in the witness chair. "Vinyl."

"Milky white vinyl, more specifically?" He nodded. "Have the record show that the witness responds in the affirmative." Lucifer was worried about the document in her hand, partly because he didn't have the foggiest notion about its nature.

"Where in Hell is vinyl manufactured, Mr. Lucifer?" Oh, the Old Foe tried his wily best to beat around the bush, but

Rita wouldn't let him get away. Just another courtroom skirt, indeed. "Please answer yes or no. Apatonium is manufactured from a substance that is neither indigenous to nor fabricated in Hell. Is that correct?"

"Yes." He hissed the word, his knuckles white around the ball bearing.

"Where, then, did your engineers get it? How was this raw material provided them?" Lucifer made a difficult witness, but Rita was relentless until she had him set up perfectly for her preemptive ploy: the document.

"This is a police report from the court house in Cotulla, Texas, Your Honor." She handed the original to Michael and certified copies to Lucifer and Hermes. Tricky hermeneutical skirmishing ensued; that is, argument over what method of interpretation should be used to ascertain the manuscript's meaning.

At first, the Other Side demanded the allegorical method but, failing that, at least the typological. Rita stuck to her guns as she fired at the literal method bulls-eye. Since this was a court of law, after all, she prevailed.

When Michael ruled in her favor, Rita proceeded to expertly establish two key points; (a) because the apatonium was fabricated from all those stolen vinyl K-Mart baggies, it lacked legitimate status as demonic property; and (b) the People of Demonic Ilk should be cited for contempt because of its attempt to "willfully defraud this court."

"So ordered," Michael immediately intoned. "Sufficient grounds for dismissal have been established by the defense. Charge one is stricken from the indictment." Clearly, Michael was impressed by Rita's courtroom skills.

"We move to consideration of charge five: alienation of affection. Six unspecified individuals. What are their names, Mr. Lucifer?"

"Objection." Hermes rose, more confident than he'd been all day. "Even the Celestial Secrets Act acknowledges our demonic prerogative on this matter. While your side lays all its cards on the table for its strategy in the ongoing war of redemption, Your Honor, our side has not done so, need not do so, and will not do so at this or any other time."

"Sustained." Michael had no choice.

"We withdraw the question, Your Honor." Rita kept her cool. Lucifer sighed with relief. A very minor victory, perhaps, but it provided a passing tad of encouragement to a demoralized amoral Other Side's morale.

Rita took the tack Tort had recommended, chastened by her impulsive tactic of getting those six names on the record. "Celestial and Earther Family Law agree on three key requirements for making an alienation of affection charge stick. First, there must be a contractual relationship document in the public record. Marriage is one example, from a government's point of view, that is. Next, said contractual relationship must be a voluntary, consensual commitment by each party to it. Third, a plaintiff must prove willful intent by the defendant to sever said relationship." She turned to Hermes. "Does the Assistant Accusator agree with this summary of the law?"

Hermes didn't bother rising. "We agree, Your Honor." Buried in his hands, Hermes' head slowly shook from side to side.

"I had them all." Lucifer hissed. "Right in the palm of my hand." When he raised his fist in a theatrical gesture, the steel ball bearing fell to the floor with a loud thunk. Lucifer's favorite cuss word could be heard in the galleries last row: "Drat!"

Rita went into her mongoose mode, as though attacking a hapless cobra. Darting in, then back out of reach, just as quickly. To a casual observer in that courtroom, it might seem she was toying with a victim much as a cat with a captured mouse. But she was in methodical earnest, getting Lucifer to fess up at every turn of the screw. Gollee, she sure was great at getting his goat.

Rita was flirting with risk, of course. Sure, at Celestial Court Lucifer was out of his element, beyond his bailiwick, a *non sequitur* without a last name, *et cetera*. In desperation, would he pull another Ruby Whammy on her? Barf brimstone—something he hadn't done since Sodom and Gomorra? Stick wads of gum under the witness chair?

The first time that tell-tale red glow of an upcoming Ruby Whammy grew in Lucifer's eyes, Michael banged his gavel, did his archangelic finger snap, and gravely intoned: "Cut that out."

"So, you demonic dissembler, where is your case on charge five now, huh? You can't prove a contract ever existed with any of these unnamed individuals. You can't prove voluntary commitment by those parties. And, you have provided this court with no evidence of the defendant's willful intent to sever these non-existent relationships. Gotcha, guy."

Angie watched him like a hawk. She'd inadvertently blinked her eyelids three times, too quickly, going to Triple-E eyeball power. Then she saw it: steam coming from his fulsome lips. "Oh my G," she gasped, "he's gonna barf brimstone on her power suit and try a Ruby Whammy."

Michael was jotting notes on his legal pad and didn't notice Lucifer's latest rising rage and congruent consternation. The heat level should have alerted him. But then, how could Michael sense actual temperatures under that polyester robe of his? And so, his polyester-induced environmental insensitivity meant only one thing: Angie had to come to the rescue.

Rita was confident, even as Lucifer's eyeballs glowered toward full laser power, staring at her prominent power suit-covered bosom. After all, she had concealed Bibles protecting them. Her confidence in the devil-defying authority of Scripture was well placed. But, she knew nothing of his brimstone-barf mode.

Angie knew as she watched for the tell-tale shift from puffs of steam to a steady stream hiss from his flaccid flappers. She'd seen it before, when her failed Mission Gal and the whole town fried to a quick crisp there on the Dead Sea's ancient *costa del sol*.

What pushed Lucifer over the edge was Rita's nailing him with: "Through this Indictment, you committed a *prima facie faux pas*."

"Nobody, but nobody gets away with calling me that. Least of all, a mere woman. Them's fighting words, Earther gal."

Angie leaped from her chair and rushed to the scene with her oversized pulpit Bible. Just in the nick of time, too. Lucifer figured he would out-swine Rita with the twin onslaught of a Ruby Whammy and brimstone barfing. His calculation hadn't counted on Angie. Too bad, for Lucifer.

Both Ruby Whammies ricocheted from Rita's bosom Bibles back to Lucifer, burning an earring hole in each lobe. His brimstone barf bounced from Angie's large pulpit Bible all over his brand new blazer.

The gallery, *en masse,* jumped to its feet, cheering, "Angie. Angie. Angie." Angel Flopsie jumped out front of the railing, doing cartwheels—her "Hi there" panties flashing—while Angel Mopsie led the yell: "Hit'm high, hit'm low, come on, Angie, go, go, go!"

Michael banged his gavel so hard that the hand-tooled Navaho silver overlay fell off the ivory shaft. "Order. Order! Please, gimme order in this court."

"Angie, Angie, Angie! Hit'm high, hit'm...."

Someone started banging a glass with a metal spoon. You know, churchy-like? Even after quiet ensued—these were angels, remember, with reflexes attuned to churchy stuff— Walter Irs, the Second kept tingling the glass on his table. "Weasel Eyes!" Greg gasped.

Lucifer was beating out the last glowing embers of barfed brimstone on his smoldering swineskin blazer. Angie was clutching her trusty large pulpit Bible and gave it an appreciative little quick kiss after noting it was miraculously unmarked and unscathed from Lucifer's brimstone gambit. She lifted it high, displaying the victorious volume to an enthusiastic gallery. That prompted a full-throated roar of "Yay." Followed by four hundred Mission Angels executing The

Wave, which prompted W-2 to bang the glass so hard it shattered.

Stubby legs hustled his flabby bulk toward the Bench as he waved computer print-out sheets. "I'm shuttin' this place down."

Michael banged his gavel. "Who are you? What's going on?"

"My name is Walter Irs, the Second, and I'm a duly sworn and authorized official of the federal government."

"Government"? Michael frowned.

"Don't play Dumbo with me, Mr. Michael Archangel." W-2 waggled at finger at His Honor. "You haven't filed a federal income tax return. Not once in the past twenty years. Scofflaw." Angels in the gallery gasped.

"And neither have these two," he gestured at the demonic duo and shuffled papers. "A Mr. Lucifer and a Mr. Hermes. What are you guys with only one name? Italian clothes designers or sumpin?"

"I'll have to order the bailiffs to remove you from this court if you don't desist disrupting these proceedings." Michael scowled at W-2.

"Ha. You wouldn't dare. I'm a government official. So there. We're the Untouchables. Y'know, like Eliot Ness on TV?" Michael signaled the two bailiffs, appreciatively recalling Raphael's hunch that something like this might happen.

"Furthermore." Walter Irs, the Second, jabbed a chubby digit at another computer printout. "Furthermore, this facility isn't listed on the tax rolls. Nowhere. You haven't paid property tax, school tax, water and sewer tax. Disgusting, I'll bet you've even got an illegal freon stash around here."

Michael banged his gavel. "Quiet in the courtroom." It wasn't just W-2's self-righteous slatherings, but the noise of four hundred hubbubbing angels that were disrupting decorum.

"Don't you bang that thing at me, Mr. Michael Archangel. I've got jurisdiction to padlock this joint and take the three of you and her," he pointed to Angie, "into federal custody. Furthermore..."

"*Jurisdiction?*" Another bang of his gavel. "This is out of your jurisdiction. Way out." Michael nodded and the bailiffs grasped Walter Irs, the Second's arms.

"You can't do this to me." W-2 screeched, trying to stomp on their toes. "I'm with the government." The bailiffs lifted him a foot off the floor and, while this terrible taxer babbled on and flailed his feet, carried him toward the nearest door.

"Turn him over to Safety, bailiffs, and get that Earther on the first available *Zap* shuttle back where he belongs." When Michael had given this order, Angie dashed over to W-2's table, retrieved his attaché case and brought it to the bailiffs. How thoughtful? Well, yeah, that too. Mainly, she wanted to make sure there'd be no further excuse for Weasel Eyes to cause trouble.

"Where were we?" Michael expertly calmed things down, restored order in the courtroom, and prodded the principals to proceed. But that all happened after he remonstrated the observers gallery. "The Bench understands your appreciation of Angela Four's timely intervention during my distraction. But really, angels. That does not excuse your behaving like a bunch of Earther rowdies, now does it?" Four hundred angels shook their heads in chastened unison.

As she returned to her seat, Angie flashed a beaming smile at her gallery gang. Most cast furtive glances at Michael before responding to her with non-verbal "Yes!" pumps of their right arms. Oh, pulling off heavenly heroics like that felt *so* good, even though she was still just "in the neighborhood."

Lucifer was excused from further testimony, and since the Accusators called no other witnesses, Rita moved into the next phase.

TWENTY-TWO

Our side's strategy called for Rita to caboose Greg's character witnessing onto Angie's graduation train. The plan was not only to have his testimony put frosting on their case's cake, but to firm up grounds for her graduation from Angel U to Heaven Angel status.

"The defense calls Mr. Greg Matthews to the stand." Preliminaries were quickly disposed of. "Would you describe for us, Mr. Matthews, the kind of life you were leading up till the time Angela Four came to your apartment in Tulsa, Oklahoma?"

Many angels in the gallery whispered to each other: "Where's Oklahoma?"

Rita drew from Greg sample details of his dissolute disarray before Angie *Zapped* into his life. A beaming Lucifer nodded vigorously while an undertone of sporadic gasps and tsk, tsks! reverberated around the gallery. Rita didn't want to overdo his naughty testimony. But she knew, from several testimony meetings she'd attended with a boyfriend in college, that the competitive objective was: the bigger the sinner, the bigger the Savior. Rather, in this instance, it would be: the bigger the success...of Angie's Mission.

Rita deftly transitioned Greg's testimony to his After Angie's Arrival experience by having him relate observations about the other five hitherto unnamed individuals. At this transition's end, she asked him, "Is it your considered opinion that, along with yourself, these persons constitute the list of six unnamed individuals in charge five?"

"Yes."

Hearing that, Lucifer's palm slammed the accusators' table. "Drat!" His secret targets had been rendered non-secrets. What worried him was the possibility there was a leak in his organization. Despite frequent warnings to his malingering minions: It's not nice to deceive the Deceiver.

Greg cast numerous warm glances Angie's way as Rita encouraged him to describe the notable progress he'd made on each of the three items on their Mission agenda. He'd been on the stand for nearly an hour when Rita asked, "Is it your estimation that her Mission with you is a complete success?"

"Success? Yes. Complete? No." Rita frowned. "It won't be complete until the roll is called up yonder, and I'll be there." She relaxed, relieved there wasn't a glitch after all. Greg was more eloquent when describing how "the biggest obstacle and yet the key to connecting all the doctrine I had up here," he tapped his forehead, "with my everyday life, with Jeely living, was making it work with Marge."

Lucifer took notes, listening intently. This soul may have slipped from his slimy grasp. But there were others. Lots of others whose thick walls of self-justifying entitlement and past hurts crippled their spiritual lives. Well, he'd just have to entice them into increasing the dosage of their poison-pill past grievances and build those walls higher, wider, and thicker. Except for folks like Greg, he thought. Earthers are so easy, including those churchy types who would rather be doctrinally-correct than treat each other the way G treats them.

Gallery angels were enthralled. Before this afternoon, they had only read accounts of successful Missions. But now, in person, here was this Earther embodying a successful Mission right before their very eyes.

Most took notes in hopes of picking up tips for their own future Missions. Rita had sensed this was happening. So, her final series of questions elicited Greg's observations on how his experience with Angie had crumbled the wall he'd built up for years under the Deceiver's wily tutelage.

"Thank you, Mr. Matthews. Your witness." Rita winked at Greg, smiled at Michael and the assembled small portion of the heavenly host, and then returned to her seat at the defense table. Meanwhile, Hermes and Lucifer flashed exaggerated sneers Greg's way.

"Having gum problems, guys?" Greg's taunt drew laughter from the gallery and a smile from Michael as he gaveled for quiet. It also defeated that demonic duo's attempt at intimidation. Nonetheless, Hermes affected a swagger as he strolled toward our successful, soteriologically speaking, servant soldier of salvation.

"Born-again Presbyterian, huh? Isn't that an oxymoron? Like military intelligence, jumbo shrimp, model husband, Lutheran discipleship?"

"Except for jumbo shrimp, your examples qualify as oxymorons only when you're stuck in stereotypes." Greg was calm but sharp. His cogent reply required Hermes to revert to a different tacky track.

"Do you really expect this court to believe," Hermes pointed at Angie, "that she's ready to soar on eagles' wings when she's full of butterflies?"

"That not for me to say, Hermes." Greg smiled at Angie. "But I would imagine I'm living proof that will be factored into Heaven Council's decision-making process."

"You think you're so eternally secure, don't you, Mr. Greg Matthews." Hermes jabbed a finger at Greg. "Let me tell you, Earther, they might move you beyond Mission Guy status. But our file on you stays open until Judgment Day. We're gonna keep comin' and gunnin' for you. You may have wriggled free of our wily ways for now, but we'll be shadowing your every step from now on. Count on it."

"I'm sure you will, Mister *Assistant* Accusator." This embarrassing reminder of his inferior status infuriated Hermes.

His eyeballs started to glow red. This time, Michael was on top of things. A quick archangelic finger snap switched off the glow.

"Once more, and I'll cite you for contempt."

"Big deal." From Hermes' disheartened mien, it was pretty obvious he knew they'd lost the case.

"You and your creepy cohorts will keep coming after me. Yipes and cripes, you don't think I know that? Sheezzz. And don't think I'll be getting smug, counting on that security you mentioned. I know that's a set-up for your kind." Greg took a deep breath. It was his turn to render a pointed warning. "We're onto your demonic devices, to your deceptions and disheartening accusations. I'm weak. I'll stumble. I'll be a sinner till the day I die. But there's a force not even the Demonic Ilk can overcome." He paused for effect. "Grace." He said it softly. Only Michael and Hermes heard it.

"Would you repeat that, please?" The court recorder looked up from his steno machine.

"Grace." Hermes winced in pain. "Grace!" Greg nearly shouted it as Hermes' and Lucifer's hands stopped their ears.

"Grace." The gallery chimed in, starting a rhythmic clapping and foot stomping, punctuating the repeated cheer, "Grace!"

Michael let it go on for awhile, relishing the anguish the mere mention of this word cause the demonic duo. Finally he banged the gavel. "Enough already. Order. Order in the court."

Visibly shaken, Hermes concluded, "No more questions of this witness, Your Honor."

Rita rose resolutely. "The defense rests, Your Honor." Michael nodded and couldn't suppress a smirk. He knew what she'd say next. Rita reached down and whispered to Angie: "Stand up now." In a firm voice, Rita resumed. "On the grounds that the Other Side has failed to substantiate the validity of its indictment, neither as a whole nor its several counts, the defense moves for immediate dismissal of all five charges."

Michael's gavel was already poised as soon as he'd heard her words, "On the grounds..." and he banged it immediately. "So ordered. Case dismissed." Then, as a signal to commence celebratory chaos, a beaming Michael tweaked his nose to switch on his halo.

The discredited demonic duo had to shield their eyes from all the holy light as four hundred halos switched on and a deep-throated roar of "rectitude restored" rattled the rafters of Celestial Court. Jigs, back slapping, hugs, tears of joy, and lots of angelic "Yippees!" did, indeed, coalesce to constitute the rare celebratory chaos Michael had convened. He knew full well how the trial's outcome would encourage Mission Angels, especially the Blondes Division. They made up most of the gallery, along with a delegation from the smaller Redheads Brigade.

If Angie could make it, so could they. Angel Charlie, for one, was so encouraged he resolved, then and there, to overcome his addiction to computer games.

Angel Peggy Sue resolved to take out her unused Madame LaFarge Knitting Kit to calm the fidgety mannerisms that had distracted too many of her own Mission Earthers at critical points.

Three others, with shortly upcoming Missions, quietly took Greg aside to seek his counsel on special circumstances posed by their intended Mission Guys.

After a while, Angie climbed onto the defense table and clapped for attention. "On to McAngel's, guys. The treat's on me."

The holy horde made its happy way to McAngel's in time for their weekly hors d'oeuvres hour, always a favorite around Mission Control. McAngel's staff was at its creative best coming up with tempting versions of mini-cowburgers for these occasions.

Our terrific trio sat with Raphael and Michael. The latter had sent a Zapfax to Heaven Council from his chambers informing them of the trial's outcome and Greg's testimony about the Mission. Whenever Michael engaged Rita in discussion about legal matters, the other four joked and talked about less important things.

"I remember when you went through your Zoot Suit phase, several Earther decades back. Raphael, you were one cool dude." Since that era was well before Rita and Greg's time, Angie and Raphael described various features of the style, including "that long gold chain looping down as far as your knee."

"At least that far."

Suddenly, Angie clapped him on the shoulder. "I've got an idea. How much does Heaven Council estimate it would cost to change Heaven Angels' robes from polyester to, say, regular silk or—um—crushed silk? How many shekels?"

"Hmm. As I recall, yes, the latest figure I got was five million."

"How much is that in Earther dollars, Raphael?"

"About the same. Five mill, give or take a hundred K."

"I'm gonna do it!" Angie shrieked so loudly, nearby angels were startled.

Greg was puzzled. "Do what, Angie?"

"My share of the lottery winnings. Buy enough bolts of silk to replace Heaven Angels' crummy polyester robes. That's what. Yesss!" She pumped her right arm. "In designer colors. Maybe—um—a few white. How many would we need in white, Raphael?"

"Hundred or a hundred and fifty should do it."

"For when we pose for paintings," Angie chimed in. They laughed and high-fived. "Plus a couple in black for Your Honor here." She punched Michael lightly in the arm.

A breathless Bert hurried to their table, cradling a very frightened carrier pigeon. "This just came in from Heaven Council, Angie. For you."

As he removed the microfiche tube from the bird's beak, Bert continued. "The Z-Mail cover note from Gabriel explained that he was meeting with the Status Review subcommittee of Heaven Council." He reached into his jacket pocket for his fold-out portable microfiche viewer. Angie held the now-cooing pigeon while Bert opened the tube and inserted the tiny microfiche square on the viewing plate. "There. Have a look."

"Dark, Bert. Nothing."

"Ooops. Sorry about that." He flicked on the viewing light and reclaimed the bird.

"Hey!" she shrieked. "Hey, listen up." She began reading aloud the memo from Hokmah, Chair of Heaven Council's Status Review subcommittee.

> CONGRATULATIONS! IN A UNANIMOUS VOTE, STATUS REVIEW DECLARES ANGELA FOUR A GRADUATE FROM ANGEL UNIVERSITY, SUMMA CUM LAUDE, MAGNUM OPUS. WELCOME TO THE RANK OF HEAVEN ANGEL, FIRST CHAIR, ALTO SECTION. MANSION READY AND WAITING NEAR ARCHANGELVILLE. ORIGINAL COPY TO FOLLOW.
> IN G'S NAME,
> HOKHMAH
> CHAIR
>
> P.S. YOU'VE GOT YOUR VOICE BACK.
> P.P.S. GOOD SHOW, ANGIE! GABRIEL.

Angie alternated between crying and laughing. She received joyful hugs from her table mates and from her Mission Angel buddies. Bert hugged her so heartily it made the pigeon squawk. Hundreds of angels whooped it up, high-fiving all over McAngel's as the great news spread. The same thought riveted into every Mission Angel brain: "Wow! If Angie can make it, there's hope for me yet."

"Graduation's next Wednesday, Angie. I'm scheduled to officiate. Although," Michael huddled with the group, "the scuttlebutt I'm getting is that M, himself, might be there to do the honors during the Grace Ring Handover."

"M, Michael?" Raphael's jaw dropped.

"No official word yet. Just scuttlebutt from a source on Heaven Council staff. You and I have talked about progress with the other five whose lives were touched by our Angie. Word is, they are all moving along so well they've been withdrawn from the pending missions roster."

"That's wonderful news, Michael." Raphael squeezed Angie's hands. "See? It's getting even better than we hoped."

"There's more, guys. Just before Dottie beamed them down, Lucifer and Hermes were observed having a heated argument with Nemesis. In the two observers' opinion, Nemesis wasn't caving in." Michael placed both palms on the table. "Now, if that's not a WOW, what is?"

The trio's takeoff slot was still two hours hence. So, before Raphael and Angie would take Rita and Greg on a guided tour of the Mission Control campus, there was time for Angie to accede to frantic pleas from *menuddeh* monotone-afflicted Mission Angels to give them a demo of her Voice-Back.

Bert punched in the code for left palm karioke instrumentation while Angie climbed up onto a table. Oh, how she had longed for this moment. She had learned all those lyrics to tunes she'd never been able to carry since that fateful Fourth Day of Creation. Now, the time had come to belt it out in all six octaves.

She began at the lowest voice ranges. A verse of Ezio Pinza singing "Some Enchanted Evening," followed by a classic Joe Williams number backed by Count Basie's band. Next came Luciano Pavarroti's stirring "Desin Norma" performance at a Three Tenors concert. For alto, she did a Sarah Vaughan interpretation of the Rogers and Hart classic, "Little Girl Blue." In her soprano mode, Angie reprised a classic Kirsten Flagstad piece from Wagner's Ring Cycle. Coloratura, of course, required the "Bell Song" from *La Boheme*.

Last, but clearly least, since no one there could hear it, she did a fun version of "How Much is that Doggy in the Window?" in her newly acquired dog whistle voice range, visually enhanced by Shirley Temple child star gestures.

Gabriel *Zapped* in for her performance and wiped more than one pearly tear from his cheeks. All those millennia of voice lessons he'd given Angie, beginning with Caveman Grunt (recently reprised as gangsta rap). He was so glad she'd regained her angelic vocal capabilities so she would no longer have to settle for rap, which requires no such capabilities.

"Practice, practice, practice," he'd told her for longer than anyone should remember, "until someday...." That day had come. He was briefly tempted to fetch his trombone to Dorsey-jam with Angie for the crowd's enjoyment. "Nahhh," he decided, "don't crowd her moment." Whew! G does work in mysteriously merciful ways.

Raphael led the trio on the guided tour. Rita and Greg were, understandably, ga-ga. Angie had seen it all before, of course, but her bubbly mood supplemented their own stupefied spirits amid the spectacular sights. "Where's earth from here?" Greg asked Raphael.

Angie's ultimate coordinator made a zig-zag gesture with one arm. "Thatta way. Your Einstein got it only partly right with his notion of curved space lines. Actually, they zig and zag. Poor fellow, he was limited by the archaic assumption that nothing moves faster than one Wink, the speed of light. You wouldn't be here if he was right. Mission Control would operate under a horrible handicap. Your Einstein was so far off from the way things really are, intergalactically."

Yes, Angie would be *Zapping* back with Rita and Greg, to shop for all that silk. Where would she find that much? What kind of deal could she make? Could she get a discount for cash? Angie's thinking patterns obviously hadn't shifted as yet to the big picture perspective that Heaven Angels have.

Angel Bert was able to get them a *Zap* takeoff slot a half-hour earlier than scheduled, to allow time for a more leisurely sightseeing pace on their way back to earth. Their time of arrival, what Zap Central called the End Times, was predestined, of course. By leaving earlier, they'd almost triple the time they had for transgalactic tripping detours.

Fond farewells all around, as our trio readied for their *Zap* at Mission Control's portico. Rita's legal stuff was in a new golden backpack presented on behalf of a grateful legal department by Angel Tort, who reminded Angie of his passionate craving to watch his beloved Cubbies play "in poysun."

> Angie did get tickets for Tort, a home game at Wrigley Field. His Cubbies knocked out twenty-four hits while their pitcher went the distance, hurling a three-hitter at the Pirates. The Bucs won. Tort couldn't have been happier, deliriously so. "It was the *way* they lost it, in such a typically Cubs way." Chicago Cubs fans are different, as Nigel Braun-Nez's Nobel Prize winning research, noted earlier, proved beyond the shadow of a doubt. *Editor.*

Arms around each others' waists, the three assumed the secret Lutheran hand grip as soon as Angie tapped her barrette's Travel bar. "Thirty seconds," Angel Bert reminded them. Just before takeoff, Angie gave the well-wishing throng her usual curled fingerwave.

"Bring back your Harley," Gabriel called through cupped hands.

ZAP! They were gone.

TWENTY-THREE

Angie's longtime shopping ally, Kristin, was an enormous support on the silk shopping spree. They tried all the usual routes. Fabric chain stores were not only too expensive but couldn't supply enough of the stuff. Two firms in Manhattan's garment district could come up with the silk but were still a tad too costly. That's when Greg remembered a college fraternity brother, a shadowy student named Josepo Paisano, whose father was in the import-export business.

The trio tracked down his establishment in a large but rundown warehouse on the Brooklyn waterfront. They were passed through several checkpoints, each staffed by rather large guys, all of whom were chewing something. They wore dark shirts, loud ties, and black suits with pinstripes. Finally, the three were led into the posh, tastefully paneled and appointed office suite of Josepo's pop, Tony "The Fixer" Paisano.

They'd lucked out. Seems that Mr. Paisano had just laid into that very warehouse a large shipment of finest quality crushed silk his boys had freshly hijacked off a slow boat from China. Stolen, you're thinking? Heaven Angels are going to be flying hither and yon in stolen goods?

Not really. Seems the Chinese government had refused our State Department's typically meekly-made request for compensation to Paisano for allowing Chinese sweatshop outfits to pirate his pride and joy, the Sweet Cakes pantyhose line, with its patented adjustable Butt Enhancer. An instant hit in China, Sweet Cakes took off on every continent around the globe. However, Tony's accountants informed their boss that the Chinese pirate shops' operations were into him for at least twenty-five million.

"Stolen? Nahhh. It's barter pure and simple. Dey got sumpin' a mine, and I got sumpin' of deirs. We're almost even steven." Tony "The Fixer" Paisano's explanation made sense to Angie. Except for her Missions with Greg and Wally Wallawash, all of her Earther escapades had happened in barter economies. Then, there was the further fact that the fabric's wholesale value was barely half the worth of what the Chinese had taken from him. Since the complexities of Far East finance eluded our trio, they had to take Paisano's word—plus what the ledger pages and other documents showed.

Fortunately for them, Tony "The Fixer" also had a current cash flow problem. Kristin did the bargaining. It took her less than five minutes to pull his asking price of twelve million down to five-point-two million, well within Angie's lottery-financed wherewithal. Hands were shaken and the check written; it cleared by the close of business that same day.

Safety sent down two *Zap* semitrailers. When Paisano delivered the goods to the now nearly empty parking lot at Louie's Place, there was more crushed silk than Angie expected. In fact, there was enough to provide each Heaven Angel with a casual robe as well as the anticipated formal version. Needless to say, the robes' delivery was to make Angie an instant heavenly hit.

Before the crushed silk-laden semi's were *Zapped* to Mission Control that afternoon, Greg helped Angie wheel her Harley into one of them. She hung a sign on the handlebars; one she'd calligraphed herself: "*Beaucoup* thanks, Gabriel! Have fun. Drive Safely, and G bless! Love, Angie."

The evening before her Graduation Day at Angel University, Angela enjoyed a boisterous *Zap Back!* farewell party with her Earther friends. Kristin hosted the event in one of Giorgio's J and G private party rooms.

Besides Greg and Kristin, the whole gang showed up. PC brought his wife, Louella. Guy Schwartz was beaming; he received news that afternoon that his research sabbatical in Madrid had been fully funded. You and I know who the "Anonymous" donor is, don't we?

Tex arrived minus his usual Stetson and affected drawl. Bert Zapfaxed Tamara's whereabouts to Angie the day before. This afternoon, Tex wired Angie's matching-funds, half of what he owed in child support, to his ex-wife. Just before he left for Giorgio's, his grateful ex-wife phoned, crying for joy. "It's been so hard for us, Stan." He'd wept when Tamara came on the line. This weekend, Tex would fly to New Orleans to see them.

When they entered the party room, Rita waved her left hand. "Lookee here, guys!" Kashi blushed as his Intended flaunted the engagement ring he'd slipped on her finger the night before. A flawless full carat, the rock was his costly but cogent concession to *goyische* cultural customs.

Angie urged Kristin to invite Nemmy, too. Unfortunately, he had not yet returned from his so-called vacation. Bert had pleaded with Raphael to *Zap* into the party, but Angie's ultimate coordinator wisely declined. "It's Angie's show. We'd only detract from the party's poignant purpose."

After Greg's announcement that he'd been selected as a finalist and had the interview this Saturday for a museum job in Texas, Kristin brought out the group's graduation presents to Angie.

First were her exquisitely crafted casual and formal crushed silk Heaven Angel robes, in designer blue hues. Kristin had them tailored by a Creole charismatic Christian, a crack craftsperson who was also a senior at a university in Tulsa. Angie felt so grand as she modeled each robe for them.

Next came a solid gold brooch in the shape of a harp, one for each garment. Engraved on back were the words: Angie, you brought heaven's music into our lives.

Finally, she received two pair of custom-fitted Ted Lapidus designer shades, which are advised for Heaven Angels and all other heavenly inhabitants because of the glare reflecting off all that shiny stuff.

It was the best of times. It was the saddest of times. Sort of. It wasn't just Angie's impending departure for her graduation. The rest of this friendly gang was heading off in various new directions. But yet, a most momentously memorable epoch in their lives was passing. "Ta-ta, Tulsa" time loomed for them all.

That time had come for Angie. Her *Zap* takeoff slot was but moments away. After lingering huggies all around, they stood in a circle and joined hands in the secret Lutheran hand grip.

Greg started them singing "G Be with You till We Meet Again." Angie chose her new Sarah Vaughan voice capability for her part.

Greg pointed at his watch. "Thirty seconds, Angie."

Her left hand slid from Kashi's grasp with one last squeeze and reached to her barrette. She watched Greg until he pointed at her. "Now."

Angie tapped her Travel bar and gave them her finger wave one last time. "G bless you."

"Five seconds, Angie." All were smiling but teary-eyed.

ZAP!

Her friends gazed into the heavens as Angie departed from their midst.

Epilogue

Our textual *Editor* converted to Melchizadekianism and accidently channeled *himself* into the future. Somewhere. He left no forwarding address.

Denise now goes by the name Sister Belle. She came upon a biker gang at a scenic lookout on I-35 in Oklahoma, liked them, and joined the group. Too late, she discovered that the gang's name, Holy Rollers, was to be literally interpreted. This group of somewhat atypical Pentecostals converted her, and Denise was immediately Spirit-filled. She makes a fair living from giving testimonies and hopes to save enough money to enter cosmetology school by year's end.

Rita Tortellini and *Rabbi Toshio Kashihara* married two months after Angie's graduation and are deliriously happy. Kashi has assumed the position as Rabbi of *Chabad ha-Hondo,* an upscale congregation located in the lush countryside west of San Antonio.

The Hadassah ladies of Kashi's new flock are not at all intimidated by their *Rebbitzin's* style and designer clothing because she makes superb *ladtke* for their frequent potluck fund-raisers.

Drawing from her expertise in coping with federal regulatory agencies, next week Rita begins working her new web site as General Counsel for Sunrise Distilleries, the variously-headquartered cooperative mentioned earlier.

Peter Chambers has gone on the straight-and-narrow, womanwise. Last week, he began work as a writer for a new public radio program, *The Prairie Domestic Partner,* sponsored by WOM (Womyn Organized for Mayhem). His wife, Louella, upon learning she's pregnant for the eighth time, joined these radical feminists. She's now bucking for fourth vice-president of WOM.

Louie's Place went belly-up within three months after Angie's departure. When the squad of faceless workpersons in unmarked vehicles was unable to effect repairs to the apatonium shroud, neither Lucifer nor Nemmy could staunch the hemorrhage of paying customers. Tulsa's IN crowd of Muppies (Middle-Aged Urban Professionals) found their fickle way elsewhere. Street drunks started frequenting Louie's, ordering only low-profit muscatel concoctions and Thunderbird. At last report, Louie's Place opens its newest franchise five weeks from now in the sub-basement of the New York Stock Exchange.

Walter Irs, the Second (W-2) never returned from lunch one Friday. Nobody noticed. After emptying his safety deposit box of bribe money and funds he'd embezzled from tax audits over the years, he disappeared. Recent reports from reliable sources locate W-2 in Montana, where he has become the Flower Child Militia's ideology expert. W-2 writes manifestoes that the Militia issues to talk shows across Montana, Wyoming, and Idaho.

In addition, he perfected a design of the group's notorious Flower Bombs; so far, three have been detonated next to IRS building dumpsters. The Militia's trademark statement against using federal tax dollars for NASA projects, each bomb is planted in the front trunk of a Volkswagen Beetle. When the bomb is detonated, the vehicle sustains some damage while zillions of freshly-cut marigold petals get plastered on windows and walls of buildings within a hundred yard radius. Aphids shun the area for days.

After years of analysis and therapy with Montana's top shrinks, traumas from his only *Zap* experience linger. Not even sticking large pins into angel dolls has helped much.

Kashi's Kosher Sushi Bar, on the beach at Miami, is doing nicely, thank you. Our intrepid Japanese rabbi met and hired a defrocked (for modifying Book of Common Prayer chanting so it would be at least "hummable") Episcopal priest, the Former Reverend Charles Herring-Bohn, who was ideal deli manager material. His superb deli-proprietor manner stems from two key physio-personality factors: an indefatigable craving to help people, which is held in check by a chronic case of hemorrhoids that stimulates his growing fame as a canny and consistent insulter of customers. His shock of prematurely gray hair also buttresses his insults with a certain aura of authority.

Because Kashi wisely changed the terms of Herring-Bohn's employment from hourly wage to commissions, the establishment's booming business means Chuck and family are finally enjoying the posh lifestyle to which Episcopal ordination entitles one.

Business is booming once again at Luigi's Pasta Specialties, Inc. *Kristin Goldfarb* has been promoted from COO to CEO on the strength of their new product's runaway success: kosher freeze-dried pasta. The product has cornered the market among Orthodox Jews, here and abroad, because its preparation entails no work on Shabbas. Test marketing results of another concept look promising, at least in redneck focus groups. "Luigi's Three Alarm" is a jalepeno-enhanced pasta line targeting the chili crowd.

Kristin and Greg kiss night-night by eleven p.m. to conclude their weekly Saturday evening dates. They're thinking of getting serious, so Greg is taking instruction to become a Lutheran. What was intended as Kristin's way of doing penance for her life in iniquitous Tulsa, becoming the volunteer youth director at her congregation, has turned into a meaningful pleasure. She's struggling with her double-decker guilt—Swedish and Jewish—over that.

Lubbock has a new curator for its world-renowned Museum of Fine and Texian art: *Greg Matthews*. Superbly melding his double-major credentials in art history and computer science, his stunning BATTI project has been fully funded by the Haigh Flootin Foundation and our Anonymous heroine. Bringing Art To The Ignorant will be available in equivalent Macintosh '88 and Windows '95 versions. Its potential has the artsy crowd sitting on the very edge of their endowed chairs.

Marge, Greg's ex-wife, upon being released from her prison of non-forgiveness for totaling his beloved Bimmer, has joined a group of topless New Age Amazons who plan to heckle Promise Keepers' rallies.

Belly has been diagnosed as pre-schizophrenic by an eminent swine psychiatrist. On the one hand, Belly "Oinks" his way into Earthers' hearts with his empathy. On the other hand, he keeps getting cast out because of his co-dependent relationship with Lucifer. On their recent inspection trip to the almost-finished Louie's Place under the New York Stock Exchange, he met a stock trader who'd lost her way looking for a ladies' room. A confrontational sort, she asked Belly: "Are you a chauvinist, pig?"

Now on his half-year sabbatical in Madrid, *Guy Schwartz* has fallen hopelessly in love with a flamenco-adagio dancer. It's a rare dance style where you stamp your feet a lot while throwing your partner around. Betsi Gabor hails from Budapest, a several generations-younger niece of famous actresses. The spontaneity she brings to their relationship has uncovered a long-repressed flair for the frivolous beneath Schwartz's rational *persona.*

If they "git hitched," as he now terms it, she will transfer to the University of Tulsa to complete her Ph.D. in Finno-Ugaritic linguistics. Fluent also in medieval Arabic, Betsi has helped Guy's research project move ahead of schedule.

With his Significance of the Year Zero module now completed, however, Schwartz's scholarly interest has shifted away from his Unified Standard Significance theory (USS Schwartz) to an inquiry into Love and Lust: Either/Or? For the paper he'll be giving at Leipzig next month, he's added a brilliant new Third Option: *Viellicht?* (translation: Maybe?)

Tex Roncowisz has moved to Branson, Missouri, where he is manager of the Donny Rickles Theater, a Country and

Western establishment. By December, he will complete payment of his matching-funds child support obligation for his daughter, Tamara. Last week, his ex-wife, Blanche du Trois (her maiden moniker), moved from the abandoned streetcar that had been home into a condo in Metairie, just outside New Orleans.

Evenings you can find Tex seated on his favorite mountaintop in the Ozarks, rocking constantly as he tries to channel his sole convert to Melchizalekianism, the aforementioned—and future vagabonding—*Editor*. It's not that Tex still believes in New Age junk. He feels he owes it to the guy to at least try.

Dr. Billie was released from the hospital after an eight-week stay. He rather enjoyed his confinement. There were cute nurses, free movies, and popcorn. Marilyn is in charge of writing his book. Writing appealed so much to Marilyn that she decided to join the Tulsa Night Writers. So TNW members beware: if you see an overweight woman blowing grape bubble gum and carrying tons of legal pads, make way.

Angie is having the time of her *very* long life. Heaven Angel colleagues adore her for replacing their polyester robes with crushed silk. That happened because lottery-advantaged Angie took to heart the Earthers proverb: "You can't take it with you." Anyway, Heaven Angels fell so in love with their new garb that M had to call a meeting to chew out the Heavenly Host for flirting on the edge of idolatry.

Angie gets invited to all their parties and Rook tournaments. Like the others, her singing voice is magnificent in all six octaves: bass, tenor, alto, soprano, contralto, and dog whistle. Since everyone can sing every part there's none of that Earther church choir problem of finding enough basses and tenors.

G be with you 'til we meet in Heaven, Dear Reader!